Dark Inspiration

Look for these titles by
Russell James

Coming Soon:

Sacrifice

Dark Inspiration

Russell James

SAMHAIN
PUBLISHING

Samhain Publishing, Ltd.
11821 Mason Montgomery Rd., 4B
Cincinnati, OH 45249
www.samhainpublishing.com

Dark Inspiration
Copyright © 2011 by Russell James
Print ISBN: 978-1-60928-669-9
Digital ISBN: 978-1-60928-656-9

Editing by Don D'Auria
Cover by Angie Waters

First Samhain Publishing, Ltd. electronic publication: November 2011
First Samhain Publishing, Ltd. print publication: February 2012

Dedication

For Christy

Yes, you were right. Someone else did want to read the stories I used to tell you during long trips in the car. Your faith and support make anything possible.

Chapter One

"Son of a bitch!" he yelled at the Tennessee countryside. Immediate and overwhelming pain arced up his arm like a lightning bolt. Dale Mabry was certain he just flattened his finger.

He dropped the mallet next to the *For Sale* sign he had forced into the cold earth. His bare hands already stung from the forty degrees temperature and that amplified the effects of the hammer's impact. He shook and then inspected his finger. It was rooster red and the nail had a white sheen destined to turn a dark, dead purple.

"Serves you right, dumbass," he said to himself. "Shouldn't be out here at all."

It wasn't just because he was underdressed for the March morning in jeans and a flannel shirt. Something inside him had nagged him from the start about putting the Dale Mabry Realty sign on the old Galaxy Farm property. But with the market stinking like a hog pen, he'd rationalized that any sale was a good sale. No matter who bought. No matter what sold.

Barren oaks swayed in the wind against the slate-gray sky. The breeze kicked up the stale scent of dead, moldy leaves. Dale had pounded his business equivalent of a tiger's marking scent where the Galaxy Farm gravel driveway met two-lane US 41. The driveway went a half mile uphill and formed a loop in front of the farm's large main house. The structure still caught the eye, as it had for over one hundred years.

The house listed as a six bedroom, four bath, but that did not do justice to its forty-five hundred square feet. The sharply peaked steel roof of the white two-story Victorian jutted into the pewter sky. Two small attic dormer windows watched out over the valley. An inviting covered porch embraced two sides of the first floor. The foundation beneath it was two feet tall, made of hand-laid dun boulders mined from the base of the ridge. From the corner closest to the road rose a round turreted room with windows around both stories. Like an aging cinema beauty, she looked stunning from afar.

But she showed her age in closeups. Her later years had been hard. The iron racing horse weathervane at the turret's peak rocked back and forth with a wailing screech in each gust of wind. Threadbare white curtains floated like spirits in the windows, unable to shield the rooms from daylight. Black paint peeled off the shutters around each window in long lazy arcs.

To the right, a low rise blocked the bottom half of the main barn, hiding its similar stone foundation. Its roofline and monochrome paint scheme matched the house. A cupola burst through the center of the curved roof, glass on every side, filthy from lack of care. The cupola was large enough to accommodate the farm's master as he watched over the acres of his domain that stretched down along the far side of the ridge.

Even with the grass in winter's death grip and the dry weeds overgrown along the split-rail fence line, the place had curb appeal. Dale wished he had the money to replace the sagging old mailbox at the entrance. If he kept the gate under the weathered *Galaxy Farm* sign locked, any looky-loos would have to go through him for a closer inspection. That would be warning enough to go in and make sure any remnants of the previous owners weren't around. Sure as hell wouldn't want to explain any of that to a prospective buyer. The bank wanted this place to move fast, and any wind of its history would stop a deal dead in its tracks.

There were folks in town who didn't think it right, Dale helping the bank sell the Galaxy. The two big Moultrie, Tennessee, realtors refused to list it. Half the small town thought it was safer to let it sit empty.

Dale figured screw them. They didn't pay for his daughter's dance lessons.

A sharp bang came from the house. Dale saw the screen door on the main entrance swing open and shut in the wind.

"Well I'll be..." he muttered. He stuck his throbbing finger in his mouth. He wasn't in the mood to go tempt the house. Not out here alone. But a good gust would tear that screen door clean off the frame and he'd be blamed.

He trudged warily up the driveway. Desiccated leaves crunched under his boot heels. He knew he had locked that door. With a new barrel bolt. From the inside.

Dale stepped on the porch and a feeling of dread came over him, thick and black and heavy as lead. The hairs on the back of his neck quivered. He'd been to the house twice before—with Darrell from the bank to inspect the place, and with Billy to walk the survey. But never alone. There was strength in numbers. Having another live person there kept you from thinking about the Galaxy Farm legends.

He grabbed the wooden screen door as it swung open again. The barrel bolt on the inside of the door was missing. Four neat white screw holes were still in the door, the grooves from the screw threads still crisp and clear. The door didn't tear open. Someone removed the bolt. Dale smelled something metallic that made him want to gag.

A dead rabbit lay in the threshold. Its eyes were wide with terror and still glassy, as if it had only been dead for moments. All that was left of its neck were two jagged edges of slick red fur. The wet blood pooled between the doors and dripped out onto the porch. Above the rabbit, finger-painted in blood on the base of the door in crooked, slashed letters it said— *NO SALE DALE.*

Dale leapt off the porch. The screen door swung shut with a muffled thud as it closed against the dead rabbit's limb. The realtor sprinted for his truck as if he were still a Moultrie High running back. As he ran through the front gate, he pulled it shut behind him. He closed the lock on the clasp in a flash. His heart pounded against his chest. With steel bars between him and the rabbit, he looked back up at the house.

"Big joke," he rationalized. "Guys in town playing a big joke or trying to scare me out of selling this place. Yeah, that's it. There ain't no ghosts. Just wives' tales. There ain't no ghosts." He caught his breath and tried hard to believe what he said.

Dale climbed into his silver Ford F-150. He fired up the engine and Johnny Cash came through the radio singing *Ring of Fire*. With another wall of Detroit steel between him and the house, Dale calmed down. It was some prank, he thought. Had to be. Vernon Pugh, probably, getting even for the bank taking the house.

Something moved in the distance behind Dale.

A gray figure stood in the second-floor window of the turreted room. It turned to face Dale. Dale's heart stopped cold. The man raised his hands over his head and struck the glass. The thump rolled down the hill like the echo of a battle's first shot. The figure vanished.

Chill bumps raced from Dale's neck down his arms. He turned and squinted hard at the empty window. A gust of wind blew and one of the window panes flexed. The sunlight flicked off the hazed surface. The glass banged in its frame.

"Jesus, Dale," he said, shaking his head clear. "Why don't you just scare the shit out of yourself? Let a damn rabbit turn you yellow."

He snapped the Ford's heater to high. Heat blasted from the vents and he rubbed his throbbing finger in it. He prayed some out-of-towner, or "outsider" as the locals called them, with a bucket of cash would cruise down US 41, fall in love with this dump and pay his commission. It would have to be an outsider. No one in Moultrie would touch the place.

Chapter Two

"Stevie Newburn, you'd better think twice!"

Laura Locke didn't turn as she reprimanded her student. She kept facing the dry erase board, writing lengthy subtraction equations with a black marker. Her SSS (Student Sixth Sense) saw everything that happened behind her back.

Stevie Newburn stood stock-still, frozen mid-pitch with a wad of paper aimed at Carrie Ramos' head. A hushed syllable of awe rose throughout the room. Stevie's eyes went wide as he slipped back down into his seat.

"She does have eyes everywhere," he whispered. He dropped the ball of paper on his desk. The boy behind him gave Stevie's head a quick shove.

"She *burned* you, dude," he said.

Laura turned to face the class. The Triple-S said things were about to begin the short, downward spiral to chaos. No one learned in chaos.

"All right!" she said with two sharp claps of her hands. "There are ten examples on the board. I want them in your notebook and solved properly. Let's get to it." Twenty-five heads bowed in unison. "The first one done with correct answers gets today's Math Gold Star." The wall chart behind her carried the name of each student, followed by a constellation of stars earned over the semester.

She paced up and down the rows of desks. The click of her high heels punctuated the rush of scratching pencils. She wore a long black denim skirt and an open black suede vest over a white blouse. She made a conscious effort to layer and lengthen her clothes at school.

The better she hid her curvaceous figure, the more seriously she found she was taken. And when it came to her kids, nothing could be more serious.

Laura glanced over the shoulders of the blue-clad students. The school district had belatedly approved uniforms for her school, which had erased the obvious income disparities between the generally poor students. The Long Island school was only minutes from Manhattan's West Side, but it could just as well have been a galaxy that separated the two islands instead of a river. Most of Laura's kids had the deck stacked against them with partial parenting and omnipresent gang influences. When she was hired, she called that Idlewild Elementary's selling point. These were the kids most in need of her help.

Laura stopped behind Tamika Washington's desk. The diminutive black girl was pulling on one of her braids, her telltale sign of frustration. Laura bent down just over Tamika's shoulder. The girl's answers were blank, though the rest of the class had several completed.

"What is it, sweetie?" Laura whispered.

Tamika turned. Laura's green eyes and long blonde hair reflected in the girl's thick glasses.

"I don't remember..." Tamika said. "If I could start, I could remember."

"It's one number at a time," Laura said. "First take four from six and what do you get?"

"Two."

"And since you can't take seven from three, what do you do?"

Tamika studied the numbers with judicial intensity. Her face lit up.

"I borrow a one!"

Laura gave the girl's back a soft pat.

"That's it, sweetie. Now you're started." She would sneak Tamika a gold star at the end of the day. It was the first time she remembered the subtraction rule on her own.

A shout sounded far down the hallway, muffled by the long distance. The principal's voice broke over the PA system. He did a lousy job hiding the panic in his voice.

"Code Red! I repeat, this is a Code Red!"

Code Red meant a lockdown emergency. Laura's first though was for her children. Someone or something in the halls had to be kept out of the classrooms.

"Everyone up against the wall!" she commanded. "Now!" Desks scraped and bashed. Kids dashed the way they had drilled and swarmed to the wall that bordered the hallway. They ducked and cowered at the base.

Laura slammed the door shut and twisted the lock closed. She glanced out through the narrow slit window, but the hallway was empty. A quick glance confirmed the classroom windows were locked. She did a headcount. Twenty-four kids.

The shouting from the far end grew louder. Her heart pounded out a staccato beat in her chest. She played out a dozen potential threat scenarios simultaneously in her head. All ended badly.

She slid to the floor and braced her back against the door. Her children radiated anxiety and she could feel the heat. A few whimpers broke the silence.

"Everyone stay calm," she said. Her whispered voice dripped with reassurance. "You are all being so brave. This will be over in just a minute."

This time the voice in the hallway was clear. Deep, throaty and filled with drunken rage.

"You can't keep me from my goddamn daughter!"

Laura's racing heart skipped a beat. She recognized the voice from six months ago. Before the man's domestic violence arrest. Before the restraining order. Before the legal separation. Before the loss of visitation rights. It was Tamika's father, Darius.

He was unforgettable. Over six feet tall and linebacker wide, his dreadlocks hung down to his shoulders. A slow-witted testament to the dangers of mixing steroids and narcotics, his dull, steel-gray eyes, devoid of emotion, still haunted Laura.

Tamika recognized the voice. She tucked her knees up to her chin and wrapped her arms around her legs. Her eyes locked closed and she began a rapid little rocking motion.

Laura wasn't letting that lunatic son of a bitch touch Tamika again.

The handle to the door thunked up and down as the lock foiled Darius's attempt at entry. He shook the door in fury. It rattled in the hinges and pulsed against Laura's back.

"Gimme my daughter, bitch!" he bellowed.

A sharp crack of something hard against the door window sounded over Laura's head. When it repeated, small glass shards fell in her hair. Laura kicked off her shoes and dug her heels in against the force.

One boy started crying. Like the fuse to a string of firecrackers, others joined in a chorus of panicked sobs.

The third assault shattered the glass. Darius thrust his thick, tattooed arm into the room, gripping the instrument of the window's destruction; an ugly black .45 automatic.

In the split second between that and the rest of her changed life, Laura had no time to think. She had only the moment to feel that combination of maternal and matriarchal instincts that anchored her existence. Those instincts saw mortal danger. This steel intruder threatened her children.

Reason washed away in a torrent of adrenaline. Her hands shot up before her mind could command them. She grabbed the barrel of the gun, her left palm nearly covering the tip.

Time slowed to a thousandth of its normal speed. All sound vanished. Everything disappeared for her but Darius's hand and the

16

potential instrument of a student's death. The split, stubby fingernail in the trigger guard shone white as a half-moon against Darius's black skin. Bright red blood smeared the nail's edge. Then in agonizing slow motion, the finger tightened around the trigger. The pistol's hammer fell with a deafening click.

The gun's blast must have echoed in the closed room, but Laura did not hear it. The bullet tore across her palm leaving a ragged raw gash. There was no pain, just the sensation of heat; the burning line along the rip in her hand, the hot pistol barrel searing her fingers.

The rest of the world snapped back into place and accelerated to full speed. The window on the classroom's far side exploded like a crack of thunder. The air reeked with the acrid scent of burnt cordite. The children's voices wailed like shearing steel. The gunshot reverberated in the center of Laura's head, though she was sure she never heard it. Her knuckles ached in the death grip she had on the .45.

The muddy echo of shouts filtered through her buzzing eardrums. Multiple shots sounded in the hallway. Three thuds sounded against the heavy wooden door.

A spray of blood and small pink flecks of flesh blasted through the broken window. They speckled Laura's arms and hair. Darius's hand jerked and then went limp. The dead weight of the .45 pulled Laura's hands to the floor, where the weapon clattered on the polished white tile between her legs. The gun lay there like a severed snake head, no longer able to deliver its venom. Darius's flaccid arm slithered back out through the windowpane.

The adrenal rush that had sustained Laura retreated like water down an unplugged drain. Her repressed terror came roaring in. She couldn't process what had just happened. She couldn't believe what she had done. All she was certain of was that Tamika and the others were all safe. Her hands began to tremble and she could not make them stop.

Chapter Three

If there was a seedier place to meet, Doug Locke didn't know about it.

The basement bar on New York's East Side hadn't had an exterior face lift since the '50s. The rusted sign still read *Mickey's* in faded green letters, even though the neighborhood hadn't been Irish for dozens of years. The steps down to the door were black and slick with whatever years of clientele had tracked out of the place.

Doug parked his car on the street a block over and wondered if his Volvo would still be in one piece in an hour. He doubted his editor at the *New York Dispatch* would sign the expense report for his insurance deductible. He should never have let Fisher talk him into meeting here.

Well, he thought, *if you do dirty work, sometimes you work in dirty places.*

Doug ran his fingers through his short brown hair and then pushed his sunglasses back up his nose. Doug was average height but still had the wiry build his college marathon days had created. He took a deep breath to prep for handling Fisher.

His phone buzzed in his pocket. It was an unfamiliar number with a Nassau County area code. It would have to wait. Fisher couldn't.

It took a moment for Doug's eyes to adjust from the afternoon daylight outside to the bar's tomblike darkness. The smell of stale beer reminded him of the morning-after frat parties at college. A rail-thin Hispanic bartender with a pencil moustache languidly sliced lemons at the bar to the right. The oak booths on the left stretched back to the rear. Amorphous wall decorations hid in the shadows. In the last booth sat Joey Fisher.

Joey had a receding hairline and a sharp nose that gave him a distinctively weasel-like appearance. That put him out of the running for political office but was practically a qualification for his job behind the scenes. He was the deputy chief of staff for the mayor, just far enough removed from the limelight to do the dirty work every politico needed done. He took a sip of whiskey from a glass and then saw Doug. He put the glass down and straightened his suit.

"Doug Locke," Fisher said. "A pleasure." He clearly didn't mean it.

"I didn't know you were a fan," Doug said.

"Nothing wraps garbage better than your column in the *New York Dispatch*," Fisher said.

"People warned me you're a charmer, but I didn't believe them."

"Let's cut the foreplay," Fisher said. "You wouldn't have wanted to meet me unless you had some hatchet job in the works for my boss."

"It's called investigative journalism," Doug said.

"Investigative journalism tells you there's salmonella in your hamburger," Fisher said. "Your 'who's humping who' shit is sub-tabloid material."

There was more truth to that statement than Doug liked to admit. His well-paid position on the *Dispatch* was due to just those kinds of stories.

"I've got proof," Doug said, "of the mayor's wife doing some shopping on the city's credit card."

The fleeting grimace that flashed across Fisher's face told Doug he hit pay dirt.

"Gracie Mansion has legitimate expenses that the city covers."

"But," Doug said, "none from Gucci or Cartier's. The mayor polishes himself up as a man of the people. A revelation like this might dull that luster."

"No one's going to give a shit about rumors like that."

"If you believed that, you'd already be out the door."

Fisher gave a defeated sigh. Doug perked up. Fisher was about to take the bait. Doug didn't have more than rumors about the mayor's wife. But a good threat would usually blackmail some sordid scoop out of the amoral Fisher.

"How about a trade?" Fisher said. He pulled an envelope from his suit pocket.

"You came prepared," Doug said.

"Your subhuman reputation precedes you."

"Coming from you, that almost hurts."

"This is Councilman Reese," Fisher said with a wave of the envelope. "Pictures and dates. The man likes to party and prefers strippers and cocaine."

Doug's phone buzzed again. Same Nassau county number. He switched off the phone.

"That ought to sell more papers than a story that says the mayor's wife is a bitch," Fisher said. "Which is old news."

The sharks always turn on each other when there is blood in the water, Doug thought. He put out his hand for the envelope.

"It doesn't hurt that Reese is opposing the mayor's taxi regulation plan, is it?" Doug said.

"Coincidence," Fisher said. He handed over the envelope and stood. "Let's not meet again."

"The pleasure would be all mine."

Doug looked over the photos after Fisher left. They were good quality. Reese at a private party in one of the VIP rooms at Boom Boom's in Brooklyn, out of a suit and looking like any other white male middle-aged New Yorker. There were enough details in the shots that he could verify the allegations, not that his boss was a stickler for multiple-source confirmation.

He looked at Reese's face in one shot, laughing as he pointed at one stripper's breasts. Reese had done a lot of good in office, standing up for the poor in his district. Yeah, well, facts are facts. Doug didn't make him take up strippers and coke, he was just telling the world about it.

He remembered he'd shut off his phone. As soon as he powered it back up, it rang. Third try from that Nassau County number. Who'd have his cell number? Doug flipped it open.

"Who is this?"

"This is St. Luke's hospital. Is this Douglas Locke?"

Hospital? Doug's mind snapped out of the world of sleazy politics.

"Yes. What's wrong?"

"Sir, your wife Laura has been admitted. There's been a shooting."

Doug's heart sank to his knees. She was dead. He knew she was dead. He was smoking out sleaze in this stupid bar and someone shot his wife. He could barely ask the next question.

"Is she all right?"

"The wounds are minor, but she wanted us to call you."

Doug was already through the front door.

"I'm on my way."

Chapter Four

Ms. Rosa Elizondo had been glued to Laura's side since the shooting. There was even a question about whether the surgical team would need to use force to keep her out of the OR. She was a short, stout, middle-aged woman with close-cropped black hair and a wide face with a permanent scowl. There wasn't a more intimidating teacher in Idlewild Elementary. The doctor breathed a sigh of relief when she agreed that her support would not be needed in the surgical theater.

Rosa had adopted Laura her first week at Idlewild, after Laura had collared a kid about to slash Rosa's tires in the parking lot. She'd more than repaid the debt with insightful advice and shoulder that absorbed tears like a sponge.

She had assumed a station at Laura's bedside. Cups of ice and water stood in formation on the bed stand and two extra blankets lay folded at the end of the bed. The room was overly bright, even though the solitary window faced the bricks of an adjacent building. Laura sat up in the bed, hands wrapped in gauze like two cartoon boxing gloves. Her eyelids fluttered.

"*¿Como esta, Mami?*" Rosa said in an uncharacteristic soft voice.

Laura managed a faint smile. "Not bad." She searched the room with glassy eyes. "Is he here?"

"Nowhere to be found," Rosa snorted. Rosa had drilled Laura enough during lunch periods this year to have the full background story on Doug Locke, Lousy Husband.

"He'll be here," Laura said.

"Are you sure?" Rosa said. "He's not at PTA nights. He's not at your award dinner...now he's not even answering his phone. You even know where he is?"

Laura didn't want to admit that she didn't. She'd stopped asking years ago why he was out at all hours all over the city. She had heard the "pursuit of the story" answer too many times.

Married life hadn't always been so fractured. When they first arrived in the city, it was an adventure. She had Doug to herself, away from the Delta Nu party scene and the online campus lit journal he'd obsessed over senior year. Their poverty created struggle, but they struggled together. They still found laughter and love amidst clipped coupons and a crumbling apartment.

But working at the *Dispatch* changed Doug. The job could take as much time as you gave it, and Doug gave all. She hated the trashy line of work he'd ended up in. She dreaded the nights she spent alone. She loathed the reek of cigarettes that he dragged home on his clothes. But the pay rate had elevated them out of the sections of town her students lived in. She had tried to bring it up a few times, see if he would move to something else, see if he remembered the literary aspirations he had in their previous life. The third fight they had about it was the last. She resigned herself to the fact that reporting sleaze was her husband's job. She didn't mention Doug's career to anyone, like some crazy uncle in the attic.

The last two years, their life together was more like two lives apart. They lived in the same place, slept in the same bed, shared the same bathroom, but now their two orbits just intersected when they used to circle each other. Between Doug being out late and Laura getting up early, there were days when under a dozen words passed between them. To Laura, what hurt the most wasn't the loss of companionship, though that was painful. It was that Doug didn't seem to miss it at all.

In the aftermath of the shooting, this sad state of marital affairs had weighed on her. Every step of the process, some EMT or admitting nurse was asking if her husband was here, like some sort of sick running joke about her marriage. Rosa was right that he had missed many an event these past few years, but he wouldn't, he couldn't miss this. If Doug Locke didn't walk through that door this afternoon, any hope of re-floating her shipwrecked marriage would be dashed.

A nurse knocked on the door. She had a wheeled tray of plastic plates, each filled with equally plastic-looking food.

"Mrs. Locke?" she said. "How about some dinner?"

Laura glanced at the clock. Five forty-two. How long had she been asleep?

"Dinner?" Laura said. "Will I be here that long?"

"Doesn't matter how long you be here," Rosa said. She took up a blocking position between the wheeled tray and Laura's bed. "You aren't eating this stuff." She gave the nurse the same glare that had literally made guilty children wet themselves. The nurse backed out of the room.

"I'll get you some real food," Rosa said. "I know what you like." She strode out the door with such determination a doctor on rounds moved out of her way.

For the first time since Laura arrived, she was alone. With the offshore breeze of others' company gone, memories of her last tragic stay at St. Luke's began to wash ashore. She pushed them back, unable to handle more than what today had already delivered. This was no time to relive that awful loss of the miscarriage.

She stared at the empty doorway and wondered if Doug would walk through it. When, she corrected to herself, not if. She had to believe it could only be when.

Chapter Five

"God damn it!" Doug cursed as a Hummer wedged itself into the tiny gap between his car and the one in front of him.

The thirty miles to St. Luke's was going to take forever. Cars jammed every bridge off Manhattan and the traffic on the Long Island Expressway crawled like a wounded soldier. A detective named Simmons gave Doug the nutshell version of the school shooting by cell phone before Doug had even crossed into Queens. Creeping through traffic, Doug had too much time to worry, too much time to think.

He pounded the steering wheel in frustration, but it wasn't just about the traffic. He had let life get to this point, the point where his wife sat in a hospital bed with gunshot wounds and a Gordian knot of automobiles kept him from her. He created their life plan seven years ago, and his sweet, supportive college girlfriend had gone along with it. A wedding after graduation, and then they'd ditch the Midwest for the Big Apple. He'd use the million stories of the City That Never Sleeps to fuel his breakthrough novel. She would put her Elementary Education degree to work teaching school. Both would achieve their dreams, everyone living happily ever after. Laura went with the plan. She trusted his judgment, believed in his potential and had faith in the future.

But the literary world ignored Doug Locke's talent. After a few months, he'd realized he needed a job to keep them afloat and found one at the *Dispatch*, one with long hours. He'd been doing mundane local stories for a year when he caught wind of a call girl ring servicing the board of directors at a local foundation. He made the front page.

One story led to another and he became the go-to-guy for any sleazy exposé and it became his niche. His pay got much better as he boosted circulation, but it was more than that. There was something a bit alluring about that dark section of society, about dipping into the smarmy side of people's character.

Laura found a job right away, but at a hellhole school. She never complained. She said those were the kids who needed her the most. But why should she have to work in a place with as much security as Riker's Island? He blamed her work stress for her miscarriage two years ago, though Laura refused to link the two.

Now as he sat in the exhaust fumes of the stalled Long Island Expressway, he couldn't believe the situation he was in. It was as if this tragedy had opened the shades and let sunlight fully illuminate the life he had been living. He was away from home all hours of the day and night, tracking down leads. And for what? One more smarmy story about some actor getting drunk at a party. What difference did it make? He'd taken for granted the woman he'd fallen in love with at college, the one who married him and said "Sure, let's give New York a try." Now the job she took to support his abandoned dream almost got her killed. What a mess he had made.

Doug dreaded returning to St. Luke's. The last time he was here, he brought three souls in with him, but left with only one. Laura had miscarried the twins here. The staff treated them both with immense compassion, but nothing could assuage the pain of having the girls they created together ripped from them. Seeing the hospital made all that pain roll back in. He pushed the hurt back, like he had in the silent months after the tragedy.

Back then, he considered his agony unbearable, yet he could only imagine by what factor Laura's was worse. He would hold her when she inexplicably broke out into tears. He wanted to console her, but did not know what to say. She did not talk about their loss, so neither did he. He thought that if they just put it behind them, the emptiness would refill. If he talked to her about the lost twins, he would just remind her of what they were missing. He buried himself in work instead. Later, when time had healed the wounds, they would talk about it. So far, later hadn't come.

His exit was two miles away. Crawling traffic stretched to the horizon. Screw this.

He yanked the wheel right and punched the accelerator. In a cloud of smoked rubber his car leapt to the shoulder. It fishtailed as Doug yanked it back straight and he blasted down to the exit. Accusatory horns honked in his wake.

Several moving violations later, he was at St. Luke's. Inside, the harried receptionist gave him Laura's room number and he dashed through the hallway maze. The tang of antiseptic and the ice-cold temperature reminded Doug of the many things he hated about hospitals. Nurses in blue floral scrubs chatted behind the central nurses' station. Doug stopped at the threshold of room 122.

Laura sat upright in the hospital bed, framed by silver rails on three sides. She wore one of the perpetually uncomfortable aqua hospital gowns. Her two hands rested awkwardly in her lap, two bundles of white bandages. She stared out the window at her brick-wall view, looking at nothing, eyes glazed and vacant.

Doug choked back a sob. This was his life, his love, his existence right here on that bed. The love he felt for her, the love that had somehow been smothered under his indulgent quest for dirt, burst out like spring tulips.

"Babe," he said.

Laura turned, and at the sight of her husband, her thousand-yard stare dissolved into a relieved smile.

"Oh, Doug," she exhaled. "You made it."

Doug sat on the side of her bed. He leaned over and hugged Laura as hard as he dared. The bandaged hands made him think she was fragile. The acrid scent of gunpowder clung to her hair. Guilt dug into him again. His wife, his lover, his college sweetheart, his future. It was as if he hadn't seen her in years, and perhaps he hadn't.

Doug kissed her lips. One of her tears rolled onto his cheek. He sat up at her waist. She laid one hand across his lap. The bandage looked like a big swollen white mitten.

"I'm so happy you are okay," Doug said with a smile of relief. "You look pretty good after your bout with heroism."

"It wasn't heroism," Laura said. "I reacted without thinking. A few sensible seconds and I might have grabbed his hand instead of the gun."

"How bad does it hurt?" Doug asked.

"Not much," she answered. "Painkillers rule."

He kissed her neck.

"You scared the shit out of me," he whispered.

"I thought he was going to kill us all," Laura said. She wrapped her arms around Doug's neck. She shuddered. "I thought I'd never see you again. You looked wonderful coming through that door."

Doug pulled away to look into her sparkling green eyes. "Not as good as you looked lying here alive."

The edges of her lips turned up in a hint of a Laura Locke smile. She touched her gown. "In this old thing?" she drawled. "I just threw it on."

"It's actually the oversized mittens I liked." He pointed at her bandaged hands. "Women should have never stopped wearing gloves."

Such witty repartee had always been their shared defense, comedy relief in those early times of canned tuna meals and intermittent steam heat. It had been awhile since they had batted the language back and forth. She sighed at the familiar tone of their banter, like seeing a friend for the first time in years. That's when Doug knew they would make it through this.

Then Laura's face went dark again, as if a black memory had come back up for air. She stared back out the window. Her arm tightened around Doug.

"It's going to be all right, isn't it?" she whispered.

Doug's love for her filled him until he thought he would burst. This was all his fault, but he could fix it. He caressed her cheek with his fingertips.

"Everything is going to be fine," he said. "I promise."

Rosa Elizondo stood in the hall with a clear plastic dome of fresh shrimp salad in her hands, the reunion's unseen witness. She shook her head and turned to go home.

Chapter Six

Six months later.

"All right, it's just around this bend," Doug said. The suspense had been murderous since they left Knoxville that morning. Finally, the Lockes were moving into their new home.

The process had taken less time than Doug had expected. The NY house sold in twenty-six days for twice what they paid for it. Laura's medical leave covered her through the end of the school year. Doug quit his job. He explained that he was moving, going to write the Great American Novel. There was enough money in the bank to cover them for at least a year. He remembered the financial weight he put on Laura when he last tried to write full time. That wasn't going to happen again.

Laura stared out the Volvo's side window. She wound an empty McDonalds straw wrapper back and forth around her index finger. Doug knew repetitive motion meant pensive emotions.

"You okay, babe?"

"You're sure about this place, Doug? I mean we bought it and we never set foot in it."

"It's been inspected by pros who know more about structural integrity, wiring and plumbing than I ever will. The location is great, the floor plan is perfect. I haven't been so sure about a decision since I married you."

Laura rolled her eyes. "This is no time to start sucking up."

Doug wasn't exaggerating, though. He was certain about this house. Not because the inspectors had certified it, not because the appraisal came in thirty percent over the asking price, not because the local schools had teacher openings they needed to fill. He was certain before all that. The moment he saw the listing online, before he even clicked on the address to see a picture of the property, he knew this was it. It was as if some benevolent force had twisted the internet's currents and eddies to direct him to this one perfect house. No, strike that. It was more like something pulled him to the listing. He had to have this place.

The house came into full view as Doug turned into the driveway. The gate under the *Galaxy Farm* sign was wide open. The imposing white house looked radiant against the blue sky. Its silver roof glittered in the sun. The lawn was lush with the unique green of Kentucky Bluegrass. At the top of the driveway, Dale Mabry sat on the open tailgate of his pickup truck. He waved and flashed an enormous "welcome home" grin.

Laura took a look at the resplendent castle on the hill.

"Oh my God. Doug, its more beautiful than the pictures, isn't it?"

Doug could barely utter "Uh-huh." He knew he was home.

"I'm calling dibs on that second-story turret," Laura said. "I'm writing lesson plans and grading papers looking out that window."

Doug was so happy Laura had continued to embrace teaching, he'd agree to anything she asked. After the terror in the classroom on Long Island, he had feared she would shrink away from the profession. No way. Laura had faxed resumes and completed phone interviews within a week of closing on the new home. If owning the second-floor turret kept that train rolling, it was hers.

Doug pulled up next to Dale. The realtor hopped off the tailgate and spun a ring of house keys on his finger like a Wild West gunman would a Colt .45. Doug got out of the car while Laura looked over at the just-visible barn.

"Welcome to Moultrie, Homeowner!" Dale boomed. "I'm Dale Mabry." He slapped the keys into Doug's outstretched hand then shook with them sandwiched between their palms. Doug had an impression that Dale was in a hurry to go.

"Doug Locke," Doug said. Laura joined them. "This is my wife, Laura."

"Pleasure, Ms. Locke," Dale said. "Gotta say, ain't never sold a house to someone I never met. This whole proxies and power of attorney thing was something else. But there's a first time for everything. Let me give you folks the tour."

They entered into the main living room. A huge, custom-built stone fireplace filled one wall. Polished light oak floors shined like mirrors. An ornate chandelier hung in the center. The room was big, but without furnishings or decorations, it looked immense. Laura gave an audible gasp.

"Galaxy Farm was designed to entertain," Dale said. "Robert Hutchington built it with the profits from his candy empire. That's how he named the place."

"Like Galaxy Bar?" Laura said. "That chocolate, pecan and coconut thing I ate as a kid?"

"Pree-cisely," Dale said. "Richest folks in the county back then."

Laura gave Doug a shove. "You didn't mention that."

"I didn't know it," Doug said. He realized how few his questions were about the place and how he'd brushed aside so many of Laura's when she asked.

"The Hutchingtons used this room for receptions or for parlor games with guests after dinner," Dale continued, pressing on with the tour. "All real high society for the 1920s. There's a stack of seasoned firewood out back for you to light up that fireplace if you want."

Dale showed them through the dining room, the master bedroom and then into a smaller first-floor room. A bay window with a window seat looked out over the expansive down-sloping backyard and across a pond. Even empty, the sunny room radiated positive energy.

"This room was the nursery when the Hutchingtons lived here," Dale said. "Still perfect for that if ya'll get the itch for children."

Doug shot Laura a quick glance to gauge her reaction, afraid Dale ripped open an emotional wound. She didn't flinch.

"Now from here you can see your property line," Dale said. He pointed out the window as he spoke. "The pond and the land on the other side are yours, right up to that cut in the ridge." The dark pond was easily a hundred yards across. Between the house and the pond stood a large natural gas tank. The ground underneath was charred and a large blackened stump nearby was cut down to the ground. "Big thunderstorm came though a month ago. Lightning hit an old oak over the natural gas tank. Tank's ground was all wrong and the thing blew a hole in the dirt a few feet deep. But Moultrie Savings and Loan trucked in some earth and fixed it up nice. That tank is brand new, double grounded and will last fifty years."

"And lightning never strikes the same place twice," Laura said.

"Especially not with that oak cut down," Dale said. "I wouldn't give it a worry. Now from the other side of the pond, just follow the tree line south to where it cuts back west and that is all yours back to the highway." The trees ran about three quarters of the way up a hill, leaving the forested top to a neighbor. The fifteen acres were nearly all pasture and dwarfed their postage stamp lot in New York. "Buddy Tucker lives down the road and he's been keeping the fields mowed for the bank while the place was up for sale. Reckon he'll keep it up for you for a fair price. You don't want to let those locust trees run wild. 'Course nothing keeps you from running a few head of cattle out there to keep things trimmed."

"I think I do," Laura said.

"Pay for themselves in steak and burgers," Dale offered.

"Vegetarian," Doug said, pointing a thumb at his wife. "Fish only. You'd best let this idea go."

Dale led the three past the renovated kitchen, which glimmered with stainless steel and green LED lights. The bank had revamped the shambles of a kitchen to pass code and make the sale enticing. The three of them mounted the L-shaped stairs that ran along the far wall.

"Four bedrooms upstairs," Dale said at the top of the stairway. "Three with a full bath." He opened the door to the turreted room that looked out over the front lawn. "This room's a real peach."

The turret filled one corner and lit the rest of the room in blazing daylight. The walls were finished in a light pine. One was all bookcase. Two doors graced the far wall.

Smiling like a kid at Christmas, Laura strode into the room alone, ready to claim the space for Queen and country. Three steps in, she froze. She turned back to face Doug. The smile was gone. In the bright room she looked pale.

"Doug," she said. "This room is yours."

"But you had a plan," Doug said. "Red pens grading tests and all that."

"No," she said. She stepped out of the room faster than she entered. "You are making the career change. You'll be writing here at the house. You need the most inspirational setting. That room is your study."

Doug didn't want Laura's burst of altruism to sabotage her enthusiastic return to work. "No, babe. You called it."

"It's yours," she said, with uncommon finality. "I insist."

Doug stepped past her into the room. His guilt at taking the room evaporated, replaced by a sense of completeness, of belonging. It was the same feeling that filled him when he first saw the ad for the house, with twice the intensity. He was glad to have this room. Standing in it now, he realized that if Laura hadn't offered it, he might have demanded it anyway. He was going to do great work in this room. He could feel it.

Doug walked to the first door in the wall and opened it to find a roomy closet, paneled in fragrant cedar. He tried the door next to it. It was locked. The old tarnished brass handle looked like one of the originals from the house, unlike the modern ones everywhere else. There was an antique keyhole below the knob.

"That's attic access," Dale explained. "We didn't even know it was there 'til we pulled the bookcase away from the front of it. The bookcase was nailed to the wall. The key to the door came up missing after the inspection. I'll give you our locksmith Jake's number and his service is on the house. Sorry."

It was agreed that they would sleep in the ground-floor master bedroom. The former nursery downstairs would be Laura's workspace. Dale walked them back to the front door.

"When do the movers arrive?" Dale asked. As if on cue, a long truck with *Empire Moving* painted on the side began crunching up the driveway. Laura's black Honda Civic was on a trailer behind it.

"Looks like now," Laura said.

Dale caught sight of the truck and looked relieved. "Well, I'll be out of your hair then. Y'all need anything, you just give me a ring, hear?" Without so much as a wave, Dale was off the porch and in his truck, as if the movers' arrival had freed him of any further obligation.

"That's a little abrupt," Laura observed, watching Dale's F-150 leave twin trails of dust down the driveway. "People leave burning houses slower than that."

Doug didn't hear her. He had the turret room on his mind; planning where to put his desk, his books, his printer. A burly, balding man in gray coveralls approached the porch from the truck.

"I hope youse guys are the Lockes," he said, thick with the Brooklynese. "'Cause if you ain't, I'm too lost to ever find 'em."

Chapter Seven

The clock struck two a.m.. Doug stood in the kitchen in his shorts and t-shirt, a glass of water in his hand. He hadn't tasted sweeter water than the well water that supplied his new home. He'd been up for an hour, inexplicably awakened at the stroke of one.

He shouldn't have been awake. He was still exhausted from eight hours of unpacking. Then he and Laura had made love that night with newlywed passion. Doug's obsession with work the last few years had sapped his fervor for all life's pleasures, even those in the bedroom. But the anticipation of the move had sparked the old ardor the last few weeks. Doug should have been mentally, emotionally and physically spent. Yet here he was, wide awake in the wee hours.

His new study sang some subconscious siren's song. It took all his self-control to pass the stairway. But there was no way he was risking waking Laura. She had an interview in seven hours at Moultrie Elementary. He walked into the old nursery. The full moon lit the backyard. Its glow sparkled off the pond beyond. Fireflies danced above the grass like neon pixies. A lone coyote howled in the distance and then the other members of its pack joined in a mournful chorus.

Something stirred by the pond. His first instinct was that the coyotes had loped down for a drink, but it was too tall. Backlit by the moon's reflection in the pond, the shape was unmistakable. A man. Tall and thin, he paced the south edge of the pond, back and forth across the fresh red clay around the propane tank. He glided along the edge of the water, head turning to scan the shore in all directions. At intervals he probed the ground with a long rod.

The figure first startled then angered Doug. Who the hell was in his backyard at two a.m.? He sure didn't move out into the boondocks to have his privacy violated. He could have stayed in New York for that.

Dormant primal programming kicked in. Another dog was on his turf. He slipped on his shoes at the back door, flipped on the backyard light and rushed out into the night.

"Hey, what are you doing down there?" he yelled.

The figure paused and looked up at Doug. Even in the far reaches of the porch light, the figure's eyes flashed like a wild animal. Long, greasy hair framed his narrow, pale face. The man's dead, unresponsive stare frightened Doug. Doug realized he was unarmed and unprotected with no clue who he was about to confront. The trespasser could have a knife. Hell, this was 2nd Amendment country. He was likely to have a gun. And that wasted expression on his face didn't paint him as the cool deliberate reasonable type.

The intruder broke left and sprinted. He sailed across the field. His long legs traversed the land with ease. He moved as if he had every dip and stone memorized. In seconds, the darkness swallowed him.

Doug walked at the edge of the pond. Rough-soled boot prints marked the shore, trampled on each other as if a stampede of construction workers had passed through. Small bore holes opened at irregular intervals where the man had probed the ground with the rod, looking for some buried secret.

By now, the intruder would be into the west tree line and long gone. Doug sure as hell wasn't going to follow him. He'd call the sheriff, but what good would that do, with the perpetrator long gone and the only descriptive details Doug had made the interloper sound more supernatural than substantial.

He'd call the sheriff tomorrow, in the daylight.

Laura woke up weeping.

The dream had been beautiful. She had been sitting behind the new house on a gorgeous spring day. A breeze sweet as honey flitted through the trees. Sunlight shimmered on the pond.

Angelic voices twittered from the side of the house. Two twin girls raced past Laura to the pond. Their long blonde hair trailed behind them, pennants of youth. They wore matching white dresses that swirled just below their knees as they ran. They could not have been more than six, all radiant smiles and sparkling blue eyes. Their bare feet hit the rich grass. Soft footfalls blended with their high laughter.

"Mother, come down to the pond!" one called. Laura knew the girl's name was Constance.

"Yes, Mother," called the other, Elizabeth. "We're skipping stones all the way across."

Laura knew their names and knew they were hers, the two girls she lost in St. Luke's ER. Healthy, happy, beautiful. Everything she'd dreamed of from the moment Dr. Cavanaugh looked at her sonogram and said, "You're having twins."

The girls flashed by and Laura tried to give chase. But she could only move in slow motion. The air felt like quicksand around her and the more she tried to force her way through, the harder it resisted. She tried to cry out after her daughters, but her voice was gone, swallowed by the stifling air. Frustration filled her as she watched her children skip down to the pond.

"Mother," Constance called. "Hurry or you'll miss all the fun."

Laura felt that void in her heart she vainly prayed would fade away, that ruptured gap where a child's death permanently robs a mother of ever being whole. As she had a hundred times over the past few years, Laura awakened crying.

How odd to have images of the house fill her dreams from the first night. There was something else unique about the dream; its digital-signal clarity. Every blade of grass was distinct, every ripple in the porch's wood grain sharp. Most striking were the girls. So much older than the other dreams and so detailed. Even now she could count the teeth in their smiles as they headed down to the pond. Such clarity only made the pain of the loss more intense.

She wiped away her tears. She hadn't cried about her lost girls in so long. So much still felt unresolved, a strong current ran under the emotional ice she had frozen over it.

She wanted from that first day to share what she endured with Doug, but he seemed resolute in some plan to just pretend that nothing ever happened. He offered quick platitudes and a change of subject when she tried, so she quickly gave up. She went to see a therapist at his suggestion, which she assumed was his way of passing the buck.

To break this spell of sadness that she awoke to, she focused on the positives as her therapist recommended. She thought about how amazing the last few months had been. As soon as Doug made the decision to quit his job, it was as if a magic wand sprinkled them with fairy dust. The rush, the energy, the lightness of their first year of marriage was back. Doug had become Doug again, not Sleazy Reporter Douglas Locke, not Distant Almost-Dad Doug. They smiled together again, kidded each other and made love like they had in college. She had no doubt that tonic sped her recovery from the gunshot wound. Her hands had healed in record time. Even the initial fears she had about being at school, or even being in public, faded quickly. Without his positive energy, she feared she would have traveled a long and dark path.

A wave of worry washed over her bright remembrances. The turret room. So beautiful on the outside, but inside... As soon as she crossed the threshold, she felt the blood drain from her extremities. Her body temperature dropped so rapidly, she felt chills. There was something unnerving about that room, something fundamentally wrong. She couldn't get out of the place fast enough.

Thank God Doug liked it. She dreaded casting a pall over their adventure by saying that a room in the new house gave her the creeps. But Doug took the room without reservation. She was sure once he made it his own, whatever bad vibe she picked up would dissipate. Too much was going too well to risk bringing up nonsense feelings.

It was two thirty a.m.. She needed to sleep. She had an interview in the morning she needed to ace. She rolled over to wrap herself around her warm husband and drift back off. She pulled herself along the king-size mattress until her hand reached the far side. Doug was gone.

Doug never got up in the middle of the night. He once slept through a house fire across the street. Laura sat straight up.

"Doug!"

"Whoa," he said, pushing open the bedroom door. "I'm right here. No need to yell."

"Where were you? I woke up and you were gone."

"Just getting some water. I woke up parched."

"Well, get back in here," Laura said. She pulled back the covers on his side of the bed. "Leaving me alone in a new house. Really."

Doug slid back in. Laura wrapped herself around him and shivered.

"You are freezing!" she cried. "Did you drink that water standing in front of an open refrigerator?"

"Just chilly, I guess," Doug said. "Warm me up like the wonderful wife you are."

Laura spooned close behind him and wrapped one leg over his. She kissed the back of his neck.

"Like that?" she said.

Doug pulled her arm up to his chest. "Just like that," he said.

She fell asleep pondering interview questions. He lay awake worried about the man by the pond.

Chapter Eight

The next morning, the sheriff's office was a surprise. It was on the south side of town, a few blocks from the quaint town square. Doug's Mayberry-inspired vision of small town law enforcement didn't fit at all. The building couldn't have been more than five years old. A fleet of new black-and-white Dodge Chargers further attested to the county's commitment to the rule of law.

Inside, a few uncomfortable chairs lined the wall of the small lobby. One door with a keypad lock led to the rest of the offices. Behind a glass window sat a matronly woman in a blue uniform shirt. The patch on her shoulder had *Citizen's Auxiliary* stitched over the county crest. The silver tag over her left pocket read *Gladys W...* The glass window had a slot at the bottom for passing documents and a circular speaker mounted in the center. She flamboyantly pushed the intercom button and shoved her face against a microphone on a stalk.

"May I help you?" she asked. Her voice echoed like The Great And Powerful Oz in the small room. The speaker clicked off like a rifle shot.

"I'm Doug Locke. I'd like to speak with the sheriff if he has a minute."

She looked Doug over like he was from Mars, a reaction to newcomers that Doug would find universal in Moultrie.

"It's about some trespassing on my property," Doug volunteered.

"You can't shoot 'em," Gladys said.

"Excuse me?"

"You can't shoot 'em. Lots of you city folks move out here and think you can shoot 'em. But you can't. We're just as civilized as anyone else."

"I didn't really plan on—"

"Well, no one does," Gladys cut in. "It's always just self-defense. Sheriff'll tell you the same thing." She pointed at the door to the parking lot. "Ask him yourself."

Sheriff Rick Mears met none of Doug's expectations. Doug had imagined at best TV's Andy Taylor, at worst *Smokey and the Bandit's* Buford T. Justice. Instead Sheriff Mears looked like a USMC recruiting poster, down to the broad shoulders and blond crew cut. He had ten years on Doug but it was hard to tell.

"Sheriff," Gladys announced through the speaker. "Mr. Locke here needs a word with you about shooting trespassers."

Sheriff Mears gave Doug a quick examination. Doug's face went beet red.

"I don't want to shoot anyone," Doug said. He extended his hand. "Doug Locke. My wife and I just moved into the old Galaxy Farm."

Gladys stifled a gasp from behind the window. Sheriff Mears gave Doug's hand an iron-gripped shake.

"Oh, the Hutchington place," the sheriff said. The phone company rep had referred to his house that way as well. He wondered how many generations of his family would have to live in it before someone referred to it as the Locke place. "So you don't have a trespassing problem?"

"No, I do," Doug said, irked that Gladys had managed to sow confusion and suspicion in a matter of seconds. "There was something strange there last night I thought you could help us with. There was someone out by the pond in the middle of the night."

The sheriff's face pinched a bit with suspicion. He took a subconscious half step back. "Are you sure?"

"Of course I am," Doug said. "Some young guy. Tall. Thin. Walking the pond probing the ground with some sort of stick. He left footprints everywhere."

The sheriff's face relaxed. "Oh, okay. Did you see his face?"

"Long, pale, wasted. White guy."

The sheriff nodded. "I've got an idea. Probably Vernon Pugh."

Doug gave him a blank look.

"Vernon Pugh," the sheriff repeated. "He was the last tenant at your address."

"I wouldn't know," Doug said. "I bought the property from the bank. Who is this guy?"

"It's a long story, but you'll find every place around here has one. Galaxy Farm was built by the Hutchingtons in the 1920s. Vernon Pugh was the last family member to live there. When his father Alexander died, the bank ended up administering the estate and selling the property. Taxes and a note came due, and Vern couldn't pay."

"So the bank tossed him off the property."

"They bought Vernon off with an acre of land south of yours and Vernon put a trailer on it," the sheriff said. "Vernon wasn't happy about it but he never turned violent because I didn't get called in. They convinced him he wasn't going to win anything suing, especially since no lawyer in town would take his case."

"Why not?"

"He's a little strange," the sheriff said. "But no history of violence."

Doug did not take that statement as a ringing endorsement.

"We busted him a few times for personal possession, DUI. Nothing to warrant jail time. But he's a loner type. Secretive. I'm certain he isn't happy with you in the house he considers his birthright. He probably thought he had a right to trespass."

"But he doesn't," Doug said. "I don't want him lurking around there. If Laura saw him out there, it would scare her to death."

43

"I'll drop by his trailer," Sheriff Mears said. "Pay the boy a little visit and make sure he understands where things sit. I don't think he'll be any trouble after that."

"Thanks, Sheriff."

"And just to be on the safe side," the sheriff added. "Post some *No Trespassing* signs at your property line. Keeps you covered and lets the neighbors who hunt know that you don't want them poaching your deer this fall."

Doug had never thought of the wildlife on his land as being his property. The idea made him smile. "I'll put them up today, Sheriff." He added the signs to the mental list of items he needed to pick up in town.

Sheriff Mears punched a code into the keypad and entered the office area. Doug turned to go.

"That's not the whole story," Gladys whispered. She was hunkered down over her desk with her mouth near the window's mail slot.

"What do you mean?" Doug asked.

"Vernon wasn't Alexander Hutchington's full son," she said. "Dirty old man was over sixty-five when his mistress gave birth. And a slutty thing she was, but you didn't hear it from me."

"My lips are sealed," Doug promised. The sarcasm sailed over Gladys's head.

"Worse, Vern was born with no hands," Gladys said.

"None at all?"

"Well, just nubs for fingers," Gladys said. "Boy could barely hold a pencil in school. Then his mother died when he was twelve and he was on his own. Of course wolves could do a better job that his mother anyhow. But Alexander's wife, a good church-going woman, mind you, had just passed, so Alexander took him in, acknowledging the boy without actually doing it, you see?"

Doug realized that Gladys's volunteerism with the police department was more to keep a thumb on the gossip pulse than to serve and protect. "So, Vern should have owned the house," Doug said.

"Alexander left Vern the house," Gladys said. "But he willed everything else to an animal rights group up in Nashville. Vern didn't have no money, so he couldn't pay even the small note the bank held against it. Taxes came due and Vern went belly-up. The bank tossed him out."

A neighbor with a serious grudge, Doug thought. Perfect. Gladys's idea about shooting him might have more merit than he first thought.

"I'll keep an eye out," Doug said.

"You do that," Gladys said. "Boy's record back here is thick, but you didn't hear that from me."

"Of course," Doug said. He backed out the front door with a little wave.

He fired up the Volvo and started to worry. To Laura, the vengeful criminal neighbor would be as welcome as a plague of locusts. If Gladys had been so quick to share the story with him, someone else in the Moultrie gossip net would be sure to give the news to Laura. But she didn't know about Vern's little midnight foray to the pond, so as far as she knew, he didn't even exist. Doug decided he could hold Vern's story back from her for now. No need to give her something else to worry about.

Damn Vernon Pugh, Sheriff Mears thought.

He sat at his desk, cowboy boots resting on the edge as he leaned back in his chair. The walls of his office were covered with grip-and-grin pictures with every county official past and present from his last six years as sheriff. He'd put away a lot of rotten apples in that time, but Pugh hadn't been one of them.

Mears wished he had been, but the boy didn't break the right laws. Mears would have been happier with him off the street, but not just because he was the epitome of white trailer trash. The county was full of that. He wanted him put away because he gave Mears the creeps, a crawling discomfort that wrapped around his spine and squeezed. He hadn't gotten that bad a case of the willies since he'd come across that Serbian fortuneteller in Kosovo during his active duty days.

Mears stood and grabbed his hat off the hat rack. Not the usual baseball cap emblazoned with the department logo, but the heavy, hot, peaked cap that exuded authority. It'd bring a little psychological edge to his meeting with Mr. Pugh. Anything to help him make his point and get away from that sewer of a trailer Vernon called home.

Chapter Nine

Laura's heart beat so loudly she was sure the students passing her on the way into school were going to stare and whisper. Her future was on the line at this interview. In this rural county, Moultrie Elementary was her best bet for employment anywhere near their home. The pressure squeezed her like a corset. She prayed she wouldn't start sweating in her best navy suit.

Moultrie Elementary was beautiful. The façade was all chiseled tan block granite with tall narrow windows and the ten-foot ceilings favored in the late '40s. The school, including the playground and parking lot, took up most of a town block. Laura stood outside the front doors and drew in a deep strengthening breath before entering. A few late kids dashed past her and inside. She clutched her portfolio under her arm and followed them in.

She unshouldered her purse automatically and realized she didn't have to. She wasn't in New York anymore. No metal detectors, no security search. She smiled like a miner seeing the sun again. Finally, a school not gripped with the endemic fear of violence. What a joy.

The principal's office was down the polished hallway to the left. Posters renouncing drugs and praising performance covered the walls. Laura swung her portfolio up against her chest and gripped it with both hands. She accidentally thumbed the catch and its contents slid to the floor like a white waterfall.

"Oh, no!" Her teaching life lay on the floor like a tossed deck of cards. If kids came barreling out of a classroom now, her work would be destroyed. She dropped to her knees and began shuffling papers together.

A second set of hands pitched in. The man crouched beside her was in his mid-fifties with wire-rimmed glasses and a full head of silver hair. His broad face carried a matching wide smile. He wore a blue corduroy jacket but his white shirt was open at the collar. He picked up one of her pictures of her old classroom.

"Looks like you need a hand," he said. "Is this your classroom in the picture?"

"Yes," Laura said. She barely looked up in her scramble to reorganize her papers. "That was my classroom outside New York City."

"New York?" he said. "We hear that those schools are close to prisons. This looks downright cheery." He pointed to the ceiling tiles that were painted in alternating primary colors. "Did you paint these?"

"Yes. I spent a Saturday with a few cans of spray paint the week before school started. I wanted the children to know right away that their classroom was a special place, different from all the others."

"I'm Ken," the gentleman said. He scooped a half-dozen papers from the floor.

"I'm Laura. Nice to meet you."

"I assume you are here for an interview," Ken said. "Lets get this stuff straight before you go in."

They laid all her papers out on a narrow table outside the principal's office. Laura quickly sorted the pages into stacks of test examples, classroom setup and student evaluations. The student evaluations were closest to Ken.

"These are pretty detailed," Ken said, looking one over. "Much more than the ones I need to fill out. I'll give the big city credit on that one."

"No, those are mine," Laura said. "I used those in addition to the standard forms. I had some serious 'at risk' kids and I wanted to make sure that their parents knew what they needed to succeed."

She collated her stacks and slipped then into her portfolio. "Okay. I'm ready. Any tips on talking to Principal Wheedle?"

"Nope," Ken said. "I've known him all his life and he's a decent man. Let me walk you in and introduce you."

Before she could decline the offer, they were past the receptionist in the outer office and through an open door into the principal's office. An imposing mahogany desk sat in the center. Laura caught her breath when she saw the name plate on it.

Principal Kenneth Weedle

"Oh my God," she whispered.

Ken laughed. "Don't tense up now, Ms. Locke. The interview was going so well." He sat down at his desk. "Let's continue by telling me about that boy's evaluation I saw. Kendrick? Tell me how you diagnosed his dyslexia."

Thirty minutes later, Laura had a job with the best principal she had ever met.

Chapter Ten

Flies buzzed in the trailer's stale air like a lazy droning chorus. The weak daylight that passed through the small dirty windows gave the interior a sense of permanent dusk. Hardened shriveled remnants of past meals clung to the dishes piled on the kitchen countertop. The hollow plop of the dripping faucet in the sink marked time.

Vernon Pugh sat on a sagging frayed couch. He stared through rips in the ragged tan curtains. He could see a sliver of Galaxy Farm through the trees. It was the only house that ever felt like home. The sight of the place used to fill him with joy, but now... He ground his teeth in seething anger. A dagger of pain lanced his jaw. A lifetime of bottled rage had ground his rear molars down to the nerves, yet he could not break the habit. But pain makes you learn, pain makes you stronger. So Mama had said between educating lashes with the big studded belt.

Long greasy hair framed his drawn pallid face. His pale blue eyes looked like life had washed the vibrancy from them. The dirt on his jeans gave them a hard, dark sheen. He wore a Joe Camel promotional t shirt. Time had cracked and faded Joe unmercifully and the phrase *Lasting Flavor* stenciled below him had been reduced to *sting Flav* through attrition. Herpes scabs lined his upper lip.

Tires crunched through the gravel outside. Vern went to the window. He brushed the curtain aside. He could barely grip the cloth. His shortened fingers lacked the last knuckle and had just an irregular spot of a fingernail at each tip. They all bent in, as if half grasping some phantom object. Doctors had blamed his mother's drug use. Momma had said it was God's will.

Outside, the menacing nose of one of the sheriff's Chargers pulled into view.

"Son of a bitch," Vernon cursed. The damn law had it out for him his whole life. Always hauling his mother off on those bullshit prostitution charges, charges usually dropped after a visit to the cruiser's back seat. Busting him for pot while the school jocks did hard expensive stuff. Even after he had inherited Galaxy Farm, they wouldn't leave him alone, hounding him about taxes and interest he knew he didn't owe. Hell, the tax assessor was cousin to Sheriff Mears. They exiled him to this acre of land and this ratty trailer. What more could they want?

The front door rattled in its frame as the sheriff pounded on it three times. "Vernon Pugh? It's Sheriff Mears. Open up."

Shit on fire, the sheriff himself, Vernon thought. He swung the front door open with a creak. Several flies took the chance to escape this circle of hell and buzzed past to freedom. Mears screwed up his face at the rank smell that rolled out of the trailer. Vernon smiled with his yellowed teeth.

"C'mon in, Sheriff."

"No, you just come out here," the sheriff answered. "That'll be fine." Vernon stepped to the doorway and leaned against the jamb. A few locks of stringy hair fell across one eye.

The sheriff gave a quick glance at Vern's twisted hands then up to his face, like everyone did. Vern found another reason to hate the man.

"You been down to the farm last night, Vernon?" the sheriff asked.

That new son of a bitch called the cops, Vernon thought.

"Just looking for some personal property I left there," Vernon said. "Had to leave in such a rush."

"Nothing down there belongs to you, Vernon," the sheriff said. Vernon knew that was true. He'd moved in with nothing at age twelve and the lawyers made sure that was exactly what he left with at eviction.

"I don't want to have to come up here again," the sheriff said. "It's a gift you got this house and land and you need to stay in it."

The idea of keeping a fraction of the land he rightfully owned brought Vernon back to a boil.

"I already warned you once," the sheriff continued, "after you pulled that bloody rabbit shit on Dale Mabry. I could have run you in for that."

"I told you that wasn't me," Vern snapped.

"Now listen up," Sheriff Mears said, his frustration uncontrolled. "I don't want to hear any of your damn ghost stories. I'm telling you to stick to your property and stay away from the Lockes down there. You understand?"

"I hear you, Sheriff," Vernon said in an unconvincing monotone. The unsettling yellowed smile reappeared.

The sheriff looked like he had more to say but he turned and retreated to his cruiser. Vernon stood in the doorway and watched the car back down his driveway. He looked down at the estate stolen from him. He'd get it back. Uncle Mabron's spirit wouldn't have it any other way.

Chapter Eleven

Laura burst in through the front door of her house, smile radiant as a sunrise.

"Doug! Doug!" she cried.

"Right here, babe," Doug said, walking in from the nursery. He had a pile of orange *No Trespassing* signs in his hand.

"You, sir," Laura announced, "are looking at the newest teacher at Moultrie Elementary."

Doug nearly dropped the signs. "You got hired?"

"Well, not right now," Laura said. She looked at her shoes in false sadness, and then broke into a smile. "I don't start until tomorrow!"

Doug gave Laura a bear hug. "You blew them away, didn't you?"

"I showed the principal my portfolio and it knocked him dead," she said. "I am a long-term substitute for a third grade teacher with a broken leg." She squeezed Doug's arm in excitement. "Third grade! My favorite. Can you believe it?"

Doug could believe it. It was their first full day and this whole move smelled like roses at every turn.

"I've got so much to do," Laura said. "All my teaching supplies are packed in boxes somewhere. I have to review the lesson plans the teacher left and start freshening them up. I've got to figure out what to wear..."

Laura's sentences ran into each other like a stampede of buffalo. Doug knew he'd be trampled if he tried to redirect that energy. But there was no need to. Having Laura back embracing the work she loved made him happy.

"Go make it happen," Doug said, but Laura was already entering the old nursery, lost in future plans.

The division of household responsibilities had been decided long before the move. Doug, working at home on his own schedule, would be the house husband as soon as Laura found work. Nevertheless, dinner prep that night was a collaborative, though far from colossal effort. Doug opened a bag of salad. Laura pushed the buttons on the microwave. Each had too much to do to spend time cooking.

"You've outdone yourself on the salad," Laura said between mouthfuls at the table.

"After hand-picking the lettuce, my back was pretty sore," Doug said. "But I knew you'd appreciate it. And your lasagna? *Molto buono!*"

"An old family recipe," Laura said. "Passed down from..." she squinted at the open container on the kitchen counter, "...Grandma Michelina. Cultured the cheese myself, but anything for you, love."

"We have had a great start here," Doug said. He raised a glass of water. "To the second phase of married life."

Laura raised her glass and they both took a drink. Laura's face twisted up.

"This stuff has got to go."

"What do you mean?" Doug said.

"This water is rank. Can't you smell it?

Doug sniffed the glass and shrugged.

"Please!" Laura said. "The sulfur! I can't believe you don't smell it. It nearly gagged me in the shower this morning."

"Really?" Doug thought their well water was the nectar of the gods.

"Oh, yes. And it is hard as a rock," Laura said. She dipped two fingers in her glass and rubbed them together. "It's slick as glycerin. I just don't feel clean."

Doug hadn't noticed any of these supposed shortcomings.

"If you say so," he said. "I'm not sure what to do about it."

"Home treatment systems," she said. "I saw the place in town that sells them. I'm guessing we're not the only ones tapped into this unholy aquifer."

Doug gave his glass of water another inspection as if suddenly he'd detect its hidden flaws. "I don't know. If you really think..."

"Great," Laura cut in. "I'll take care of it on the way home tomorrow. This water needs to stop stinking before I wash my first load of clothes. The kids will snicker one long 'rotten egg' joke if I smell like sulfur."

Laura dropped her empty plates in the sink and then hugged Doug from behind his chair. She kissed his cheek. "Got work to do for tomorrow. Did I mention I got a teaching position?"

"No, but it was on Fox News," Doug said. "They broke in with a special bulletin."

Laura gave his ear a playful, disciplinary yank and she left for her study. Doug wasn't going to complain. He was happy she was eager to work. But he also wanted some time to himself. His fingertips itched to start crafting the written word.

The turret room was ready. While dishes, towels and other necessities were still entombed in boxes in the living room, he'd spent this afternoon unpacking what he needed for writing. His laptop and printer were set up on his desk and his reference library filled the bookshelves. The shelf closest to the desk held books he'd long forgotten. A dictionary of synonyms, *Style and Substance*, his favorite writing text from college and all of Strunk and White's works. At graduation he saw these old friends guiding him through a literary career. They'd gotten lost in the maze of writing about graft and hookers. But now they were rediscovered and ready to help Doug fulfill his destiny. Better late than never.

Doug took a seat at the desk and flipped open his laptop. He called up the pristine white space of a blank Microsoft Word document. The cursor blinked at him like the staging lights at a drag race. He took a deep breath and stared at the keyboard.

Nothing. No inspiration. No hook. The cursor mocked him from the empty expanse. Doug had been sure his muse was in this room. He'd felt it. This place was going to be the threshold to his success. Where did it go?

He snapped the laptop shut and pulled a legal pad from a desk drawer. He picked up a pen, one of the fine-point rollers he loved the feel of. This was what he needed. The old-school approach. Ink on paper. Just like college, when he'd write on anything available when inspiration hit. He once outlined a great short story on toilet paper in the john.

Still, no ideas surfaced. He though about conflicts, he trotted out themes. He started filling the page with a stream of consciousness collection of ideas; characters, places, periods of history. Two pages in to he knew it was all crap. He tore the page from the pad, crumpled it into a ball and swatted it across the room.

What happened to all the ideas he used to have? Before he started shoveling mud for the *Dispatch*, he had so many ideas each day he used to carry a note pad to scribble them down on the fly. Had that part of his brain solidified into a block of Jell-O?

What if it had? What if he was out of inspiration? It would be one long lifetime sitting here every day staring at blank reams of paper. He'd bet it all on his belief that he could generate a blockbuster novel. If his creative well was dry...

He dropped the pad and pen on the desk. He went to the bookcase and picked a random volume. *Great Expectations*. He plopped back down at his desk. He remembered how this book had entranced him in junior high, made him want to read more than his English teacher had assigned. The more he read, the more he thought he could write. He'd see if the story of Pip would spark that fire again. He opened to page one.

My father's family name being Pirrip, and my Christian name Philip, my infant tongue could make of both names nothing longer or more explicit than Pip. So, I called myself Pip, and came to be called Pip.

Chapter Twelve

Downstairs, Laura sat on the floor, her legs folded to her side. Boxes of half-packed school supplies lined the walls. A sheaf of lesson plans sat in front of her, two different open text books bracketed each side. She wielded a blue felt-tip marker like a surgeon, lining through whole sections of the lesson plans, annotating others. She sang along softly with Sting as he crooned from the clock radio on the dresser. The local FM station sounded as if it stopped buying music sometime in the '80s.

As Laura crossed out a particularly redundant class exercise, she felt a presence in the room. She turned, expecting to see Doug in the doorway with that you-are-so-cute-when-you're-a-teacher look on his face. But the door was closed, just as she left it. The temperature in the room dropped suddenly as if an air conditioner kicked on. Bewildered, she turned back to her stack of lesson plans.

The stack was upside down. The two textbooks were closed.

Goose bumps rippled up her bare legs. Her faithful Student Sixth Sense sounded an alarm. She scrambled backward in a panicked crabwalk until she crushed a moving box against the wall. Her pulse thudded a salsa beat in her head. She grasped in vain for a plausible explanation.

The song on the radio faded to static, followed by snippets of words and music, as if someone were thumbing the tuning dial. But the red tuning needle didn't move an inch. Then, like the whisper of rustling leaves, came a sound unmistakable to a seasoned teacher; the twittering laughter of two little girls. The laughter's volume oscillated as if the girls were flying back and forth between her and some distant place.

Laura leapt to her feet and flung the door open. She screamed, "Doug!" and lunged toward the stairs. On the second floor, she could see Doug at his desk through the turret room doorway, book open in his lap, no reaction to her cry. Halfway up the steps, the turret room door slammed shut with the crack of a thunderbolt. She jumped the last three steps to the top. Laura pounded on the door and yanked at the frozen handle.

"Doug!"

Doug opened the door, bemused. "What do you need?"

"In my room," she panted. "Just now. Something's in there."

She grabbed Doug's hand and pulled him down the stairs. At the doorway, she stopped dead in her tracks. The textbooks were open, the lesson plans in a neat pile, blue pen on top. Billy Joel sang a capella on the radio, static free.

"It didn't look like this," she said. "I felt something, or someone, in the room. I thought it was you, but... Then all the lesson plans flipped around and the textbooks closed. The radio went bonkers. There were voices and I ran."

Doug took a scrutinizing walk around the room. "You're sure about that?"

Fire flashed in Laura's eyes. Doug winced at the stupidity of his statement.

"No," she said. "I saw it happen I a Wes Craven flick and just wanted to share. Of course I'm sure."

"Okay," Doug said. "There must be an explanation. This house is almost a hundred years old. It's going to be drafty and make some strange noises. I've got the windows open in my room. The breeze could have swept in here by you and ruffled some things around."

Laura rolled her eyes. "Through a closed door? No way. And the radio?"

"This house has wiring from the 1930s," Doug said. "The inspectors told me it was safe but replacing it would be a great idea. They told me it was all poorly shielded and we'd have RF leakage that would play hell with radio and TV reception on occasion. That little radio would be prone to it. It doesn't even have an antenna."

Laura wanted a rational answer. The radio explanation was reasonable. Wind could blow under the big gap at the base of the door. It also could have blown Doug's door shut as she ran down the hall. It would be a forced fit, but that reasoning could explain it, except...

"No way," she said. "I heard voices."

"What did they say?"

"They just laughed."

"Like kids?" Doug asked.

"Exactly."

"Babe," Doug said. He took both hands in hers. "Don't get all defensive when I say this, okay? Maybe your mind over interpreted some things. The wind rustles some papers. A mouse scurries through these old walls. You are pretty keyed up about school and your last day in a classroom you almost died. It might be completely natural for your imagination to put a little supernatural spin on everything, a little anxiety release."

Laura clenched her jaw. That condescending brush off of an answer triggered memories of Doug's avoidance after the miscarriage. A vehement denial leapt to Laura's lips.

But she paused. Maybe he had a point. She remembered the flash of fear in the school hallway. She thought she'd conquered it, but maybe it made a little return appearance, one last curtain call. The trauma therapist warned her about this type of post-stress manifestation. It made more sense than spooks. What was wrong with her? She squeezed Doug's hands.

"Maybe you are right," she said. "I want you to be right." She hugged him and gave him a passionate kiss on the lips. "Say, didn't you hear me yell your name?"

"No," Doug answered. "I was reading for inspiration. I must have been in a trance."

"Well, go back and finish," Laura said. "I'll be done here soon and then I intend to rock your world for being such a hero. Be prepared."

"Hey, if you think you can ply me with pre-fab lasagna and then take advantage of me, forget it," Doug said. "I'm not that easy."

"You are twice that easy," Laura said. "I could get you in the sack with crackers and cheese whip." She spun him around, sent him out the door and shut it.

Laura sat down in front of the lesson plans. She took a deep breath and wondered how much of that little experience really was in her head. A lot of it, she guessed. It would be better tomorrow. Once she got in front of a class, everything would be back to normal. No more pseudo-spooks.

She picked up a lesson plan and then dropped it. She opened the door and slid a packing box in front of it. It probably *was* all in her head, but an open door still felt better.

Chapter Thirteen

Laura left for work early the next morning, barely able to sleep the night before. Once she was gone, Doug picked up a hammer and a handful of nails from the top of an unpacked brown box and left to perform the homeowner equivalent of marking his turf with his pee.

Fifteen acres was a lot more territory than he thought. He walked south first, toward the ridgeline Vernon Pugh disappeared into early that morning. If only one *Keep Out* sign got posted, he wanted it to be facing the trespasser as he crossed the property line. As Doug trudged across the field, he realized he had yet to walk his property line, something every rancher in every Western always did. He never even asked to when they moved in. Fifteen acres with who knows what in the nooks and crannies and he just bought it. What a dope. He plunged most of his net worth into an eighty-five-year-old-house sight unseen, basing his decisions on some gut feeling from a picture on the internet. What the hell had he been thinking?

At the edge of the trees, a fence delineated his property line. It was simple, just crooked posts set about twenty feet apart with three strands of barbed wire strung between them. The posts appeared to have once been stout tree branches, pressed into service to defend the homeland. Doug leaned over and nailed one of his big orange signs to the far side of one post. Crazy Vern couldn't miss it.

The forest on the other side of the fence ran thick up the gentle hill. The sheriff said ole Vern put a trailer on his acre, but Doug couldn't see it for sure. He thought that was just as well. He was happy having the trees, and the sheriff, as buffers between him and Vern.

He walked the fence line west, posting another sign where he estimated the halfway point on this side of his property line would be. There the fence ran through the woods, returning to the tree line a short distance later, cutting off a peninsula of trees on his side. The patch was about the size of the barn, which he realized he also hadn't set foot in. Something low and rectangular protruded from the leaf litter in the thicket, almost a clearing in the center. Walking in, Doug kicked away some debris and uncovered the corner of a low stone wall, just a foot high, handmade from the same stones that made up the house and barn foundations. He stepped over the wall and its rectangular perimeter became clear. Doug walked across it and his foot hit something hard and heavy. He scraped away the leaves with his signs. The plastic made a mournful moan as it rubbed against the hard surface beneath. The dull, dead leaves parted to reveal a toppled white marble tombstone.

The stone had an unhealthy mottling of black mildew and a jagged crack severed it from its base. Time or vandals had broken it off at ground level. Doug pulled some moss from the center and could read the inscription. The neat hand-carved block letters had thin serifs on each edge.

Rutherford Hutchington

1865-1928

Beloved Father and Husband

It took Doug a second to place the name. It was the man who built Galaxy Farm, the candy baron. It must be a family plot. He thought Realtor Dale should have mentioned that in the listing somewhere. A few of the older farm houses near by had small plots on them, though none were in this state of disrepair. Doug scraped away leaves inside the tiny battlement protecting the Hutchington clan. Four more gravestones emerged, each toppled from its proud vertical position. Two of the smaller ones were facedown. He pulled them back up to the vertical position to see the inscriptions. The headstones read:

William A. Hutchington , 1895-1931, first son of Rutherford

Sarah Hutchington, 1900-1931, his wife

Constance and Elizabeth Hutchington, 1925-1930, daughters.

And at the end lay *Mabron Hutchington 1900-1959, second son of Rutherford*

How sad to see a whole family laid to rest together, especially such a tragic cluster of deaths; the patriarch, followed within two years by the twin girls then their parents. How much grief could one family stand? Worse, they were tucked into this corner of the property and forgotten by family and friends. Even the woods worked to obscure these permanent residents, snaking burrowing roots and shedding faded leaves to subsume the remains of these mortals and their markers.

Notable by his absence was Vernon Pugh's father, Alexander. Did he abhor joining the family in eternal repose, or did the legal wrangling over the estate keep his wish from being executed? Or did Vernon bury him elsewhere out of spite for his mercurial commitment to fatherhood?

There are the seeds of a story in there, Doug thought. For the first time since deciding to write, he had an inspiration. Even when he drove home from St. Luke's after Laura's shooting and knew that the time had come to write the Great American Novel, he had no idea what that novel would be about. He had no concept, no characters, no plot. Now he did. It roiled around in his subconscious, dammed water rising toward the spillway. He'd need to rush to be ready to catch it all on paper when it started to flow.

His pulse quickened and he shed the macabre mantle the family plot had draped over him. He had writing to do. He hopped over the cemetery wall and ran back to the house.

Inside the plot, a few leaves shuffled at the base of Mabron's tombstone. A swath of blackened mold peeled away from across the name, as if an invisible hand brushed the surface clean.

Chapter Fourteen

Doug turned on the laptop in the turret room but couldn't abide the wait for it to boot up. He grabbed a pen and a pad of paper. He started to write.

The story swirled inside him, bits of ideas caught up in a tornado that only showed him glimpses of each piece. He couldn't slow them down, couldn't get them in order. He jotted down the snippets he could extract from the maelstrom.

Slaveholder family.

Pre-Civil War.

Crazy son. Murder.

He already knew the setting of the story. It sprang up in his mind full grown in exquisite detail. A plantation. The immense main house, two stories tall with a dual level porch and a central, pillared portico. Snow-white paint gleamed in the sun and the shutters and metal roof were a brilliant red. Blooming magnolias lined the driveway. Chirping birds flitted from branch to branch.

Doug's whole body pulsed with excitement. This minor epiphany was the reason he moved out here. He hadn't felt that rush of creativity since his college days. Nothing he wrote for the *New York Dispatch* ever gave him this reaction. He felt ten years younger.

His lack of faith last night embarrassed him. How could he doubt that he had a story inside him? He just needed to jar it loose.

His untouched laptop rolled over to a screensaver as his pen flew over the paper. Notes and ideas flashed faster than he could transcribe them. Sentences came out as fragments, words became abbreviations.

He'd backtrack and add detail to previous thoughts. The tip of his pen became a bottleneck for a torrential creative flow.

He scrawled page upon page of notes. Some of it looked like it was in the same convoluted format favored by the Unabomber's manifesto. No matter. Doug would clean it up and make it coherent later. The point was to channel as much of the inspirational lightning bolt as possible as it struck. He could adjust the amps and voltage later.

He hunched closer to the paper. This was what he quit his job for, the chance to surrender to creativity. No better way to make a living.

Chapter Fifteen

Laura's first day could not have gone better so far. From the moment she stepped into the classroom, she felt complete. She slipped into the teacher role like a pair of well-worn slippers. Mrs. Matthews had been her kind of teacher. Her students were disciplined and behaved. They figured out in the first twenty minutes that Laura was no pushover substitute and toed the line. Laura beamed as she entered the teacher's lounge after fourth period.

Austere would be a kind word for the teacher's lounge. The district must have funded the room as an afterthought. Two mismatched castoff couches sagged against the wall. One was gold and one red, but their faded colors didn't add a glow of festivity. A male and a female teacher sat around a central table borrowed from the cafeteria, sipping coffee and eating out of Tupperware. They chopped their conversation as Laura entered. Their heads swiveled to face her like the rifles of a firing squad.

Laura's face went red. She could see their eyes passing judgment. By seven thirty this morning she realized that by wearing a long skirt and heels she was overdressed by a factor of five compared to the rest of the jeans-clad staff. She had so hoped that fitting in would not be an issue. Based on the looks she saw now, it was going to be a struggle.

Best defense is a good offense, she thought. She looked for the face with the most contempt. The woman on the left was in her mid-forties with too much makeup and artificially black hair in a short wedge cut. Reading glasses perched on the edge of her nose like a hawk on the hunt. She'd be the leader. She had the air of a bully. Laura went straight for her and stuck out her hand.

"Hi there," she said. "I'm Laura Locke, filling in for..."

"Sherri Matthews," the woman said. "We know." She gave Laura's hand a look of bemusement and than offered a limp shake. "I'm Patrice, sixth grade. This is Danny, fifth grade."

"Nice to meet you both," Laura lied.

"So where you from?" Danny asked. Danny had a middle-age spread barely restrained within a blue-checked button-down shirt. He had the world's most obvious comb-over. Laura sensed the onset of an Inquisitional interrogation.

"We just moved from outside New York City," Laura said. "I taught there for three years." She hoped describing her experience might garner some points. No luck. From the looks on their faces, she could have just announced she spent a year at a leper colony. She struggled for a local connection that might help. "My husband and I just moved into Galaxy Farm." Their looks moved from disdain to disbelief.

"That was you?" Danny said. "You got some courage."

"Courage?"

"That house has a history," Patrice said. "Nothing but death and bad luck on that property since the Hutchingtons bought it. Don't tell me Dale Mabry left that out of his listing?"

Laura flashed back to the feeling she had when she stepped into the turret room. That foreboding, heavy, dark sensation that set her fear center firing.

"Oh, yes," Patrice said, relishing being the bringer of bad news. "From the time the house was built it has been one awful event after another. The owners who didn't die ended up certifiable."

"Buried 'em right there on the property," Danny added. "Hutchingtons were too good for the county cemetery, not that anyone was extending any invitations anyhow."

Laura worked hard to keep a fake smile on her face. People had died in her house and were buried in her yard. What the hell was all this? Did Doug know any of this, the king of the "I feel this house" method of internet real estate purchases? Whether Doug knew it or not, Lauren wasn't about to give these two the satisfaction of knowing she didn't.

"Well, if you buy into that kind of stuff," Laura said. "We're not big believers in curses and bad luck."

Laura needed an excuse to get out of there without having it look like a retreat. She shoved change into the soda machine and punched the first button she could reach. A cream soda rolled out at the bottom and she forced herself not to cringe. She would rather dehydrate than drink cream soda. She picked up the can and headed for the door.

"Not staying?" Patrice asked, peering over her reading glasses.

"I'm still finding everything in the classroom," Laura said over her shoulder. "I'll see you both later. Nice meeting you."

As the door closed behind her, she could just hear Danny's voice saying, "Don't think she's a gonna make it."

Laura gripped the soda can hard enough to dent it. She didn't need this crap. She was a good teacher. No, she was a *damn* good teacher. Those two didn't have the right to judge her. "Not gonna make it?" She'd show that paunchy know-nothing who would make it.

And don't think Doug wasn't getting a special prize when she got home. Move her into a house with such a history. No wonder she felt creepy last night making lesson plans. Her Student Sixth Sense was never wrong. There would be an earful waiting for him.

She missed Rosa Elizondo, her mentor and defensive line at Idlewild Elementary. It was a long shot, but she had hoped to find someone like her at Moultrie. If Patrice and Danny were a representative sample, it didn't look like that was going to happen.

Chapter Sixteen

Downtown Moultrie was postcard perfect. It had a classic small town design with a central square for the county courthouse, a domed turn-of-the-century sandstone masterpiece. A weathered bronze statue of a Civil War soldier stood at attention on a pedestal in front of the main entrance. Retirees in seed company caps and thick glasses sat on the green benches along the perimeter, commenting to each other on the events of the day.

Two- and three-story brick buildings lined the streets around the courthouse. Relentless advances in transportation and technology had long stripped away the businesses that once made the downtown a microcosm of big-city commerce. Each shop carried a bit of its history on it façade, like campaign medals on an old soldier's uniform. The vertical sign that once advertised the Rialto Theatre in neon letters still jutted over the entrance to Bumby's Furniture, though now it was just pained a solid blue. The marble cornice over the flower shop still had *Union Bank 1912* carved into it in block letters. The ghostly white letters on the side of Mabry Realty read *Harrison's Dry Goods and Livery* if the sunlight was just right. Only two businesses had history on the square. The Moultrie Luncheonette was an honest-to-goodness soda and sandwich shop kept on nostalgic life support by the fifth generation of family owners. The other was Randolph's Hardware, where you still walked on a hardwood floor and brought a half pound of nails home in a brown paper sack.

After work, Laura entered Randolph's. The narrow aisles were crammed with building supplies and farm implements she could not identify. The place smelled of polished wood and had a hint of light machine oil mixed in. She went straight to the back counter. An older gentleman with half-moon reading glasses on his nose stood by the register. He wore an apron with *Lon* and *Randolph's Hardware* stitched on the front. Laura put on her biggest smile.

"Hi, I see you sell and install water treatment systems?"

"Sure do," Lon said. He looked her over top to bottom. "You must be the new substitute at the elementary school."

Laura was stunned. "How could you...?"

"Word travels," Lon said.

Laura imagined the hardware store as the gossip nexus of the town.

"So you need a home system?" Lon continued.

Laura explained the situation, the sulfur in the hard water.

"We got a standard system that uses salt as the catalyst," Lon said. "But we also got a newer, smaller one that doesn't need salt. It's a lot easier to use."

Laura felt an imperative come over her, an overriding need to instantly decide the system to take, and which one to choose.

"We'll go with the standard system."

Lon gave her a bemused look. Apparently the salt-based systems didn't sell as well as they used to. He filled out a purchase order and showed Laura the price.

"Now that includes installation and the one-year warrantee," Lon said.

The price was immaterial. Laura needed the system. She needed *that* system. "How soon can we get it put in?"

"I guess we could do it tomorrow," Lon said. "Happen to have one in stock."

"Fantastic," Laura said. "We're at 2143 Hwy 41 North."

Lon took a half step back from the counter.

"So you bought the Hutchington place?"

All the anger about the house's history came flooding back. She held it back. "So what time can we expect you in the morning?"

"About eight, I'd say," Lon said. "Wait. Make it eight thirty so my boy has time to load the truck."

"My husband will see you then," Laura said. She turned to leave the store, ready to avoid any discussion about her supposedly haunted house. A box of matchbooks sat on the countertop, giveaway books embossed with *Randolph's Hardware*.

Laura didn't smoke and didn't need matches. But she had an instant craving for these. Before she knew what she did, she had of book of them in her pocket and was out the door.

The "Are-you-nuts?" look from the owner when she told him her address got her mad at Doug all over again. Even the good news of the promised morning installation didn't quell her anger at Doug for buying a house with so much backstory. Her fury ran in an amplifying feedback loop on the drive home. Only the need to talk to him face to face kept her from calling him immediately.

Unaware of the coming storm, Doug was pacing the kitchen, dying to tell Laura about his novel's progress.

Laura yelled Doug's name as she blew in through the front door. He wandered in to the living room, smiling with a blueberry muffin in his hand.

"Welcome home, teacher," he said. "I got these muffins at the Piggly Wiggly. You've got to try—"

The fury in Laura's eyes froze him mid-sentence, muffin in his outstretched hand. He'd seen that look before, the time he inadvertently bought Yankees tickets on their wedding anniversary. He braced for impact.

"When were you going to tell me we bought a cursed house?" Laura said.

Doug nearly dropped the muffin. "What do you mean?"

"The people who built this place, the Huntingtons—"

"Hutchingtons," Doug corrected.

"Whoever!" Laura snapped. "A busybody at work told me that the whole family died here. The whole county knows the place is cursed, choked full of bad mojo."

Doug's jaw went slack. "I have no idea what you mean. I told you everything I knew about the house when we bought it. No one said anything about people dying here."

"What about the onsite graveyard?" she said. "I suppose you didn't know about that either?"

"Not when we bought the place," he said. He couldn't conceal the "oh shit" look on his face.

"*'Not when we bought it?'*" She was flabbergasted. "When *did* you know we owned a graveyard?"

"Not until today," he said. "I stumbled across it, literally, when I was posting the no trespassing signs..."

"And you didn't tell me?"

"I was afraid you'd overreact." He was losing ground fast.

"Overreact? I have corpses buried near my home. Who lives like that? How normal is that?"

She yanked the muffin out of his hand, stomped into the kitchen and pulled a bottle of water from the refrigerator. She went straight to the nursery. As she disappeared, she called back.

"I've got prep to do for tomorrow. We're going to have to finish this later when I'm not so furious." The door to her study slammed shut.

Doug waited over an hour before launching his apology. He nudged open the door and crept into Laura's study. A plate of shrimp primavera steamed in his hands. Laura sat on the floor facing the door, lesson plans laid out in front of her.

"Hey, babe," he said.

Laura looked up. Doug put on a penitent look. Delivering one of her favorite dishes had to be a good start. She looked like she had cooled off a bit.

"How about a little dinner?" he said.

"Bribing yourself back into my good graces?"

"For a start," Doug said.

"Luckily for you I'm famished," she said.

Doug sat down next to her and handed her the plate of shrimp. She took a bite.

"Well, it's good. One point for you."

"I had no idea about the history of this house," Doug said. "It didn't even occur to me to ask. As long as it was structurally sound, that was good enough."

"I believe you," Laura sighed. "Today was just so stressful. All the teachers were a bit standoffish to say the least. That put me on edge, then when that royal bitch Patrice dumped the 'cursed history' info on me, I went over the cliff. You were the first person I could vent to."

"Tomorrow, I'll go downtown and do some research," Doug said. "I'll find out the Hutchington story in extreme detail." He paused. "You don't have problems with the house now, do you?"

She hesitated.

"No," she said without conviction. "Patrice just brought out the worst in me."

"That's good," Doug said. He stole a shrimp from her plate and popped it into his mouth. "Because we have twenty-nine years and eleven months of payments to make, so we are going to need to live here."

Chapter Seventeen

"It's kinda big."

The next morning the installer from Randolph's Hardware stood on the front porch. The young man had a gift for understatement. Doug looked past the installation tech's shoulder. A large fiberglass cylinder rose from the back of his pickup truck.

True to his promise to Laura, Lon Randolph had sent his son Charlie out to install the water filtration system. He volunteered that he had installed over twenty of them when Doug gave him a disbelieving look at their introduction. The thin sandy-haired twenty-something seemed earnest, his blue jumpsuit was clean and his tools looked professional grade, so Doug gave him the benefit of the doubt.

"Most folks put it in the basement," Charlie said. "Y'all have a basement?"

"Afraid not."

"Well, how about a pump house? Where's the well?"

"Couldn't tell you," Doug said. "We just moved in."

Charlie gave his eyes a little "another city boy" roll. "Well, we'd best go find it. You don't want me putting this thing in the house if you can help it."

Charlie found the main waterline entering the house. It angled out to the barn. They walked that way. Charlie pointed to a shallow metal box a hundred yards past the barn.

"Now there's your well head," he said. "The line runs under the barn on the way to the house. I could tap in there and set the whole thing up for you if you don't mind losing a little space in there."

Doug didn't mind. He wasn't planning on filling any of the horse stalls. He rolled open the heavy wooden barn door.

Seven horse stalls lined one side of the barn. Old man Hutchington had spared no expense. The rich dark boards looked like some South American hardwood. The walls were all beautiful tongue-in-groove construction. In the center of the stalls, a circular stairway led to the barn's cupola, a six-sided, well-windowed affair with room for two, or one if that person brought a chair. Doug imagined old Hutch watching his horses work out from there. The view of the estate was perfect.

The open space at the end, formerly occupied by an eighth stall, had undergone some kind of conversion. The waterline entered here and fed a porcelain sink, vintage 1920, with cast iron legs. It looked like a prop from a movie set hospital with doctors treating the Spanish Flu. A covered wooden barrel stood next to the sink.

On the other side sat a white cast iron bath tub, complete with leonine clawed feet. The feet rested on two-foot blocks that brought the edge of the tub up waist high. A homemade heavy-gauge mesh covered the top, as if someone had used the tub to rinse vegetables. But no water was piped to the tub. Severe brownish-yellow stains coated the tub's bottom third. Hairline cracks spider webbed across the old fixture.

"Looks like the wrong half of a half bath," Charlie quipped.

"What good is a bathtub with no water?" Doug said to himself.

Charlie ran a bit of water from the sink into his cupped hand. He sniffed it, and then took a sip. He looked surprised. "Don't mean to lose my Dad a sale, but you sure you need this system?"

"My wife sure is."

Charlie nodded in understanding as if the two had just shared one of the truths only men know. He gave the exposed water pipes a quick inspection.

"Here's what I can do," Charlie said. "If you want, I can drag that old pallet over there to this corner, route the water through the treatment system then to this here sink and the house. I can tap power from the lights in the stalls and we'll be in business."

Doug agreed and Charlie went to work. Doug nosed around the barn. It looked like Vern had as much interest in horses as Doug had because the stalls were filled with crap. Old boards, rusting tools, a half-dozen bags of lime fertilizer, canvas tarps; all guarded by a billowing screen of spider webs.

But in the corner of the last stall, he found something of interest. It was a full set of fireplace utensils. They looked old and custom forged, a project the Galaxy Farm blacksmith whipped up in his spare time. They were heavy black iron and the handles were globes emblazoned with the Galaxy Candy logo. Doug lifted the poker. It had to weigh at least ten pounds. The estate scavengers must have skipped searching the barn for anything of value.

After lunch, Charlie showed Doug the complete system. There was a pump and two tanks and some kind of filter. Doug had no idea what he was looking at.

But Charlie patiently explained how the bleach pumped into the holding tank and how the salt adjusted the PH. Laura had ordered several gallons of bleach and three fifty-pound bags of salt. Apparently she was taking no chances on sulfur-scented clothes.

Charlie showed Doug how to refill both catalysts and how to test the water and adjust pump settings. Doug thought about how much fun it would be out here in the winter. He thanked Charlie for all his help and took out a credit card for payment.

"Oh no, Mr. Locke," Charlie said. "It's on your account. Y'all just come on down and settle up sometime this week."

Doug smiled at the simple trust you could find in a small town. "I'll be down this afternoon, Charlie."

Chapter Eighteen

Doug did pay that bill after lunch. But he owed it to himself and Laura to do his promised background research on their house and the five deceased residents. An internet search earlier in the day had yielded a few details on Rutherford Hutchington but nothing Doug didn't already know. Self-made candy baron, dabbled in horseracing. Not even a mention of Moultrie. He cursed Wikipedia for its unfulfilled promise and dubious provenance. He was downtown now to do it the hard way.

The county library sat one block off the town square. An anonymous rectangle of a building with narrow window slits around the roofline. Doug guessed it was some standard government building design, adapted to a library in this instance. Inside, rows of bookshelves carried mostly paperbacks. People of all ages surfed the internet at kiosks along one wall. A teenager sat at the checkout desk. Her long black hair was blonde halfway down where her last trip to the salon marked its passage. She was so thin Doug thought the weight of her nametag might be hard for her to bear. The tag said *Monica— Volunteer.*

"Hi there," Doug greeted her. "I'd like to look into some local history. Have you got a section for that?"

Monica sized him up with the "outsider" look he'd grown to know so well. "The County Room is back there," she said. "You down from Nashville?"

Doug still hadn't adjusted to the Moultrie residents' uninhibited quest for personal information from strangers. It was one hundred and eighty degrees from the mode he learned in New York City where you avoided even eye contact with people on the street.

"No," he answered. "I'm looking into the history of some property I just bought."

Monica's eyes lit up. "Don't tell me. The Hutchington place."

Doug officially gave up hope of ever escaping Galaxy Farm's legacy. "Yep, that's it."

"We have lots on that place. It's famous, you know."

"You don't say."

The sarcasm sailed past Monica. She led Doug back to a small room labeled *Archives*. Inside, dusty leather-bound books filled the walls. There was a single desk in the center.

"There are all sorts of records and county history," Monica said. "No one has ever converted all this to digital. Those there," she pointed to one wall, "are bound copies of the *Moultrie Appeal*, the county newspaper. Have fun!"

Doug remembered most of the dates from the gravestones but figured he would start with the house. He was certain it was built in 1926. He ran his finger along the rich leather bindings of the *Moultrie Appeal* until he found that year.

He took the oversized volume to the table, sat down and cracked it open. A stale, dusty smell wafted out. He flipped through the pages. The dry newsprint had a fragile, brittle feel.

He couldn't miss the first big reference to Galaxy Farm; a front page article under the headline:

TYCOON OPENS GALAXY FARM

To the right was a picture of his house. Of course, in the whole town only he thought of it as his. An impressive collection of men in suits and women in long drop-waist dresses stood at attention on the porch, models of the reserved fun the Roaring Twenties were destroying. In the center stood Rutherford Hutchington in proper tails with his top hat cupped in the crook of his arm. A full handlebar moustache covered most of his rather grim smile.

A doll-like woman caught his eye just to the right of Rutherford. Her dark hair was cut short to just below her ears. Behind a wall of broad shoulders, only the curve of a string of pearls across her delicate neck was visible. The grainy old photograph could not diminish her captivating eyes.

Another man stood out far to the other side of Rutherford, dressed to the nines, with a shock of unruly black hair and a thick droopy moustache. While the rest of the group stared at the camera, face forward, his eyes cut left, fixed on the beautiful woman in white pearls.

The photo caption carried the names of everyone on the porch, the local attendees proud to be documented at Moultrie's event of the year. The woman was Sarah, a name familiar from the family graveyard. He assumed the man eyeing her was her husband William, but he was wrong. William was at her side, a taller strikingly handsome man with short-cropped hair and a razor-straight part. The other man was Mabron, second son and brother-in-law.

An odd set of poses, Doug thought. Probably just one of those stray seconds the camera catches where someone has their eyes closed or their face in a bizarre contortion. He imagined how embarrassed Mabron had to be when the family saw the picture published the next day.

The fawning article that followed described the party in excruciating detail. The writer, no doubt influenced by the society columns from the East Coast, thought the town waited breathlessly to find out who ate what hors de oeuvre.

Hutchington had spared no expense in setting up his farm. The article mentioned the finest horses had been imported, Thoroughbred and Arabians. The Arabians had been brought in from Arabia itself, including a trainer from Egypt. Hutchington had cleared the land and sown it with rich Kentucky bluegrass. Apparently a practice course used to encircle the pond, though no trace of it remained now.

Doug now had pictures for the graveyard names. He paged through the rest of the year, but there was no mention of the farm until the next year. The article was on the editorial page.

Doug was certainly no stranger to the newspaper business and had even done some editorials for the *New York Dispatch* during his tenure. He had to follow all the rules of persuasive writing and heed the *Dispatch*'s dictates about not offending those readers who might disagree with his position. The *Moultrie Appeal* apparently had no such restrictions.

STRANGERS GO HOME read the headline. Mincing words wasn't on that editor's agenda.

The quarter page tirade that followed excoriated the Hutchingtons. Apparently the hospitality from the welcome party had dried up. The Hutchingtons were depicted as cold and clannish. They imported almost everything they needed from Nashville. Even local beef wasn't good enough for these self-centered snobs. Visitors to the farm from town became fewer as the Hutchingtons had the rich and near-famous from out of state fill the guest rooms.

But worst of all, the anticipated hiring of locals to work on the farm never materialized. Hutchington hadn't promised as much, but the townspeople had just assumed the tycoon would be spreading some of his wealth via payroll. Instead, the groomsmen and jockeys were all from an upstate New York farm run by a board member of Galaxy Confectioners, Inc. But even worse than having those *Yankee carpetbaggers* the actual description, on the farm, was having a *godless foreigner.*

The editor singled out the Egyptian trainer. With a rich history of equine husbandry in the county, the editor couldn't fathom why *lesser races, who weren't even Christian,* he added, needed to be imported. The editor alluded to rumors of strange rituals and sacrifices but stayed vague enough to avoid a libel lawsuit. Doug had observed that present day Moultrie accepted strangers about as well as a body accepted a cold virus. Things were no different in 1927. Once it became apparent that the Hutchingtons thought that they were a cut above the locals, (imagine that) the bloom was off the rose.

Doug returned the volume to the shelf and pulled out 1928, the first date from the graveyard. Rutherford Hutchington's death had to have made the paper. Doug assumed he died here since he was interred on the property.

Sure enough, old man Hutchington's obit was front page news. He spent the last six months of his life at Galaxy Farm, afflicted with a debilitating illness the reporter appeared to root for. From the description, it may have been a combination of high blood pressure and diabetes, but since the attending physicians were from New York (of course), no diagnosis was available. Morticians from Nashville prepared the body and as one parting slap to the town, no public service was held before burial. From the triumphant tone of the article, Doug doubted anyone would have attended anyway.

A public notice a few pages later announced that Galaxy Farm ownership had passed on to the brothers Mabron and William and that all debtors and creditors should note the fact. Apparently old man Hutchington's wife was not enamored of the country life and returned to their New York City home with their youngest son Alexander.

Now that name rang a bell. That was Vernon Pugh's father. The third son was at least thirty years younger than his older brothers. Doug caught scent of a second, younger wife in old man Hutchington's life. His creative process imagined little Alexander being a surprise result from a dalliance that old Hutch had to legalize with an expensive divorce and a marriage. The older sons must have hated her. That scenario would also explain why Alexander would avoid claiming illegitimate Vernon until later in life. Who wanted to admit repeating the sins of his father?

In the 1931 volume, tragedy continued to unfold for the Hutchingtons. One cold winter afternoon, William and Sarah's twin girls Constance and Elizabeth went out to the pond to go ice skating. They broke through the ice. Between the weight of the skates and the crumbling ice, they couldn't escape from the bone-numbing water.

William rushed out to rescue them, but the ice closed in over them. He dove in and, after repeated attempts, pulled the two lifeless bodies ashore. A local doctor arrived, but all he could do was sign death certificates.

In deference to the girls, no doubt, the gloating tone of Rutherford's obituary was missing. The article treated this tragedy as just that, the accidental loss of two five-year-old girls. Whatever enmity the town had against the parents, the innocents were immune. Doug remembered the hollow ache he felt after Laura's miscarriage and imagined the unbearable pain of the father's failed rescue.

But Doug knew the dates on the gravestones and, like a movie trailer that told too much, the inscriptions warned him that worse scenes were yet to unfold. The next issue had a short article that announced the death of William Hutchington. Pneumonia was the primary cause, caught during his extensive time in the frozen pond. Though he appeared to be recovering, his brother Mabron found him dead one morning. Heart failure, Mabron had told the reporter. Doug wondered if he meant failed or broken. William's guilt must have been agonizing.

In twenty-four months, the grave of Rutherford Hutchington had become a family plot.

The next Hutchington tragedy unfolded at the end of 1931. The compounded tragedies of losing her daughters and her husband were more than Sarah Hutchington could bear. One morning Mabron found her hanged in the barn. There was no note, but any written explanation would have been superfluous. She joined the rest of her family, buried in the space she had made sure to leave open between her husband and the twins.

Doug sighed. This little history lesson wasn't going to assuage Laura at all. Drowned children and a suicidal parent were horror movie material, not the backstory to a dream house. He couldn't sugar coat this, not after her reaction to the graveyard's existence. Maybe impulse purchases of real property weren't such a good idea after all.

Then again, what difference did it make? The house had some history. What eighty-five-year-old house wouldn't? Sure it was more dramatic than most, but unless you believe in the spirits of the dead walking the night, so what? The locals probably had a collection of bogus ghost stories about the house, but that was the way small minds sifted through tragedy, especially if the victims could be rationalized to deserve it. What better punishment for old man Hutchington than to walk the house he built for all eternity?

But there were no ghosts, no cold spots in the rooms, no full-torso apparitions floating in the halls. In fact, Doug felt nothing but comfortable everywhere in the house. Why tell Laura about something that would just put her on edge, add grist to her active imagination. Even knowing nothing about the history, she had given herself a serious case of the creeps the second night here.

He resolved to tell his wife the minimum, slant the story a bit. Laura didn't need to know all of it anyway. What harm could it do?

Chapter Nineteen

Laura could smell the spices cooking from the porch when she got home that night. Cayenne, red pepper, ground chilies. Only one thing smelled like that. Doug's homemade chili.

"Something smells good," she said as she rolled in through the front door.

Doug stuck his head out from the kitchen doorway. "¡Si, Senora, la comida es muy bueno!"

The kitchen table was set for dinner. Laura dropped her bag at the door, walked over and gave him a kiss. For an instant it felt wrong. Something about his lips...the texture, the fullness...she couldn't nail it down and then the feeling vanished. She wrapped her arms around Doug's waist.

"Is that the famous chili I smell?" she said.

"You used to call it infamous," Doug said.

"That was when we had it eat it every other night because it was all we could afford," Laura said.

"And only through one hundred and eighty attempts in one year could such magic be perfected." Doug dipped a wooden spoon into a pot simmering on the stove and put it to Laura's lips. She blew across the top and then tasted. The inside of her mouth caught fire and her eyes watered.

"That's the good stuff," she said.

"Check out the fireplace," Doug said.

"Wow!" she said as she spied the fireplace utensils. Doug had cleaned them after pulling them from the barn. The logo handles were now sprayed a gloss black. "Where did you get these?"

"Hidden down in the barn where we put in the filtration system."

Laura grabbed the shovel. She underestimated its weight and nearly dropped it. "Are they heavy enough for you?" she asked.

"More than enough," Doug said. "But they clearly belong here. Maybe we'll buy a new set to actually use once the weather gets cold."

"There's an interior decorator in you screaming to get out," Laura teased.

"Another cheap shot like that and those go back in the barn," Doug said. "Are we going to eat dinner or are you going to keep insulting me?"

"Hey, why choose?"

Doug filled the dinner conversation that evening with as many details about the water filtration system as he could, but after a while that well went dry. Out of a combination of guilt and altruism (he was afraid to know the ratio) he had to bring up the Hutchington history.

"So," he said. "I did some research today on the Hutchingtons."

Laura stuck her spoon straight up in her chili. "And you waited this long to tell me? Let's go, out with it."

"Well, the patriarch, Mr. Candy Baron, died of old age and good living," Doug said. "His two eldest sons lived here after that. One, William, was married with two daughters. One winter the girls went out skating on the pond. The ice was too thin. They broke through and drowned."

"That's an awful story," Laura said. "The poor parents, they must have felt... How old were the girls?"

"Five years old."

Laura flashed back to her dream the first night they were here. Two girls wanted her to come down to the pond, two girls who were about five years old.

"Were there pictures of them?" she asked.

"I didn't find any."

"What were their names?" Laura already knew the answer.

"Constance and Elizabeth," Doug said. Laura recited the names along with him in her head, syllable for syllable. Her body made an involuntary shudder.

"Remember that night," Laura said, "the first night after I was hired, when I got spooked in my room? I heard girls laughing."

"C'mon, babe," Doug said. "That noise was nothing but wind blowing through eighty-five-year-old siding. I knew if I told you about this, you would blow it up into something big."

That condescending comment punched the wrong button in Laura. She knew what she heard that night. She knew what she experienced. Most of all, she knew what she dreamed. Twins names Constance and Elizabeth came in her dream and called her "Mother". She was about to blurt that out to Doug but cut herself short. He'd made up his mind that what she'd experienced had been in her head. He'd just say that the dream planted the seeds for her hallucination or some such psycho-babble nonsense. She wasn't in the mood for that.

"Never mind that," she said. "So the girls are buried in that little cemetery?"

"Along with their parents," Doug said. "By now it's just gravestones out there. After over eighty years, what could be left? There's no such thing as ghosts or spirits of the dead or cursed houses. It's all just local superstition and bullshit. You should have read how much the townspeople resented the rich folks up here on the ridge. They would be quick to make up all sorts of nasty stories."

There were a few more things she wanted to know, but she knew she couldn't stomach much of Doug's dismissive attitude. He wanted to just glaze over this and move on. Like every major trauma they had endured. She threw her napkin at the table.

"Well, I have to get set for tomorrow. Those history tests won't grade themselves."

"Fail one of them for me," Doug said, but Laura wasn't in the mood for banter.

Later in her study, she was halfway through the stack of exams. She had tweaked the test Mrs. Matthews had left. The last two questions morphed from multiple choice to written answers in paragraph form. The multiple-choice section graded quickly, but reading the last two questions was like walking through a minefield of grammatical errors. That was okay. She also taught the kids English every day. By the end of the year, she would have them up to speed.

She caught herself again, treating her position as a permanent job. She was the *substitute*. Long-term substitute, but substitute nonetheless. Ms. Matthews would be back since broken legs are not fatal. She felt so guilty every time she caught herself rooting for complications to set in.

Her Student Sixth Sense flashed a warning and she dropped her red pen. The clock radio, which she had kept off since the night it went haywire, clicked on. No station came on, just a hiss of static. Laura felt her heart hammer in her chest. She got the same shiver she did before the room went *Amityville Horror* on her before.

She remembered the little girl laughter from last time. She recalled the smiling blonde twins from her dream. Her SSS told her this was Constance and Elizabeth visiting. These girls wouldn't, couldn't be evil. How could she be scared by them? She took a deep, cleansing breath.

After all, what had they done last time? Closed her books and shuffled her papers? That was hardly threatening. It wasn't diabolical. It was a prank. Two girls playing a prank on the teacher.

The room temperature dropped like a blast from a freezer. Laura slowly turned to see the room. She kept her history tests in the corner of her eye. At the edge of her peripheral vision, a paper started to flutter. She spun back and slapped it down.

"Ha, ha," she said. "I was too quick for you this time." She was certain she was not talking to herself. She rolled open a desk drawer and pulled out a bright blue ball. It was the exercise squeeze ball St. Luke's had given her as part of her hand rehab.

"You want something to play with?" she said. "Here you go."

She tossed the ball against the far wall. It hit the floor and rolled to a stop.

"Go ahead," Laura said. She would treat them just like two of her students. "You can make the papers move, so you can make the ball move. Or are you only good behind someone's back?"

Laura stared at the motionless ball on the hardwood floor. "Go ahead. Let's see you play."

The ball rocked back and forth a few degrees.

"Very good!" Laura said. "Go ahead, show me what you can do."

The ball took off like it had been swatted by a tiger. It raced a third of the way across the room and stopped as abruptly as if it had hit a wall. Then it rocketed back across the room and slammed to a halt right where it started. The soft, ethereal laughter of two little girls floated through the room.

The next instant, Laura knew their presence had disappeared. The girls were gone, moved to a different location or even a different dimension. Laura broke into a smile. She wasn't scared at all. It was just the twins. What a treat this would be, sharing her house with spirits. This was going to be fun.

She rose to tell Doug about this amazing experience and stopped herself short. She remembered his trivializing response to her last paranormal experience. This one wouldn't be any different.

The hell with that. The girls came to her, not him. He didn't want to believe, fine. She could have her own secrets.

Chapter Twenty

The next morning flew by before Doug knew it. From the end of breakfast until noon he sat in the turret room and wrote. Characters came to life so vividly he swore he knew them. The patriarch of the Southern family was austere and demanding. His two sons vied to run the plantation upon his death, each wishing they could hasten it. Intrigue begat intrigue and the Civil War loomed on the horizon. It was so good, even Doug wanted to know how it ended. He didn't have an outline. He didn't have character notes. The story just flowed out of him as if he picked up the words like radio waves.

His throat felt dry and he glanced at the clock. One p.m.. What the hell happened to the morning? He straightened up from behind his keyboard. His brain felt like it had been through a wringer. He was done writing, but he wished he didn't have to stop. In fact, he didn't want to leave the room. He was certain this inspired energy he felt came from within these four walls. That initial attraction he had for the turret room had amplified. This space belonged to him or maybe that he belonged to it. Whichever way it was, it gave him what he needed to write.

He rose from his desk and noticed the locked door to the unexplored attic. A key protruded from the antique lock. Laura must have come across it and left it in there for him. That saved him a call to Dale's locksmith pal, another chore he was now glad he had put off. His hunger abated immediately, replaced by an insatiable curiosity, a gravitational pull to that undiscovered country beyond that door.

The trefoil head of the iron key was warm. The lock turned grudgingly. A series of heavy clicks sounded inside the door. The door creaked as Doug pulled it open, as if the room were issuing a welcome. A set of rough wooden steps rose up into the gloom of the attic.

Doug crept up the stairs, hoping his eyes would adjust to the darkness. Unseen cobwebs caressed his face and he batted them away. The air smelled stale, mildewed with a trace of musk. The force that pulled him forward grew.

At the top of the steps, his head struck an exposed rafter. He ducked and turned right to where the roofline rose. A few feet in, a white string lamp pull glowed in the dim light. Doug grabbed it and yanked. A bare overhead bulb clicked to life and swung back and forth.

Dozens of eyes stared at him.

Doug took a startled step back, but he was surrounded. Taxidermied animals filled the room. On the floor, squirrels perched on logs. A bobcat crouched in the corner, ears back, yellow slit eyes blazing. A bear rug covered part of the floor to the right. The animal's jaws were opened wide to display two sets of gleaming sharp teeth. Animal heads hung from the walls; a ten-point buck, antlers rising in perfect symmetry; a snarling boar, hair coarse as a scrub brush; an immense buffalo, black shaggy mane almost covering its eyes. Other smaller animals were scattered or piled around the room, a mummified Noah's Ark.

Wax figures and mounted museum displays usually gave Doug the willies, but oddly these creatures didn't. He examined some of the larger animals up close. They were old. Small patches of tan leather showed where fur or feathers had fallen out over time. A few eyes lolled askew in their sockets, giving the animal a panicked, crazed expression.

The dormer windows should have let the afternoon sun fill the attic, but they were boarded up, so hastily covered with cheap pressboard that many of the nailheads were exposed and bent at odd angles. Whoever did the work wanted out of here in a hurry.

Doug picked his way through the shadowy attic. The swinging light bulb made the long rafter shadows roll up and down the walls. Each dusky band swept across shelves of mismatched earthen jars, their tops sealed with mottled wax. The floorboards creaked beneath him with each step. That feeling he had in the turret room, that this was the place to be, was stronger here in this still-life zoo. He stroked the head of a horned owl as he passed it. The bird was so soft. A pin feather shed and fluttered to the floor.

At the far end of the attic, a cedar chest sat against the wall. Doug thought women used to call these "hope chests" but he had no idea why. He pulled up the lid and dust cascaded down it like a minor avalanche. The tray on the top of the chest held two matching ribbons, white with lace trim. Next to them lay a locket, silver with fine turn-of-the-century engraving. Its silver chain coiled around it in a precise spiral. Doug popped it open.

In the right side was a picture of a beautiful woman. He recognized Sarah Hutchington. Even miniaturized, the detail of the black-and-white photo was striking. She wore a close-fitting hat with an upturned brim. A long pattered scarf hung around her neck over a white blouse. In the picture, the locket in Doug's hand hung just above her breasts. Her alabaster-white skin glowed in the photograph's lighting. Soft brown eyes looked off to the left, searching for the face in the locket's other half.

On the left side of the locket, a man stared straight out at Doug. He remembered Mabron from the porch picture in the library. In contrast to the perfectly coiffed queen to his left, this man was practically unkempt. A tangled mess black hair refused to be tamed. His moustache drooped over his mouth but still could not mask his prominent overbite. He had a strange, crooked half smile. His ill-fitting shirt left a large gap around his neck and made him look like a turtle peering from its shell. While the angelic woman on the right gazed adoringly left, the man on the left stared straight ahead, a haunting gaze that hinted at a mind as barely controlled as his hair. And while the background of the woman's picture was a neutral photographer's backdrop, what little background was visible on the man's photo was busy and jumbled. His off-center head nearly filled the frame, as if the picture was cropped to force it into the locket half.

The pairing in the locket at first struck Doug as odd, but he shrugged it off. He replaced the locket in the tray. He followed an inexplicable compulsion and twirled the chain back into a symmetrical spiral. He removed the tray from the chest. Inside lay two books and a black canvas roll tied with a string in the center. The book titles were imprinted on the black leather spines in gold letters. The first read *North American Fauna*

The second book's spine was coated in mildew. Doug licked his thumb and swept the spine clean. The title read *Methods in the Art of Taxidermy*

He untied the canvas bundle. It unrolled like a carpet runner. Inside a collection of bright silver instruments glittered in the overhead light. Each had its own custom sewn sleeve. The knives, scissors and scrapers had all types of edges from straight and sharp to sickle and serrated. Needles of all sizes pierced the last few inches of the kit.

One of the previous owners must have done all this taxidermy himself, Doug thought. Probably not Psycho Vern on the hill or all of this would be gone. Besides, the books were old enough to have hand-sewn binding and the instruments looked like props from a 1930s Frankenstein movie. From the level of dust on everything, no one had been up here in years.

What was this place? A last retreat for Mabron, the long-dead taxidermist, a secret place to practice his hobby, later forgotten? Or were these things forced into the attic and locked away by someone else, someone with the strength to collect these artifacts but too weak to dispose of them? Whatever it was, the last act was to nail the bookcase over the doorway. Trying to keep everyone out or trying to keep everything in?

Doug carefully replaced everything within the chest and closed the lid. He picked up a stuffed red-tailed hawk. The bird stood on a short branch, wings tucked up, as if surveying a field for prey. He brought it down to the turret room. The eyes of the bird sparkled, almost alive. As the bird passed into the daylight, the mounting base quivered. Doug put the bird on the corner of his desk, facing him. He stepped back and swung the attic door shut. He twisted the lock and pocketed the key.

The hunger Doug felt earlier returned with a vengeance. He left for the kitchen with a vision of a rare hamburger filling his mind. He hadn't craved rare meat as far back as he could remember. With the slam of the turret room door, he missed the soft sound of feathers brushing together.

Chapter Twenty-One

It was the third week of her Tennessee teaching career when Principal Ken Wheedle stood in the doorway of Laura's classroom. He'd left his ubiquitous jacket in the office and he was down to cuffed shirt sleeves.

School had let out twenty minutes ago and Laura was taking advantage of the calm to grade some pretty depressing essay answers. She caught the principal out of the corner of her eye.

"Principal Wheedle," she said as she stood up.

"Do you have a moment?" he asked.

Her heart sank. Mr. Wheedle hadn't been to her classroom since she'd started. She hadn't given him reason to, of course. She handled her own discipline and hadn't had any questions she couldn't get answered by one of the less frosty teachers. There could only be one reason for his arrival. The sands in her employment hourglass had run out.

From her first day at the school, she had dreaded the inevitable final day. If she had been a daily sub, the everyday transition from one class to another or the unavoidable days between assignments would have been easy to take. But she had spent weeks with these kids. During the first day, she had pegged each one's strengths and weaknesses. By day two, she had considered them hers. Every time it surfaced, she pushed the idea of her temporary status back underwater and hoped it might drown and never rise again. Now it looked like her time was up.

"Come on in," she told the principal.

Mr. Wheedle slid a short table over next to her desk and sat on the edge of it. His feet dangled down like a kid's and she saw that his socks were a bizarre red plaid.

"Are you having fun at Moultrie?" he asked.

"Fun?" she said. "So much fun, I'd do it for free, but you are really not the person to tell that to."

"I've been impressed with your lesson plans," he said. "And I admit to some clandestine eavesdropping during the day and like your classroom control techniques."

Laura smiled but grimaced inside. *C'mon*, she thought. *Knock off the snow job. Just lower the ax so I can start packing.*

"You remember that Mrs. Matthews was scheduled to be out for a few weeks while her leg healed."

Laura nodded. She held back a sigh. What was she going to do when she woke up in the morning with no children to teach?

"Well," Mr. Wheedle continued, "she realized the number of sick days she had accumulated over the years and decided to rest up completely and stay out the rest of the semester."

"You mean..."

"I mean that the class is yours until then if you want it."

"Want it?" Laura could hardly contain her joy. "Absolutely!"

"Now in all fairness, there's something you need to know," Mr. Wheedle said. "Your third graders have to take the TCAP at the end of the semester. That's the Tennessee Comprehensive Assessment Program exam. It's their first state standardized test. It grades them but it also grades the school. A lot rides on the results and, fair or not, everyone will give you the credit or the blame."

"Then they'll just have to ace that test, won't they?"

Mr. Wheedle smiled. "That's what I knew you'd say. That's why I didn't try too hard to talk Mrs. Matthews out of her decision." He got up and extended his hand. "Pleasure to have you here."

Laura ignored his hand and gave him a quick hug. "It's great to be here."

Mr. Wheedle left and Laura's mind began racing. So much to do. She needed to start reviewing the TCAP. She needed practice tests. She needed a TCAP prep plan. She would have to make *months* of lesson plans! Some kids needed tutoring. She knew which ones. Parent/Teacher conferences were this week.

Seconds ago she feared she was about to be unemployed. Now she was instantly weeks behind.

And it felt great.

Chapter Twenty-Two

It just stunned him sometimes. Over the last three weeks, Doug had turned his afternoons into a personal version of *This Old House*.

He had definitely bonded with the building. Maybe it was the hours he spent writing in the turret room that caused the feel of the house to seep into his bones. Whatever the reason, he had adopted this house like nowhere else he had ever lived.

He remembered the picture from the old newspaper, the one from the gala party, the one with lovely Sarah on the front porch. He remembered it with more detail than it could possibly have contained. Then as he walked around the property, he cringed at every sign of age the way a super model bemoans each facial wrinkle. The guy who paid a local kid to clean his gutters in New York was now out painting trim, replacing rotted boards and weeding flowerbeds. He'd even spiffed up the Hutchington graveyard, resetting all the headstones. An eighty-five-year-old house, a barn and fifteen acres of property made for a lengthy list of chores. He had become a regular at Randolph's Hardware downtown.

He was on his way back from Randolph's when he yanked his car to a stop at the end of the driveway. He jumped out of the car, furious.

An early project had been to replace the rusting, door-less mailbox at the road with a more respectable version. Doug had purchased a beautiful wooden version and painted it in the same contrasting colors of the house and detailed the top to match the shingles. Someone had turned it into a collection of shards and splinters. A few pieces clung to the wooden mounting post, but the rest lay in a pile at the base.

This hadn't been some joyriding kids driving by with a bat. The destruction was deliberate and determined. Whoever did this had a serious grudge, and in his three weeks here, Doug only knew one person who did. Vern.

His first impulse was to drive up the hill and confront the son of a bitch. The sheriff said he had warned the redneck but apparently that hadn't sunk in. Someone needed to explain property rights to him again.

But Doug had no proof. Vern would deny it. They would both shout at each other. In the end, Vern would see he had pissed Doug off and feel good about it. And he would not be deterred.

Doug got back in the car and slammed the door. He yanked the gearshift into reverse, spun the car around and headed back to town. One more trip to Randolph's for a new mailbox. But he wouldn't forget this. Someday Vern would get what was coming to him.

Chapter Twenty-Three

Laura noticed the new mailbox as soon as she approached the house. The old one had certainly met her needs, but if this was part of Doug's *Home Improvement* tear, she was fine with it. She parked by the side of the house and pulled her bags from the front seat.

She approached the house and stopped short of the front steps. She had thought about the ghost girls on and off all day, though it had been weeks since their last encounter. Now an idea struck her. They had come to visit her. Were they waiting for her to visit them?

The Hutchington graveyard was out there somewhere. She guessed it was in the cluster of trees at the far end of the open field. Doug could wait a few moments for her return. She dropped her purse and book bag on the porch and headed for the grove.

The deceptive expanse of lush grass disguised a ragged potholed surface. Laura's ankles twisted awkwardly with every step. Flights of buzzing insects launched as she shuffled through the calf-deep growth. Minutes later, her slow progress and the rolling beads of sweat on her back made her question her impulsive expedition. But those girls *had* come to her... She slapped a mosquito and pressed on.

She stepped into the shade of the grove and it was like entering another world. The temperature dropped ten degrees. The drone of insects disappeared. In the shade she stopped squinting against the low-lying sun and her face relaxed. Far from being the haunted place she feared, the tiny burial ground had a calm, cathedral-like quality.

She saw the grave markers immediately since Doug had cleared much of the debris away. She made a beeline for the twin smaller headstones. She stood between them and read Constance's and Elizabeth's names.

The years engraved on the stones were so long ago. It was a different world back them when food was always fresh and electricity a rarity in rural Tennessee. The girls were probably quite different from the students she had now. They had no television and probably no radio to baby-sit them. Their imagination had to spin their entertainment out of the wisps of their experiences. Many of her students now had so little creativity that she had to jump-start their creative writing storylines or describe the locations they were going to paint. These girls wouldn't have been like that. Building off each other's ideas, they no doubt had hosted imaginary tea parties, played the roles of kidnapped princesses and envisioned secret worlds beneath the surface of the pond.

She knelt between the headstones and placed one hand on each. She felt that twinge at the base of her neck, the warning shot from the old Triple-S. But it was faint, not the jolt she got from the girls' last visit. Were they farther away? Were they weak? Was it because it was daylight? The idea that they did not plan on returning crossed her mind and she was filled with disappointment. She gripped the top of each gravestone.

"You can come back anytime," Laura said. "I'll be here for you. You won't be alone."

The oak she was under shed two leaves. They dropped in two lazy symmetrical spirals like helicopters on a slow approach. One came to rest on the top of each of her hands with a soft caress.

Laura broke into an excited smile. She slipped the leaves into one hand and held them to her heart. The girls knew she cared. She was sure they'd be back when they could. She would be waiting.

Chapter Twenty-Four

Cast-off crap.

That's what her rat bastard ex had called the contents of Theresa Grissom's antique store, Treasured Things. Cast-off crap, salvaged shit, Dumpster debris. He was too stupid to know a business opportunity. Hell, he was too stupid to know he was being alliterative. But it wouldn't have mattered if Theresa had planned to sell permanent weight loss pills, dollar-per-gallon gas or next week's winning lottery numbers. Bobby would have told her every idea she has was retarded. Not because they were but because they were hers. To hear him tell it, marrying him was the only good decision she ever made. So once a day, Theresa Grissom stood in the front door of her successful store, scanned her inventory, smiled and said, "Cast-off crap." She loved to remind herself of one more time that her jackass former husband had been wrong.

Theresa tucked her short red hair behind her ear. She was thin with fair skin and delicate features. A score of faint freckles brushed her cheekbones. Her petite height made her appear just over twenty instead of past thirty. But telltale wrinkles already creased the corners of her eyes and between her brows, vapor trails left by the public trials of marrying a jerk and the private burden of her psychic gift.

"Premonitions" her grandmother called them, though Theresa wished they were as precise as that name implied. Usually it was just a feeling, a vague fear, a wisp of foreboding. First one event would trigger the sensation, and then later another. Each was a sensory event (touch, smell, hearing) and she would experience them in a string over time, like putting extra letters on the little ledge from a Scrabble game.

The problem was the letters were never in order and she never knew how many there were supposed to be. All she had was a nonsense word until the letters marched into the right order and her premonition made sense. But often it was too late to do anything about it.

Her gift first manifested at age fourteen. A colossal oak shaded the family trailer outside of Moultrie. She'd grown up around the tree, climbed in its branches with her sister, played in its shade in the summer and jumped in its leaves in the fall. Then one day, leaning her bike against the tree after school, the touch of the tree terrified her. The branches turned menacing, like a witch's outstretched arms. The ripples in the gnarled bark of the trunk sneered at her. The leaves rustled in the wind like whispered warnings. Gooseflesh rippled across her arms and every fiber in her being said the tree was one supernaturally poisoned oak.

Try as she did to rationally douse the flames of this unsubstantiated fear, they only burned hotter all week. She avoided the tree, fearful even to cross its long shadow in the late-day sun. Of course she shared her trepidation with no one, afraid to sound like a scared child when she wanted to be considered on the edge of adulthood.

A few days later, her second Scrabble letter went face up. Her mother was making breakfast, frying eggs for all. She had a gift for cracking the egg against the edge of the cast iron skillet and pouring its contents into the pan while demolishing the eggshell. Other cooks ended up with two eggshell halves, but Mom had a handful of eggshell crumbs and none of it ever made it into the pan. At the crack and crush symphony from the first egg, Theresa felt a chill race down her spine. She wasn't even watching her mother cook. All she sensed was the sound, one snap and crumble of the splintered shell, a faint noise that inexplicably pushed itself to the foreground, past her sister's panicked rant about her fuzzy hair, the blare of the *Today* show on the kitchen micro-TV and the cascade of the shower running down the hall. Crack. Crush. Panic.

It wasn't the eggs she was afraid of. When her mother slapped one sunny side up in front of her, Theresa didn't flinch. It was the sound of the shattering shell, the concept of a durable surface instantly pulverized, that made the terror race through her like a thousand volts. Nothing else tripped her premonition sensors that day, or the next. But the image of her mother's one-handed crush was never far from her mind.

That Friday, rain fell in sheets as the school bus dropped Theresa at the foot of her driveway. Thunder rumbled close by. She grabbed the mail from the mailbox and dashed through the torrent to the trailer. She entered dripping wet. As she moved to toss the mail on the table, she felt her hand grow cold, as if there were a chunk of ice imbedded in the mail. That same sense of impending evil filled her soul. She flipped through the sheaf of envelopes and tossed discards to the floor. Her fingers went numb as she held the last one.

The return address was the County Clerk's Office. This was the registration renewal for her mother's minivan.

Rain pounded against the tin roof of the trailer. Lightning cracked overhead so close that Theresa could hear raindrops explode in its path. The flash lit the envelope in her hand and the room went white.

A vision flashed through Theresa's mind and all the clues fell into place. The tree, the egg, the letter, the storm. The vision lasted but seconds, but it was all Theresa needed. *Her mother's van, wipers slapping against the blinding rain, barrels up the driveway. Lightning strikes the tree beside the house, splitting the mighty oak in two. Half the tree shears away, too quickly for Theresa's mother to react after the blinding flash. The oak lands across the roof and bends the car into a V around the driver's seat. The windshield explodes outward, showering glass nuggets into the pounding downpour. No one survives.*

Dread engulfed Theresa. She had no doubt that what she saw would come true. She had to act now.

She ran out the front door. The white minivan was yards from the driveway and closing fast. A snap of cloud-to-cloud lightning announced the thunderhead's arrival. Theresa's hair stood on end as the ground swelled with static electricity, ready to pull down the next lightning bolt.

There was no time for thought. The van had to stop. Theresa grabbed her bicycle from beside the door. The van turned into the driveway and Theresa ran.

The air was thick with the blinding rain. The van defroster wasn't worth a crap and between the windshield fog and the worn wipers, Theresa's mom would never recognize her daughter trying to flag her down.

Feet from the van, Theresa launched her bicycle in front of it. The van grill snapped as a handlebar speared the plastic. The bike rolled under the front tires. Metal twisted and the bike seat plowed wet gravel into a grinding pile. The van rolled over the bike and Theresa's mother screamed. The van's brakes locked.

A bolt of lightning two feet wide leapt from the clouds overhead. True to Theresa's vision, it blasted the mighty oak down the middle. Sap boiled in the doomed tree and the trunk exploded. The right side of the tree crashed on the driveway with the staccato snap of dozens of branches. The tree missed Theresa by inches. She did not flinch.

Theresa's mother burst from the van. At the sight of the mangled bicycle, she screamed Theresa's name then cut it off midway when she saw her daughter standing in the pouring rain. Strands of Theresa's red hair were plastered against her face like dripping candle wax. Theresa's mother looked back and forth between the bike, her daughter and the exploded oak, unsure where to begin her questioning.

Theresa was never able to fully explain her gift to her mother, but saving her life was all that was important. Though her first experience at "prophesy", as her mother took to calling it, let her change a horrible future, the gift was not always so generous. Sometimes the pieces only came together after the event transpired. Sometimes they never amounted to anything, as far as she could tell.

So the gift doubled as a curse. Theresa's debilitating guilt at understanding too late about the impending fire at the County Animal

Shelter was one thing. But the frustration from all the unsolved sensations of dread was even worse. Did the anxiety she felt when she touched an antique bowl mean something nefarious was about to unfold, or was it just a stray thought that coincidentally passed by? Most times, she never knew.

Another disappointment was her lack of control. She could not select what her premonition was about. The vision seemed to select her. God knew, a few visions of her future with Bastard Bobby Grissom would have been nice the week before their courthouse wedding.

The good news was Treasured Things had been a hit from the start. And it was a good thing since Bastard Bobby's child support was as reliable as his toilet bowl aim. Sympathetic folks had let her sell their heirlooms on consignment, so she needed little investment to get up and running. Most of the sales were to outsiders, folks passing through or out for a weekend drive. The visitors paid top dollar. Since the day the judge ordered Bobby to move out, Theresa hadn't missed a mortgage payment.

The store fronted on the west side of Moultrie's town square, staring at the main entrance to the county courthouse and it's ever vigilant bronze son of the Confederacy. Rooting through the second-floor storage when she first opened up, Theresa found lost reminders of the shop's previous lives as a shoe store, a sporting goods store, and even hat blocks from the bygone era when men would not dare go out bareheaded. The relics all joined the jumble of antiques that filled the narrow store to overflowing.

On the shelves, anachronisms abounded. Sewing machines, typewriters, hand farm tools (some with traces of dirt in their tines). Theresa made sure the store had the proper scent of mixed must and polish so the customers knew the items were old yet taken care of.

The bell rang at the front door of the store. Theresa looked up from behind the desk she was dusting. Ruby Broadway strode in, cradling a large open box in her arms. She wore a bright red dress that, over her three-hundred-pound frame, made her look a bit like a barn. Theresa knew that dress. Ruby did estate sales and auctions in this county and the next, and she always wore red when she was selling. She said she didn't want the buyers to miss her. Her dark skin amplified her already dazzling white smile. Her hair had a new style, processed straight and pulled back and up, with ringlets at each ear.

"Girl," Ruby announced as she muscled down the tight aisle. "Have I got some wonders for you!" Ruby made back the bulk of her investment in each estate from the furniture. Most of the remainder sold for small sums too small for her to worry about. Ruby donated these orphans to Theresa.

"Ruby, you have no idea how much some of the things you give me are worth," Theresa said. "You have to take a percentage."

Ruby dropped the box on the desk. The impact rocked a small, empty crystal vase off the edge. Theresa caught it with a snap of the wrist. The averted calamity didn't register with Ruby.

"Don't need no percentage," she said. "My percentage is seeing that cute boy of yours well fed and away from his loser of a father." Ruby had more than one ax to grind with men from her past. "You got after him about those support payments yet?"

Theresa was ashamed to admit she hadn't. She avoided confrontation in general, but with Bobby in specific. Part of the reason was his capacity for violence, especially with a few under his belt. Also, his presence was a reminder of the mistake she'd made marrying him, the only positive outcome of which had been her son Dustin.

"I called my lawyer about the support payments," Theresa said.

"You need to call the cops," Ruby said. "Get his ass tossed in jail for a while."

Theresa wished it were that easy. She hated that the son of a bitch still intimidated her.

"Gotta run, doll," Ruby said, already mid-turn for the door. "Kids'll be home soon and I gotta be out of this dress before *that* storm hits. Tell me, girl, what do you call a man who's lost ninety percent of his mental skills?"

Theresa smiled as she delivered Ruby's punch line for the thousandth time. "Divorced."

"Amen, sister." The door shut behind Ruby.

Theresa glanced at the clock. It was almost four thirty. She had to pick up her son Dustin as well. She gripped the box on the desk and the feeling hit her. Black, cold debilitating dread. She pulled her hands away as if she had touched a hot stove.

"Damn it," she whispered. This had been such a good day, such a good string of days, now about to be ruined by the Gift That Keeps On Giving. The box had some pictures in it, a few small boxes that probably held cheap jewelry, and some books. Theresa reached inside to find the source of the premonition, and then yanked her hand back.

"No way," she said. Not now. It was too late in the day to start solving that nasty little enigma. The search could go on forever, looking for the other puzzle pieces, and once she started, she lived in fear every minute, wondering if she would crack the secret code in time to derail disaster. She wasn't starting that at this hour. She tossed the box onto a low shelf on the wall. She turned the shop lights out. Whatever it was, it could wait.

Chapter Twenty-Five

One woman stick figure. One boy stick figure. One cat. Those were the three decals in the back window of Theresa Grissom's Ford Explorer. There was a space on the left where Bastard Bobby's little stick figure had been last year. The residual adhesive had attracted a coating of dirt Theresa refused to clean off. She thought it was fitting.

The Explorer rolled to a stop in front of Moultrie Elementary. A customer had kept her late and kids were already streaming out from extended after care. The program was the county's recognition that the majority of the families were dual income or single parents struggling to get by on one. Theresa kept a sharp eye out for Dustin's bright blue jacket.

The last year had been tough on the boy. To say the divorce was messy would be like calling 9-11 an aviation mishap. Throughout it, Bobby got drunker, louder and more abusive than usual. Nothing Theresa said could get him to shield his son from his rages. Dustin, like any boy, had idolized his father. But the hero worship ended the night Dustin watched his drunken dad rant outside their house and crap on the hood of his mother's SUV before the cops dragged him off. In the downward spiral over the eight months between filing and finalizing the divorce, Dustin became silent, withdrawn. Theresa did all she could, but she had to admit the divorce drained her. There were days she knew she was no help to her son.

She expected to see the crowd of kids dissolve and Dustin complete his usual head-down shuffle to the car. Her jaw nearly hit the steering wheel when her son burst from the school, smiling from ear to ear. He had short blond hair and ears that protruded just enough to qualify as cute. He raced to the car, little backpack slamming back and forth with each stride. He gripped a large rolled up paper in one hand. He threw himself in the backseat without closing the door.

"Look, Mom, look," he panted. He shoved the thick artist's paper at her. "Look what I made."

"Whoa, whoa," Theresa said. "Let me see." She unrolled the paper. It was a watercolor scene of a forest by the lake. She recognized it as the state park they went to two summers ago. She was stunned because most of Dustin's works were strictly crayon-based primary school efforts with stick figures and yellow circle suns. This painting had a hint of style.

"You did this by yourself?" Theresa said.

"Yeah. Ms. Locke brought us in paints and showed us how to hold the brushes." It had been three weeks since the long-term substitute teacher for Mrs. Matthews had taken Dustin's class. "They're called 'watercolors'. And look at the top of the picture."

A gold star glittered in the afternoon sun. Next to it in perfect penmanship it said *Wonderful job, Dustin!*

"Wow," Theresa said. "Your new teacher really liked it." She passed it back to Dustin who unrolled it again.

"And I really like it," he said.

That substitute Ms. Locke found something new Dustin enjoyed, Theresa thought. The withdrawn boy had a way to express himself, and it had nothing to do with his father. This activity was going to be one hundred percent Dustin. Just what he needed.

"Can we get some watercolors?" Dustin said.

"We'll get some at Walmart on the way home if you're good."

"Yesss!" Dustin slammed the Explorer's back door and put on his seat belt. It was the first time in months he hadn't needed a reminder.

Parent/Teacher Night was tomorrow. Theresa couldn't wait to meet Ms. Locke. With a great deal of guilt, she gave thanks that Mrs. Matthews had broken her leg.

Chapter Twenty-Six

"Three doors down on the left, Ms. Grissom."

Theresa nodded a thank-you to the PTA volunteer at the main entrance to Moultrie Elementary. She already knew where the third grade classroom was. She sat in it as a student for a whole year. Nothing like Parent/Teacher night to remind you how fast life could pass you by.

She entered the classroom and slipped into one of the pint-sized desks. Being petite paid yet another dividend as she found she could still breathe. Most of the dozen other parents couldn't say the same. Wide butts and potbellies were shoehorned into the desks around her. She recognized all the parents—Cassie Lutz's mom, Nicky Clark's dad, Barry Levin's chronically overprotective parents. This was the group's fourth year together shepherding their children through the public education maze. But it was their first experience with an outsider teacher none of them knew. Theresa wasn't as xenophobic as the Moultrie locals. She couldn't wait to meet the woman who had brought her son back into the world through art.

The classroom décor should have melted the other parents' concerns. Ms. Locke had made it her own in Ms. Matthew's absence. Bright, engaging cartoon decorations covered the bulletin boards. Posters encouraging the kids to do their best hung on the walls. It was a far cry from the oppressive grays and blacks Theresa's third grade teacher had favored.

When Laura Locke entered, Theresa instantly liked her. Laura looked sharp and professional in a calf-length navy dress and short red jacket. But the treat was her smile; dazzling, engaging, honest. This was a woman who loved to teach.

Laura introduced herself and started with handshakes all around. With each, she delivered a positive comment about the parent's child. She extended her hand to Theresa in turn.

"Theresa Grissom," Theresa said. "Dustin's mom."

As their hands touched, Theresa's world went dark. The Gift delivered like a pile driver. Pain. Suffering. Fear. Loss. It was as if four speakers surrounding her head blasted four separate dirges simultaneously and the sound waves crashed together inside her brain. The classroom returned in a disorienting flash.

"Danger," Theresa muttered.

"Excuse me?" Laura said.

Theresa realized she had spoken out loud and her face turned red.

"Nice to meet you," Theresa said. She snapped her hand back to avoid a second dose of psychic downloading.

"Dustin has done so well this year," Laura said. "Especially in Math. He may have a gift we can cultivate if I get him away from painting"

Theresa gave the compliment a wan smile. All the wonderful things she planned to say washed away as the black emotions she channeled cut a path through her consciousness.

While Laura addressed the group on how third grade would unwind that year, how she would there until the end of the semester. She explained the TCAP exams and their importance. Her mention of tutoring got a low rumble of a response from the room until she added that it would be free after school in the classroom. Smiles blossomed everywhere.

Theresa could barely focus. Her first maternal reaction to the overwhelming sense of danger was that Laura was a threat to her son. She dismissed that idea as soon as it appeared. The feeling was all wrong for that. It wasn't her son who was in danger, it was this new teacher.

112

The emotional encounter brought back the memory of her last psychic blast when Ruby Green brought her the box from the estate sale. The two feelings were different but related, as if they resonated at the same frequency but with different amplitudes. Theresa gritted her teeth. The quest had begun.

At the end of the session, Laura handed out cards with her address and phone number on them. On the back of each was a bright yellow smiley face. On the way out of the classroom, Theresa fiddled with her purse to avoid a parting handshake with Laura and another round of physical contact.

Theresa had been in this cursed position so many times. She knew something bad was on the way, but not enough to prevent it. She didn't even know enough to convince potential victims trouble was brewing. Much as she wanted to warn Laura, she knew that first she had to complete the quest, turn over those last few Scrabble letters and solve the puzzle. She had to go back to Treasured Things.

Theresa called the sitter and extended her for an hour. She pulled her car into a spot in front of Treasured Things. The deserted block around the courthouse testified to the small town's missing night life. She looked at her store, her second son, with unaccustomed dread. The sight of the shop in the morning sun each day always made her smile. But tonight in the shadows and fuzzy vapor lights, the dark store engendered fear. The black block letter sign said *Closed* and the dark interior reinforced it. But Theresa had to know what was in the box. The clock had started. The riddle had to be solved before it solved itself.

She punched the pass code into the burglar alarm's keypad, then went straight to the box. Bottom shelf next to the old armoire. Funny how in the crowded store she knew exactly where each of her treasures rested.

She pulled the box out with one quick, clean jerk, like a chef trying to pull a hot pan from an oven without a pot holder. She dropped it to the floor. She sat cross-legged in front of it and passed her left hand over its contents. She got to a wood picture frame and her fingertips tingled.

Bingo.

She took a deep breath closed her eyes and grabbed the frame. Fear lit her fingertips and spread across her body like an army of biting fleas. She pulled the picture from the box and dropped it on the floor. The fear evaporated and she looked at the black-and-white picture.

A sleek ebony thoroughbred stood at a racetrack's inside rail. He stared at the camera with haughty pride, a garland of first-place flowers around his glistening neck. A diminutive Hispanic jockey with a narrow moustache sat straight in the saddle wearing what looked like red-and-white-checked silks. The attire of the gawkers behind the steed placed the picture in the 1940s.

Theresa wrapped her hand in the tail of her blouse. She used it as an insulator and flipped the picture on its back. She pried the back off the frame with a butter knife from a nearby set of silver.

A notation on the back of the photo, handwritten in the perfect penmanship the world no longer practiced, read *Challenger's Fancy— March 28—Nashville Raceway*

Piece of cake, Theresa thought.

She went to her office and clicked her computer to life. In minutes she found the Nashville Raceway Historical Society website and knew more than she had ever wanted to know about the long-defunct track. She clicked on the loving cup icon and the winners of each race were listed by year. She wondered who had the time to get all this data together.

She flipped from March to March each year looking for Challenger's Fancy. There he was in 1946, in first place at the annual Vanderbilt Cup, Jorge Hermosa riding. Nice information, but none of it clicked until she read who owned the horse.

Mabron Hutchington, Galaxy Farm.

That was the connection. Theresa remembered something, a fragment she hadn't thought important at the time. She pulled Laura

Locke's card from her pocket. The big yellow smile face greeted her. She flipped it over and read the address. 2143 Hwy 41 N. The address made her shudder. Laura hadn't printed the name on there, but the whole town knew the address of Galaxy Farm.

Theresa had heard that a writer and his wife had bought the old place awhile back but didn't know she was her son's teacher. Outsiders would have to buy the house. Just knowing Vernon Pugh lived there would keep the average person away from it.

Theresa gave the computer's mouse a frustrated spin on its mouse pad. She had a handful of threads, but no idea what tapestry they were supposed to form. Dustin's nice teacher was in danger. It would happen at home. A fire? An accident? A heart attack? Theresa didn't have enough to warn her. But she'd keep up the search and pray she would know the answer before it was too late.

Chapter Twenty-Seven

A week after Parent/Teacher Night, Laura awoke before the alarm. The rich smell of perking coffee filled the dark bedroom. Visions of Doug serving fresh fruit, hot coffee and a steaming croissant came to mind and she cracked a sleepy smile. She rolled over and into Doug's back. He was still asleep. The coffee was on a timer. Her smile faded.

There had been a subtle shift over the first month at Galaxy Farm. The first week or so, Doug had been up early with Laura's alarm clock. They shared a hot breakfast on the front porch in the morning sun and dinner awaited when Laura got home. By the second week, Doug wasn't up until after she showered and breakfast had devolved to cereal and yogurt. This week he wasn't awake at all before she left. He'd also begun rolling into bed later, working into the night on his novel. At first he'd knock off when Laura was done with her school prep, but last week she was asleep before he crawled into bed. Their sex life had died on the vine.

Laura slid out of bed. Doug didn't stir. She wondered what time he'd turned in. When she had awakened briefly at one a.m., she was sure he wasn't there. She pulled on her robe and padded out to the kitchen. The sun just crested the horizon and the low golden rays set the kitchen aglow. She poured herself a cup of coffee and headed into the bathroom.

While she drank her coffee and let the shower water heat up (another sacrifice for living in an antique house), she mulled over Doug's recent behavior. He did nice things for her like setting up the coffee, doing the shopping while she was at work, taking care of the house. These were things he never did back in New York. Even cutting their postage stamp lawn had been a burden he hated to shoulder. She should be happy as hell.

As to his sleep schedule, he'd always been a night owl. God knows, his work at the *Dispatch* tended to be all late nights. Was she unreasonable to expect him to revert to punching a rooster's time clock?

She *was* coming home later from school with TCAP tutoring every afternoon. School had been consuming more of her waking hours. Did he feel neglected and this was a subconscious reaction?

She shook off her unwarranted guilt trip. No, the situation didn't feel right. There was a distance in Doug, even when he was right next to her. The outside was Doug, but the inside was something else. Not way off inside, just a bit out of phase. She had no proof of it, no actions she could point to that were bizarre. There was something going on. Her old Student Sixth Sense didn't work well on adults, but it wasn't completely shut down. Like the bruise under the skin of a ripe banana, there might be a wisp of something amiss in Doug.

She banished the thought. Living in this isolated house in the country, with most of her colleagues giving her the cold shoulder, Doug was all she had. She had to be able to count on him.

An hour later, when she headed out the door, Doug was still asleep. She grabbed her purse and did the usual pre-departure check. Keys, cell phone, wallet. She rooted around for one more thing. Matches, check.

She had carried that book of matches from Randolph's every day since she had picked them up. She couldn't explain the fixation. At first she thought that having them in her purse was just because she forgot to take them out. But when she had taken them out, she felt incomplete, vulnerable. The feelings went away when she put the matches back in.

Good luck charm? Talisman? She didn't know. Whatever the reason, the habit was harmless. On her list of things to worry about, the inclination ranked way below TCAP practice tests and Doug's

117

shifting schedule. Besides, in a few months the chill air would make that big fireplace in the living room look pretty inviting. She could always use the matches there.

Chapter Twenty-Eight

Doug woke later to the heat of the sun cooking his bedspread. He rolled over and pried open an eyelid. The clock read *10:25.*

Doug had perfected his routine this week. He got up late, well after Laura left. A leisurely brunch would be followed by work, usually an hour or two pounding out a chapter of his unfolding Southern saga. He had to write in the turret room, and he got the feeling the room didn't want Laura to know its inspirational abilities. He never even left the door open anymore, afraid to have to explain the taxidermied hawk from the attic.

He'd do his afternoon errands then share dinner with Laura. Afterward he'd retire to polish the words he'd scribed in haste earlier in the day. He knew Laura understood. She was working on her class work for the next day anyway, and she had some tutoring thing going on after school that kept her out until after five p.m..

This morning, after checking the internet news as he ate brunch, he took the laptop back up to the study and dropped it into the base station. When the AC power hit, the screen lit up to full intensity, as if saying, "Now let's get some real work done." Doug parked himself at the desk.

The family in his tale of an 1850s Southern plantation had come to life. Patriarch Nathan Edwards ruled the cotton plantation with an iron hand and raked in profits from the burgeoning trade with British textile mills. His sons Randall and Samuel vied for control of their father's estate as his health declined. The two brothers courted Veronica, the beautiful daughter of the town's mayor. The plantation's evil overseer hid the truth of the plight of the hundreds of slaves from the father, but the sons both understood plantation life. Doug could feel the characters, knew their motivations. It was like they were alive in his head. Novelist nirvana.

Later, his shoulders ached from hunching over his keyboard. He pulled himself back one hundred and sixty years and rolled his chair back from the desk. His back creaked as he forced himself upright. The sun had gone from shining in the east turret window to the west. Where did the day go?

He had written a lot but still felt pressed to do more since he'd have to forsake his morning ritual tomorrow. His agent had scheduled him for a slot on *Good Morning America* as an example of either the penitent face of reformed trash writers, or the latest high-profile exile from city stress. He wasn't sure which. Whatever it was, it was good publicity for his novel. So Doug was going to sit in the local affiliate in Nashville, stare at a camera and pretend he was talking to George Stephanopoulos. Not bad except he had to do it at seven a.m., which meant spending the night tonight in the city.

The hawk on his desk caught his eye. It certainly grew on him, this proud, regal bird. Quite a feat of skill, making it so lifelike, down to the tilt of its head, which he thought was cocked a little more to the left when he first brought it down.

He hadn't explored the attic once since that first time. His absence wasn't because he hadn't thought about returning. The attic had an allure he could not explain. He had just been so busy with household chores and this novel aching to be written. But today he'd done several thousand words, a personal record. He rated a break.

He pulled the key from a desk drawer. He couldn't explain why he thought he had to hide it, or why he had to lock the door at all.

At the top of the creaking attic stairs, he shuffled through the dim room to the chest at the end of the attic. Doug went straight for it, through the gauntlet of taxidermied creatures and their glassy, staring eyes.

He lifted the chest lid and the silver locket caught his eye. He opened it again and marveled at the exquisite detail of the lovely Sarah's picture. She had an aquiline beauty ideal in any era.

He realized he may have given short shrift to Mabron, the man in the other half. On second look, he had a dignity about him, a sense of purpose. There had to be a great story that ended with sharing a locket with your brother's wife. An illicit love affair, perhaps?

Doug returned the locket with the same delicate spiraling of the fine chain as before. He set the inner shelf aside. A tray of different-sized marbles blocked access to the books. Doug set them aside on top of a box. From that position they literally looked straight at him. Six pairs of various pupils sparkled in the sunlight. They were glass eyes for the mounted animals, different sizes for different animals. Fascinating.

A larger eye sat in the end position, a yellow iris with a narrow black slit pupil that that seemed to open onto infinite darkness beyond.

Doug pulled out the *Methods in the Art of Taxidermy* volume. The leather creaked as he opened the cover. The copyright on the first brittle yellow page read 1900. He flipped through the pages. The first paragraph read:

The art of embalming was invented by the Egyptians for the purpose of preserving dead bodies from decay by means of aromatics, antiseptics or desiccation. It was an art created by the demands of the religious superstition of the times, and was practiced by the ancients from the earliest periods, but, unfortunately, was not calculated to enlighten and elevate. In their sepulchers, tombs and pits are found not only countless bodies of human beings, but also myriads of dogs, apes, crocodiles, cats, ibises, sheep, oxen and other animals.

There followed a history of taxidermy through the nineteenth century, followed by instructions on setting up a workshop. Then came chapter after chapter on how to mount an animal skin. A few sheets had illustrations of recommended tools of the trade. All of them were in the canvas bundle Doug unwound the first day in the attic. Now he knew their specialized missions; cutting, scraping, sewing, even a specialized melon-baller designed to slice socket joints apart.

Doug sat under the light and flipped back to page one. He began to read with slow deliberation, pulling apart every paragraph of the author's stilted English. The more he read, the more intriguing the techniques became; scraping bones, tanning hides, molding clay mounts. The most gruesome references inspired reverence rather than revulsion.

The illuminated edges of the boards over the windows grew dim and reminded Doug he needed to suspend his education. He repacked the chest.

On the way down the stairs, Doug caught a glimpse of a mounted bobcat near the top of the steps. He scooped the diminutive feline up from around the waist like a housecat. He carried it down the stairs and put it on the floor at the apex of the three turret windows. When it hit the afternoon sun, Doug swore its yellow eyes glowed brighter. The fur seemed to ripple, the skin draw tighter on the body. Doug though what amazing things the right lighting could do.

He shut the attic door and spun the key to lock it. This time he didn't just drop the key in his top desk drawer. He approached the bookshelf.

He slid out a copy of *Keys to Creative Writing.* He slipped the key into the binding and slid the book back. The motion left a clear trail in the dust. He cursed and wiped down all the shelves with the edge of his T-shirt. No evidence, he thought. No clues. The last bastion had to remain inviolate.

"Where the hell did that come from?" he said to himself and gave his head a shake.

As he closed the door to the turret room, he thumbed the handle over to the locked position without even knowing it.

Chapter Twenty-Nine

Half a dozen watercolors lined the wall behind Theresa Grissom's desk in the rear of Treasured Things. Dustin had put his home set of paints to good use, creating something every day after school. Some were pictures of happy times. Some were memories of the dark days of the divorce. The happy ones made the cut to the wall.

But Theresa didn't care if he painted *Dogs Playing Poker*. He found an outlet for the thoughts that raced around in his head. Dustin's therapist had fruitlessly talked himself hoarse trying to get Dustin to say anything about his feelings. But as soon as he had a paintbrush in his hand, it all came rushing out of him. Then when he showed the picture to his mother, all she had to do was ask, and they could talk about everything he felt. Theresa wondered if Mrs. Locke had any idea what an impact she had on Dustin.

Treasured Things had a slow afternoon and Theresa sat with her shoes off and stocking feet on the stool next to her chair. It was funny how she could gauge the day within the first hour and a half of opening. This morning had been dead as road kill and she knew the rest of the day would be no better. If she had paid herself by the hour, she would have gone home to cut costs. She had balanced the books earlier, but now she was part of the way through a marginal novel called *Retroactive*, about a serial killer obstetrician who murders criminal adults he helped bring into the world. There were some strange books that made it into her shop when friends donated boxes of castoffs.

A near-drained glass of lemonade sweated onto a coaster on her desk. Without looking up, she grabbed it and finished the remainder.

As she finished, the ice clumped in the bottom broke free and slid down. A chunk hit her front tooth with what Theresa swore was the sound of a cannon. She felt a numbing cold spread from her mouth to her extremities. A sudden rush of claustrophobic panic gripped her. The air felt thick, almost chunky. She spit the ice out of her mouth and leapt to her feet. She shook her hands and then rubbed them together. They were stone cold.

She stomped to the front of the store to distance herself from the location of the experience and to absorb some of the warm afternoon sunlight. She passed the box on the shelf where she left the picture of the Galaxy Farm champion horse. A feeling of dread hit her in the stomach like a prizefighter's punch. She doubled over but kept going forward, now trying to outrun two premonitions. She grabbed a display case for support and nearly launched herself out the shop's front door.

The little bell on the door tingled behind her as if ending the round between her and her gift. She stood shoeless and gasping on the sidewalk. With her hands on her knees, she took deep breaths of the afternoon air until she felt her lungs warm up. She looked up just in time to see a little girl staring at her from the curb. The pigtailed girl was about five and had on a faded souvenir shirt from the Nashville Zoo.

"You don't look good," the girl said.

She gave the kid a scowl and went back in the store. There was no doubt about it. Another Scrabble piece just flipped over. And the way the premonition intertwined with the one from the Galaxy Farm picture, there was no way they were unrelated. She knew more than enough of the Galaxy Farm history to know its most famous connection with ice. The drowned twins in the frozen pond. Stories of them haunting the Galaxy Farm grounds had circulated since their deaths.

She didn't have enough information to see the whole vision, but she had enough to be scared. Something supernatural was stirring at Galaxy Farm, and whatever it was, it had evil intentions for her son's new teacher. She could wait for more clues to surface and see the entire story, but she had the feeling that time was of the essence. She was going to need help.

Theresa flipped the sign on the door over to read *Closed.* School was out in under an hour. She hoped Laura Locke would have time to talk. She also hoped Dustin's teacher wouldn't think she was crazy.

"Mrs. Locke?"

Laura looked up from her desk in the empty classroom. She gave Theresa a smile of recognition. Theresa was relieved. Her first fear was that Laura wouldn't recognize her from Parent/Teacher night last week.

"Ms. Grissom!" Laura said. "Dustin is already over in after care."

"I came a bit early to see you," Theresa said.

Laura smiled. "Come on in and please call me Laura."

Theresa approached Laura's desk, feeling uncomfortably like a school kid before the teacher. She looked around for somewhere to sit and ending up leaning back against a pint-sized desktop. "I'm not interrupting you, am I?"

"No," Laura said. "I've been planning to talk with you about Dustin. His grades have turned one hundred and eighty degrees in the last few weeks. He also plays with the other kids at recess now. You must be doing something great with him at home."

"It's the painting," Theresa said. "You got him hooked on it. He paints every night at home and it's become a way for him to work through some issues he has around my divorce from his father. He's turning back into the little boy I used to know. How did you know he would take to it?"

"Sometimes I just get a sense for what flips a kid's switch," Laura said. "Something about Dustin said 'artist'."

Theresa got a ray of hope. At least this woman has an appreciation for intuition. Maybe she could take her belief just one step further...

125

"I came to talk about something else," Theresa said. She'd only have one shot at this, one test well to strike oil. She thought carefully for a moment. "The address on your card is the old Galaxy Farm, isn't it?"

"Yes, though it seems to be more of a conversation stopper than the starter you've made it."

Theresa was afraid she'd lose her nerve if she beat around the bush.

"Have you seen the girls?" she blurted out.

Laura's eyes went wide. Her pen went limp in her hand. Theresa hit a gusher with the first well.

"What girls?' Laura said with a complete lack of conviction. Theresa pulled the student desk up along side Laura's and sat down.

"You've seen the ghosts of the Hutchington twins," Theresa said.

"Who told you to..."

"This is going to sound strange," Theresa began, and she told Laura a short version of her life with her "gift" and how it worked. Through it, Laura nodded and listened, the opposite reaction Theresa got from the few locals she had ever told. Theresa finished with the two clues of the racehorse picture and her encounter with the ice.

"But what connects those two premonitions to me?" Laura said.

"At the Parent/Teacher night," Theresa said. "We shook hands and I got the feeling that, well, you were in danger. Tell me about seeing the girls."

"Well, I didn't see them actually," Laura said. "They came to me in a dream. Then later I felt their presence in my study with me while I was working. Trust me, there wasn't anything malicious in their visits. They rustled my papers. It was more like a prank. They even rolled a ball back and forth for me. They don't pose any danger. I liked having them around."

"What does your husband think about these visitors?"

"Doug?" Laura hesitated, as if weighing how forthcoming to be with the answer. "Let's just say he's a nonbeliever. Thought I was imagining things."

"We've ruled out this being your imagination," Theresa said. "But I'm not ruling out that there's something dangerous. I felt it and my premonitions are never wrong. I might take too long to figure them out, but they are never wrong."

There was an uncomfortable pause and Theresa knew she was failing to convince.

"I've spoken a bit with Dustin on how things are at home," Laura said. "You two have had a rough time of it recently. Maybe some of the stress there triggered your feeling of—"

"No, no," Theresa said. "I know the difference. You have to believe me. I wouldn't expose myself like this if I wasn't sure. If I could get closer to the source, I would probably get much better reception. I hate to be forward, but perhaps if I came to your house..." This was the big moment, she thought.

"Sure," Laura said without hesitation. "Doug is away tonight, come on over. You'll find that there is nothing to be afraid of and you can rest easy."

They agreed on seven p.m.. Dustin would have to be looked after, but Theresa knew her mother would be happy to have her grandson spend the night with her.

Theresa walked over and picked her son up early from after school care. That made him happy, but not as happy as the opportunity to spend the night with Grandma, who always had the best desserts.

Theresa wasn't sure whether to be excited about the evening or apprehensive. The night would either confirm or contradict her theory about a threat to Laura. Laura felt that the girls' spirits were not evil, so maybe Theresa's premonitions weren't right. At the farm tonight, she'd probably find out she had nothing to worry about.

Theresa found her rationalization completely unconvincing.

Chapter Thirty

Theresa had a distinct feeling of foreboding as she drove up Galaxy Farm's driveway. The setting sun left only a pink ribbon along the western horizon. Her headlights lit the main house and she had to admit it was classically beautiful with its turreted upper room and wraparound porch. A few of the shutters even glistened with a fresh coat of black paint. But there was nothing inviting about the place. She didn't get the big slam she got with a premonition, but she felt an underlying current of evil.

Laura met her at the front door with a big smile. "The first night I'm here alone and I invite over a neighbor," she said. "You'll think I really am scared of spirits in the house."

"No," Theresa said. "I know I'm the one with issues there."

Theresa crossed over the threshold and felt no different. She looked around the main room and the impressive stone fireplace with the wrought iron tool set caught her eye. The sparse modern furniture looked like it would be more at home in New York City, and she guessed it had been. Laura took her on a tour of the downstairs. They ended up outside the old nursery.

"Well," Laura said. "Any bad vibes?"

"Can't say that there are," Theresa answered.

"I hope you stay as disappointed all evening," Laura said.

They entered Laura's study. "This was where I met them," Laura said. They both stood in the room. Laura watched for a reaction from Theresa. "Anything?"

Theresa shook her head. She was starting to feel ridiculous. "What were you doing when they came the last time?"

"Grading papers."

"And you felt them here before they manifested themselves?"

"Absolutely."

Theresa silently cursed the lack of control she had over her gift. She'd have to try a less passive tack.

"Let's try what attracted them before," she said. "I'll sit over there and you go do whatever it is you need to do for school."

"You are going to watch me grade spelling and math quizzes?" Laura said. "I though the nightlife in Moultrie might need a shot in the arm, but if you think test grading is entertainment, things are worse than I thought."

Theresa sat in the recess of the bay window, her knees tucked up to her chin. Laura put a red marker to work against the stack of quizzes. The clock radio crept through ascending digits as the stack of tests diminished. A coyote howled somewhere far across the pond.

Suddenly, Laura gave a little shake and dropped her pen on the desk. She shot a quick glance to Theresa and mouthed, "They're here."

Theresa felt nothing, but she was sure Laura did. Even from across the room she could see the hairs standing up on Laura's arms. The door to the room slammed shut. Tiny footsteps slapped against the floor outside.

"They're gone," Laura said. She jumped up and yanked the door back open, Theresa right behind her.

Two sets of glistening bare footprints led from the study to the front door across the polished hardwood floor. The prints were wet but evaporated before their eyes, prints closest to the study first, like the spirits rolled up their trail behind them as they left.

"Isn't that amazing?" Laura said. "Have you ever seen anything like that?"

Theresa shook her head. She may have lived her life beset by paranormal visions, but she'd never seen ghosts manifest themselves.

"See," Laura said. "They just play games. You were in the room with me waiting, so they just shut the door and ran away. Nothing to be afraid of. Did you feel threatened?"

"Not at all," Theresa said. She really hadn't. In fact, she felt no response as jarring as her visions engendered. She felt a bit spooked, but nothing like the flash of dread she got when she first shook hands with Laura that night. If there had been something dangerous about the girls, it would have tripped a premonition, wouldn't it? Maybe her feeling of dread driving up to the house was just there because she expected it to be there. "I'm sorry to put you through all this. Sometimes these premonitions are hard to translate. I'll stop intruding and head home."

"First the ghosts leave," Laura said, "and then you? I think not. I'm putting on coffee and we're going to have a few cups. You are my first friend in town and I'm going to pump you for all the dirt here. Besides, we need to make a plan to get Dustin to the top of the class and this is the perfect time."

Theresa's embarrassment at her stuttering premonitions disappeared. She smiled. "That sounds like a plan."

That evening, Laura told Theresa about teaching in a big city and Theresa told Laura about growing up on a farm. Together they laid out a plan to reinforce and reward Dustin in and out of school. By the stroke of ten they were friends for life.

Theresa left with a swirling mixture of emotions. She was happy to add Laura to her short list of friends. She felt confident that the two of them would turn Dustin from the dark place the divorce had led him. But she could not shake the oppressive feeling of dread that had first infected her back at Treasured Things. The twin ghosts seemed unthreatening, but Theresa was still not at ease. She calmed herself with a reminder that the house did not trigger any apocalyptic visions.

If only she had gone upstairs.

Chapter Thirty-One

The morning's trip to WSEH had been as uncomfortable as Doug had imagined it would be. He was herded from reception to makeup to green room by a retinue of harried assistants who could not spend sixty seconds without checking their watch against a ceaseless march of approaching deadlines. He sat in front of a camera with an ill-fitting earplug spitting static-filled instructions into his brain. Then on came the voice of a New York anchor and he tried to stare earnestly into the black void of the camera lens as he chatted about his change in lifestyle.

And it was all crap. He spoke about how there was more to life than the pressures of the big city, but he didn't tell them what that "more" was. He didn't tell them about the fascinating attic full of animals with the gravitational pull of the sun. He did plug the novel he was crafting and drop a few tantalizing bits of the storyline, hopefully enough to get his agent some interest from publishers.

Five minutes after his segment, he was blasting down I-65 at twenty over the speed limit on a beeline home. He hadn't liked staying in a hotel last night. It was five-star quality, but he felt alone and incomplete. It was like he left a part of himself back at Galaxy Farm. He told himself that he missed Laura but still went to sleep without calling her. Now all he wanted to do was walk through his own front door again.

He audibly sighed with relief when he saw the spire of Galaxy Farm's turret room as he barreled up the driveway. Doug went straight upstairs, his fingers itching to type out a new chapter of the darkening love triangle between the brothers in the Old South. But he just stared at the blinking cursor, bereft of inspiration. His morning muse had pulled out of the station without him and all he could see were taillights. He stared at yesterday's half-finished paragraph and couldn't summon the first word to complete it. He uttered a quick curse for WSEH and shut down the computer.

The attic's siren song sounded in his head. He looked across the room at the mounted bobcat. The glass eyes sparkled in the sunlight. He rationalized that he had abandoned hope of working, so he might as well play.

He settled in on the floor of the attic. The bright sun outside warmed the roof and made the attic a perfect temperature. He opened *Methods in the Art of Taxidermy* in his lap and thumbed through the yellowed pages.

The more he read, the more intrigued he became. A process he once thought abhorrent had an elegance to it, an inherent respect for the beauty of the subject and the desire to preserve that beauty. If only the creature understood the honor bestowed upon it. The taxidermist ended the animal's life that it might be preserved forever.

Then the realization struck him. He could do this. He could bestow that immortality on a creature. He had the tools, he had the instructions. There was a box of wire and excelsior in the corner. He would need to buy modeling clay and some chemicals, but that was all available at Randolph's Hardware. He had the time in the afternoons, so why not?

Laura, that's why not. He'd kept the attic discoveries secret for a reason. This collection of critters would send his animal-loving vegetarian wife over the edge. And the idea of her husband adding to the frozen zoo would go over like kazoos at Carnegie Hall.

Well, she didn't have to know. There was enough room up here in the attic to do the work, and all the tools were here. He could experiment during the day while she was gone. What she didn't know wouldn't hurt her.

Doug just needed a subject to immortalize.

He closed the book and stood to look out the window. Two rabbits sat in front of the house, munching grass.

He smiled. Perfect. Soft, small. And he had seen cage traps in the last stall in the barn. One hundred percent under Laura's radar. The idea caught fire within him. He made a mental list of the things he would need for this project.

He left the attic, double checking the lock on the door as he closed it. He felt the same thrill he did when he began to write, that euphoric rush of energetic adrenaline. He checked the clock and figured he would have time to set the traps before Laura got home. Then tomorrow would be something special.

That evening, Laura told Doug that Theresa had dropped by the night before. She left out the ghostly encounter. Doug told Laura about the morning at WSEH. He left out his afternoon attic exploration.

After dinner Laura retreated to the nursery to review her TCAP sample test. Instead she stared into space and wondered where her ghostly girls were that night.

At the same time, Doug returned to the turret room, ready to embellish his tale of doomed Southern aristocracy. Instead he stared at the locked attic door and wished tomorrow was already here.

Chapter Thirty-Two

The next morning, Doug rose minutes after Laura left for work. He had set two traps in the high grass behind the house, baited with a medley of fresh vegetables, at least some of which would be irresistible to a rabbit, if his weaning on Bugs Bunny cartoons taught him anything. He dashed out the back door before he even poured himself coffee.

The wire mesh traps were about the size of a gym bag. A door snapped shut behind the prey when it tripped a pressure plate in the enclosure. Doug had spent the previous afternoon scraping rust and oiling hinges to get these aged models working again. They didn't look old enough to have trapped the animals in the attic, but they still looked vintage 1970s.

Doug's heart pounded as he approached the first trap, and then stopped when he saw it. Empty. Even the bait food was gone, so something had eaten it and escaped. He picked up a stick and stuck it through the cage wall. He pressed down on the pressure plate and nothing happened. The broken trigger spring dangled from the trap door.

"Shit." Maybe these traps were just too old.

He walked to the next trap with low expectations. He might have to go to town and buy a new trap, which would be another trail Laura might follow to uncover his clandestine activity. As he approached the next trap, the cage thumped against the ground.

He made the last few steps at a bound. Inside the cage, a brown rabbit huddled in one corner. Panic bulged in her soft brown eyes. Her whiskers rowed the air as she sniffed with machine gun rapidity.

Doug slipped a pair of work gloves from his back pocket and put them on. He blocked the trap entrance with his body and lifted door. His pulse quickened as he reached in and gripped the panting bunny. It offered no resistance as he extracted it. In fact, it huddled up against his chest.

Realization dawned. He had to kill the rabbit. Doug hadn't killed anything bigger than a cockroach in his life. Worse, this was a mammal, one of the good guys. This defenseless doe-eyed creature would be his first victim.

He hadn't even thought about how he would kill it without damaging the skin. The thing would twitch too much to suffocate it. He could break its neck. Just a little twist and it would be over. Simple and quick.

The rabbit looked up with pleading eyes. Doug felt the power Roman emperors must have felt determining gladiators' fates in the arena. He considered releasing the bunny.

But the pull took hold again. The pull that made him buy the house. The pull that drew him into the attic each time. The pull that made his fingers itch to pull the rabbit's skin tight over a wire frame and set glassy eyes into its darkened sockets.

He gripped the rabbit, one hand on its head, one around its body. The feel wasn't right. The gloves muted his sensation. He slipped one off. The rabbit's pulse hammered against his fingertips. He smiled. A vision of a hooded executioner wielding a battle ax flashed through his mind. He held his breath.

Twist. Crunch.

Tiny bones crushed between his fingers. The rabbit's eyes bulged and went still.

Doug lifted the rabbit by its ears. Its limp body hung like becalmed sails.

The remorse did not come. Instead of empathy, Doug felt empowered. He had held life in his hand and snuffed it out. He pushed a creature from one realm of existence to the next. What a rush! Mounting the rabbit would not be an homage to its existence, as he thought before, but a tribute to the power Doug exercised in its execution.

The rabbit's body was still warm when Doug laid it on the attic floor. He rolled out the taxidermy tools and the overhead light made stars along the sharpened edges. He had laid out a plastic drop cloth to contain the mess. He flipped the taxidermy instruction book open to the third chapter. He picked up a small knife. He reviewed the instructions, but somehow he already knew where to cut. He could see the whole process, the bleeding, the gutting, the delicate inch by inch skinning process. He had read the procedure over many times, but now he understood the steps in more detail than the book related, as if someone had played a movie of the process in his head.

He flipped the rabbit on its back and, without hesitation, punctured the animal just under the chin. He slit the corpse open down to the tail.

Doug smiled an odd, crooked smile. Not one of his smiles. It was more like the one on the face of the man in the hope chest locket, the man with the unkempt hair and the wild look in his eyes.

Chapter Thirty-Three

Laura had been distracted through the day at school. The whole experience with Theresa and the little girl ghosts was two days old, but many facets of the whole event kept filling her mind.

Her interactions with the staff at Moultrie Elementary had worried her. In New York, she had made lots of friends among the staff, but the cold shoulder she got at work made her afraid she'd spend the semester alone in the crowd. Add in the unnerving isolation of living out in the country, and Laura feared she wouldn't have the opportunity to make friends at all. So the ease with which she hit it off with Theresa dispelled a dark cloud that had settled in over Laura's future.

Then there were the girls. Her only contact with the supernatural before this had been though the gaps between her fingers at bad B-movies. The idea of living in a haunted house was as appealing as a bucket full of rats. But the girls' playful presence was more like Casper than something from *The Shining*. Theresa's assessment further convinced her that the permanent residents of her new home were no threat.

During her afternoon prep period, she sat alone in the Teacher's Lounge. A file of practice math quizzes downloaded from the common computer to her USB drive. When the process blinked that it was complete, she let her curiosity take over. Laura wanted a better way to communicate with the girls, to make them feel at home in the house, to trust that she would not hurt them. She logged on to the internet and Googled *Ghost Investigations*.

Thousands of hits lined up for her attention. Professional paranormal investigators, amateur groups, ghost hunting outfitters claiming to be the REIs of the paranormal world. The list seemed endless. She found an informational website and hit the link.

The reading was fascinating. The theory was that spirits were a type of leftover energy the deceased left behind. Most hauntings were residual, just an echo of someone that played back over and over, like when people saw a figure walk across the room and through a wall every night. The second rarer, and more powerful, type was an interactive haunting. One hundred percent of whatever energy that person had was still bound here on earth, likely in a specific location.

Want to send the pesky spirit packing to the great beyond? The site didn't recommend using a creepy short woman and a rope like in *Poltergeist.* Instead, *Find the remains of the ghost, salt them and burn them. The spirit now has no anchor tying it to the location, think of a hermit crab without its shell. It would be pulled off to the other side without a replacement home.*

The site explained that malicious hauntings were the exception rather than the rule. Spirits had some sort of electrical attribute, causing them to drain batteries or disrupt electrical appliances when they were near. That explained the clock radio going haywire when the girls manifested. Laura scrolled down to the section on communication.

Apparently, visual and auditory manifestations weren't as common as the movies would lead people to believe. But there was a way to hear them speak using electronic voice phenomenon, or EVP. The theory held that the enormous amount of energy needed for spirits to speak across whatever void separated us from them was more than most could summon. But their voices could be heard on audio recordings, soft and irregular, like the spirit was miles away.

That idea made her pulse quicken. Perhaps she *could* talk with the girls. She owned a digital audio recorder she had used to record events at school. That would be the proof she needed to convince her skeptical husband. Maybe one night while Doug was working upstairs...

Patrice burst into the Teacher's Lounge like Wonderland's Red Queen entering court. She gave Laura a contemptuous look. Laura snapped the internet browser shut.

"I knew you'd be here." Patrice practically hissed as she said it.

Laura was ready to praise her Holmes-like deductive skills that let Patrice find Laura in the break room on her break, but Pat didn't look receptive to sarcasm.

Patrice stomped over to the computer. She stared down with a gaze that could ignite dry timber. "What do you think you're doing?"

Laura tried to think how to explain her ghost research without admitting to a having a haunted house. She pointed to the screen. "Well I just..."

"Just what do you think your little tutoring sessions are going to accomplish?"

Tutoring?

"You know you won't get paid for those hours."

"I never thought I would," Laura said. "Some of the children were behind grade level. I thought if they had some practice, got comfortable with the test format..."

"That then you could make Mrs. Matthews look bad," Patrice said. "Probably try to squeeze her out of her job while she's home recuperating. Well forget that plan."

"I didn't want to make anyone look bad," Laura said.

"No, you wanted to make *everyone* look bad. There are other grades that take TCAP exams. Are all supposed to put our lives on hold and join your little crusade?" She pointed an index finger in Laura's face. The red nail polish had a few chips around the tip. "Listen, dear. You keep this up and you won't even sub in this district after this little show comes to a close. I guarantee it."

Patrice had worked herself completely red-faced with rage. She snapped her chin up in disdain and stormed out of the lounge.

Laura was at the point of tears. Her interactions with the other teachers had been restrained, a shade frosty maybe. But she knew they would thaw once they got to know her, saw that she shared the same passion for teaching that they did. But if this is how they all thought…well, even if it wasn't, she was sure Patrice would make sure it *was* the way they thought.

She checked the wall clock. Her students were back from Music in ten minutes. She pulled a napkin from a dispenser and blotted her watery eyes.

The hell with Patrice, she thought. The hell with all of them. She was there to teach the kids. She would do what needed to get done to make that happen. If it made the other teachers look lazy, too damn bad. Maybe she would only spend one semester here. But she would make sure the kids were more than one semester smarter for it.

She held her planning book across her chest like a knight's shield and set out for her room.

Chapter Thirty-Four

That night, the earthy spiced scent of homemade chili rolled over Laura as she opened the front door of the house. She sighed and smiled. She'd had one long day. After her encounter with Patrice, she'd had a frustrating TCAP tutoring session. Several kids, the ones most in need, of course, were not making every session and their lack of progress was frustrating. One of her favorite dinners would be just what the doctor ordered. It was as if Doug had read her mind.

She dropped her bags at the door as if they weighed a ton and went into the kitchen. Two pots simmered on the stove. Doug stirred one with a wooden spoon. He had an odd, concentrated look on his face.

"¿Una comida buena?" Laura asked.

Doug jerked as if awakened from a dream. The spoon flew out of his hand and onto the stovetop. Droplets of red chili splattered the stove backsplash.

"Jesus!" Doug said. "You startled me. I didn't hear you come in." He spun to put himself between Laura and the pot he'd been tending. He gave her a quick hug and a kiss on the cheek.

"Was that some new Zen cooking method?" she said.

"No, just a bit distracted."

"Plotting out the novel in your head?"

Doug gave his head an affirmative shake that seemed relieved. "Yep, tying up loose ends. Dinner's ready." He tried to lead her out of the kitchen. "Have a seat before I burn it."

She looked over his shoulder to the stove. "What's with the second pot?"

A guilty little look flashed across Doug's face. "One with meat, one without."

"Meat? You never used to put meat in the chili."

"Because back then we couldn't afford it," Doug said.

"And because I wouldn't eat it."

"That too. Hence, two pots a simmering."

Laura pushed by him and scooped up some of the chili in the second pot. Stringy hunks of gray meat swam around with the beans. They smelled gamey. "Ugh, what is in here?"

"Chicken," Doug said. He pulled the spoon from her hand and dropped a lid on the pot.

"Chicken doesn't look like that," Laura said, he nose wrinkled up in revulsion.

"And what do you know about chicken, Vegetarian Girl?" Doug said. He gave her a gentle push out of the kitchen. "No one's asking you to eat it."

"One strand of that nasty stuff hits my plate and you *will* be wearing it," Laura said with a smile.

"One more complaint from you and I won't just cook chickens," Doug said. "I'll start raising them."

Laura sat at the table and Doug brought in two steaming bowls of chili. It was delicious and she enjoyed every tear-inducing mouthful. Laura filled Doug in on her encounter with Patrice and her tutoring frustrations, but Doug nodded and swallowed more than he spoke. He finished his chili before she was half done.

"Hungry, dear?" Laura said as Doug scraped the bottom of his bowl.

"Famished," Doug said. "Must be the country air." He flashed his empty bowl at her. "Sure you don't want to try my version?"

"Keep your poultry to yourself, Colonel Sanders."

"Don't say I never offered," Doug said. He got up and tossed his bowl in the sink. "I'm going to go up and finish some writing. okay?"

"Uh, yeah, sure," Laura said. "I've got a test to prep for tomorrow anyway."

Doug smiled an odd little smirk of a smile. He bent down and kissed Laura on the cheek. The smell of the greasy chili on his breath made Laura shudder. Doug bounded up the stairs behind her.

Laura felt completely out of sorts. A waiting dinner was a happy surprise, but Doug's actions were a shade past bizarre. Chicken chili? And he was in a hurry to get away from the dinner table. He had some of the normal lighthearted banter...but still there was an undercurrent she didn't like, something like...

Black water under silver ice.

She wondered where that image came from. The twins. She'd been thinking about the spirits of those two poor girls most of the day. Time to get cracking. She had an internet-inspired experiment to conduct.

She wadded up her napkin and tossed it in the trash under the kitchen sink. The cupboard door slammed shut, and in the darkness, the napkin came to rest next to an empty can of tomato sauce and a few stray tufts of rabbit fur.

Chapter Thirty-Five

She couldn't complain about Doug writing tonight. Dinner had given her a slight case of the creeps, and besides, she wanted some time to talk with the girls alone. She didn't want to clue in Doug on her plan. He'd just dismiss it as her imagination again. That was exactly the reason she hadn't told Doug anything about the girls' visitation the night he was in Nashville. She didn't want to hear some explanation about two women with fertile imaginations.

Laura pulled open her bag at the desk in the nursery. She took out her planning book and the math test she had to grade. At the bottom of her bag lay the digital recorder, small as a pack of cigarettes. She took it out, pressed *Record* and a tiny red light blinked on. She set the recorder on the corner of her desk. It had two hours' worth of recording time. She hoped she wouldn't need that much.

She turned on the clock radio and set the volume low. An ad for Moultrie Ford told her she could get a great deal leasing an F-150. If the ghost website was right, this little power source might help the girls manifest. She wondered if electrical appliances attracted them like moths to a light.

As she graded the papers, Laura kept losing her place, distracted by the subconscious ear she had tuned to her Student Sixth Sense. But half an hour later her math papers were finally graded with no sign of the twins. She shook her head in disappointment and cracked open her English book to the section on adverbs. She began to write out a study exercise.

She felt a tingle near the top her spine. The hairs on the back of her neck went to attention. She caught her breath as her SSS kicked in. The radio warbled and the digital display faded to black. Laura checked the red LED on the recorder. Still rolling.

Laura smiled and spun in her chair. She could feel the girls in the room, sense a warming inside her, a lighting of the flame your heart burns around family. She wished so much that she could see them.

"Constance?" Laura said. "Elizabeth? Are you here?"

A floorboard creaked near the nursery window.

"I know you're here, girls," Laura said. "Talk to me."

A short hushed little noise responded, soft as the rustle of leaves in a breeze.

A floorboard creaked near Laura's chair. Laura had a charm around her neck, a cheery silver sunburst she picked up in the city years ago. The charm rose off her chest and floated.

"Do you like that?" Laura said.

The charm bobbed once and then sank back against her blouse. Tiny fingertips traced a path down her breastbone and disappeared.

Laura sensed the girls were still there. She had to reach out to them. "What do you need?" she asked. There was a minute of silence. "What can I do for you?"

Then they were gone, like their presence had been vacuumed out of the room.

Adrenaline surged as Laura spun around to the recorder. She rewound the last few minutes and hit *Play*.

She heard her own voice say "I know you're here, girls. Talk to me." Did she really sound that nasal?

The reply was ethereal, soft and high pitched. It faded loud and soft as if the speakers were bouncing from one corner of the room to another, but it was unmistakable. Two little girls spoke in unison. "Hello."

Laura's skin prickled into goose bumps.

145

"Do you like that?" Laura said on the recording. She remembered the charm floating off her chest.

The girls' voices returned, tinged with a sense of wonder. "Sooo pretty." The first word was drawn out like a piece of stretched taffy. The last word seemed to fade off into the distance.

Once more Laura spoke. "What do you need?" No answer. "What can I do for you?"

The answer came back as a mournful dirge, a cry etched with the raw emotion only children display without dilution.

"We've lost our mother."

Laura's heart shattered. Waves of anguish washed over her as she imagined the loss of her own mother and relived the loss of her unborn daughters. These poor spirits didn't know they were dead, only that they were no longer with their mother.

She hit *Stop*.

In her wildest expectations, she never imagined contact like this. So personal, so moving, so undeniably real.

She couldn't wait to tell Theresa tomorrow. The idea of telling Doug didn't even occur to her.

Chapter Thirty-Six

The next morning dawned crisp and clear in downtown Moultrie. The sun turned a slight frost into steam on the roof of Theresa's little box of a house several blocks from the town square. Theresa had Dustin packed and ready for school. They were headed for the car when she froze in the doorway.

"Damn it," Theresa cursed under her breath. Her adrenal glands kicked into gear. This was not how she wanted to start her day.

Bastard Bobby's black primer Dodge Ram sat at the end of her driveway. The tailgate was open and sat low on the sagging rear springs. Chunks of brown mud arced along the sides behind the wheel wells.

Bobby Grissom, ex-husband and current parasite, sat behind the wheel, staring into space. He was a stocky guy with a head like a block of wood. His black hair was shaved to stubble. His arm stuck out the open window, a lit cigarette pinched between his first two fingers. Two spent filters lay on the curb under his hand.

"What's the matter, Mom?" Dustin asked from behind her.

"It's nothing," Theresa answered.

Dustin stuck his head out the door. "Hey, that's Daddy's truck." Dustin scowled. "He's not supposed to be here."

The restraining order was crystal clear. One thousand feet from the house and on weekends only Bobby's parents picked Dustin up. Even the boy knew the rules.

"Stay inside," Theresa said. Dustin gave a series of rapid, serious nods.

She stepped outside and closed the door behind her. She pulled her phone out of her purse and flipped it open. What the hell was he doing here? A restraining order was a restraining order, damn it. Anxiety churned in her stomach.

All she had to do was call to the cops then go back inside and wait. She'd give them twenty minutes to sweep that loser off her street, and then get Dustin to school. She punched in the sheriff's department number to her phone.

Theresa paused before hitting send. The cops would take too long. She was sick of living like this, physically free of her husband but still mentally enslaved. Had she fought through divorce and custody hearings to live like this? No way. She was sick of his crap. And he was going to hear about it.

Theresa clutched her phone in her right hand. She strode across the yard. She could smell the stink of burning tobacco wafting from the truck and remembered the dark days when the stench permeated their house. She stopped a few yards from the truck.

"What the hell are you doing here?" she demanded.

Bobby's head rolled over in her direction. His black eyes were rimmed red from who knew what. He pointed his smoldering cigarette at Theresa. "You mean what am I doing at my own house?"

"Look, you aren't supposed to be here and you know it," Theresa said. She flashed her cell phone at him. "Get out. Or do I need to call the sheriff?"

"I have a right to see what my child support is paying for," Bobby said. "See that my boy has proper clothes and such."

Theresa saw red. "When the hell was the last time you made a child support payment? Where do you get off acting like a parent? You didn't even show up at your parents' house on your last scheduled weekend with Dustin."

"I was working," Bobby said.

"Working your right arm down at Slim's Place, maybe," Theresa said. "But I know for a fact that the mill was down all weekend."

148

Bobby gritted his teeth and his eyes narrowed. "Listen here, I don't need this shit from you." He popped open the door to his truck.

Theresa flipped open her phone. The sheriff's department number was still programmed in. Her thumb hovered over the *Send* button. "One foot touches ground and I'll have every deputy in the county here."

"You bitch," Bobby hissed. He swung the truck door full open.

"C'mon," Theresa said. "Give me an excuse. No, give *them* an excuse. There's a few of those boys still looking for a reason to get rough with you after your drunk and disorderly a few months back."

Bobby bit his lower lip. His hand trembled as he gripped the armrest of the truck door. Fury burned in his eyes. Then he swung around and slammed the door shut. Theresa took one step closer, thumb still poised over the keypad to call in the cavalry.

"Now get out of here," she said. "If I so much as see your truck within a mile of here, I swear to God you'll be back in county jail."

Bobby gave his cigarette nub a defiant flick onto the front lawn. His truck barked to life. Bobby's eyes never left Theresa's.

"It ain't over," he said. "Only so much shit a man can take."

"If only you were a man," Theresa said.

Bobby slammed it into drive. It chirped the tires and squealed away with a belch of black smoke.

Theresa felt her knees grow weak as the combat rush of the moment receded. She'd done it. Toe to toe with Bastard Bobby and she came out on top. She realized she was still holding the cell phone in front of her like some futuristic weapon. She snapped the cover closed and headed for the house.

The front door was open. Dustin stood in the doorway, face blank, school backpack at his feet. Theresa ran to him.

"Are you all right, honey?" Theresa said.

"Yeah, Mom," Dustin said. He reached out and squeezed her hand. "Way to go."

Chapter Thirty-Seven

The stuffed rabbit didn't look half bad in the late-morning light.

Of course, Doug might have been enamored of his own work, but he could honestly say that the bunny looked good. The stitches were hidden, the fur groomed, the body contours were correct. Even the little glass eyes looked lifelike. It sat on the trunk of the attic, nose permanently sniffing for fresh clover.

The positive results weren't a surprise. As soon as Doug had started working on this little project, he'd felt infused with the skills to do it. Back in New York, Laura had once talked him into a tennis date with a friend from work and her husband. Doug hadn't played since high school, but as soon as his feet hit the clay, it all came back to him—how to serve, how to backhand. It was like his old friend Tennis Skills had dropped in for a visit. Mounting the rabbit was just like that.

Except that Doug didn't know Mr. Rabbit Skills. He had read *Methods in the Art of Taxidermy* cover to cover a half-dozen times, so he rationalized that was why he was so comfortable. But deep down he knew that was crap. He'd picked up tools before he knew he needed them, stitched a seam pattern he hadn't even selected yet. It felt like someone else had put on Doug's hands like a pair of gloves and went to work.

Good as the little mammal looked, something was missing, some kind of icing on the cake that the other animals in the attic had. Whatever it was, *Methods in the Art of Taxidermy* didn't cover it. But Doug hadn't skipped a step.

He moved the rabbit to the floor and opened the chest. Maybe there was another, more advanced text in there with an answer. He removed the top tray and the wrapped set of tools. He pulled everything out, all the books, all the old taxidermy supplies. Nothing new.

Then he noticed the trunk seemed too shallow. He held it on end and sure enough, there was at least an inch between the floor of the trunk and its external bottom. The sides and the top had no such insulation.

He dropped the trunk back down. He pressed on the bottom. A loud click sounded and he felt the bottom recess a fraction of an inch. He released it and the bottom popped up on one edge. His pulse quickened and he pried the open edge up.

Inside, coated in dust, lay a book. The binding was of mahogany-colored leather, riven with deep cracks. The edges of the thick pages were rough and uneven, a telltale sign that this ancient edition hadn't been mass produced. On the front, in gold leaf was a line of Egyptian hieroglyphs. There were several different bird images and a bunch of geometric shapes.

Doug opened the book and the binding wailed in creaking protest. Inside, the text was in Arabic, hand copied in quill-delivered ink. Perhaps this book couldn't be trusted to a publisher. Or couldn't be published.

The title page had one line of Arabic text. Underneath, in crooked block print pencil letters it said *The Book of the Dead.*

Doug had seen every film in the *Mummy* franchise. If he remembered right, this was the Egyptian cook book for how to send spirits to the afterlife as well as how to hold them back. There was no copyright, no author, no publisher's imprint. The book was obviously older than the house, even older than every house in the county. From the looks of it, Doug wouldn't be surprised if the book was older than anything in the nation.

He flashed back to the story on the old newspaper he read in the library. There was that Egyptian trainer who worked for the family, the one the welcoming townsfolk had threatened to ride out on a rail, tarred and feathered. This book must have been his.

He turned to the next page. It was a broadside of Arabic. The page after was the same. This little discovery wasn't going to be worth much if he had to learn Arabic to read it.

After a dozen incomprehensible pages, the penciled translation reappeared. The chapter translation read *Taming the Power of the Beasts.*

Between each line of Arabic, smudged penciled letters spelled out a stilted English translation. Between the references to appeasing Osiris, it explained that the life force of an animal could be captured after its death and bound to an object on Earth. Its essence would fill the object, give it the power the animal had in life.

Doug thought of the uncannily lifelike statuary he'd always seen around Egyptian burial sites. He remembered reading about the thousands of mummified cats found in tombs along the Nile. Did the bound spirits of the mummified animal donors make the carvings look so real?

The text continued with specific instructions on how to extract certain organs intact, like the heart, kidneys and liver. The brain came out through the nose with the help of a long screw-type device Doug recognized from the taxidermy kit, but not from the taxidermy book. All the organs needed to be placed in separate jars.

Next followed a description of the preservative mixture to add to the jars. The list made little sense to Doug. Other than cinnamon, the names meant nothing to him. He recognized myrrh from Christmas stories but had no idea what it was. The units of measurement were just as obtuse.

A slip of ruled notebook paper tucked into the next page was the key. In ink, in a different hand, a rougher jagged cursive with a decided backward slant, was a list of the Egyptian ingredients. Next to each was a more familiar name like turmeric or saffron, and a measurement for each. Sometimes the amount was struck through and a second or sometimes third amount followed, as if trial and error had found the correct recipe.

The face of the next page had the final instructions. After putting the organs and the mixtures into earthen pots, there was a solemn incantation to be read. Under it there was no English translation. Instead it was phonetic, as if Osiris needed to hear it on ancient Egyptian if he was going to understand it. Doug sounded out a few words. They reminded him of the Hebrew from the bar mitzvah of one of his New York coworker's sons.

After the ceremony, as soon as the animal was touched by the light of the sun god Ra, its essence would revitalize the body, as Ra had once returned Osiris body to life.

Doug remembered how the hawk and the bobcat had seemed so different when they came down into the turret room. It wasn't that they appeared more lifelike in the daylight, the daylight actually made them more lifelike.

As soon as he read it, he knew that this book contained the missing piece, the extra push that would enliven the rabbit at his feet. The taxidermist had sprinkled a little of that Egyptian black magic on his creations.

He had to test his theory. He went to the window and grabbed the edge of the board that covered it. He pulled and the old wood peeled away from the window frame. Light poured into the room for the first time in decades.

The menagerie of creatures shuddered as daylight hit their bodies. A collective stretching sound rippled through the room as old hides stretched tighter. Feathers and fur straightened and fluffed, sending a cloud of dust into the air. Glass eyes flashed to life. The edges of the bear rug's jaws curled up and its teeth glowed brighter.

Doug understood the attic now, the blocked windows, the animals jammed into all the corners. Alexander had shuttered them in here, away from the light that let their essences bridge the divide between this world and the next. With some type of life still in them, the man who donated a bulk of his estate to the local humane society could not bring himself to destroy them. Instead he just put them to sleep.

Mabron had accomplished the amazing. Doug now had the instructions to do the same. What a rush it would be.

He replaced the board over the window. The room went dark and a soft communal sigh sounded as the creatures shifted back to their less lifelike mode. Doug didn't need Laura noticing the change in the attic window. It might prod her to investigate and this was no time to share his secret hobby with her.

He glanced at his watch. Three thirty. Laura would be home soon. But this idea had become a compelling imperative. He'd need a new subject since the entrails of Thumper here were long gone. He'd also need the items on the list. He copied them over onto the back of a receipt from his wallet. If he hurried, he could set the traps before Laura got home, and with a bit of luck, he'd have his volunteer in the morning.

Chapter Thirty-Eight

The day couldn't end fast enough for Laura. The last bell rang and she beat everyone to the parking lot. She found Treasured Things on the town square.

From the moment she entered, she was impressed. The jumble of antique furniture and curios begged to be explored. There were period things here that would look great in her study.

One item on a shelf caught her eye, a thin boxy gold lighter. It was barely larger than the cigarette it was supposed to light. Engraved roses covered the outside.

"Don't you have a good eye," Theresa said from behind her.

"Theresa!" Laura let loose a wide smile. She gave her new friend a quick hug. "What a great store. This lighter just jumped out at me."

"A ladies model from the 1940s," Theresa said. "When it was sexy to smoke. The market for it has kind of dried up."

"I think I'm a latent pyro," Laura said. "Since we moved here I've been collecting matchbooks. Maybe I'm graduating to lighters. Anyway, I've got a little ghost update that should enliven your day."

"Another experience?"

Laura took her recorder out of her purse. "And it's on tape."

Theresa's eyes lit up. She grabbed Laura's arm. "Well, let's hear it!" She dragged Laura back to her desk and pulled a folding chair over.

Laura told her the story of the encounter from the previous night, about the charm floating off her neck, about being able to hear the girls recorded but not live. She played the recording. It rolled on to the point where the girls admired the charm.

"Hello," said the girls through the speaker.

Laura's skin went to goose bumps again, even though she had played the recording a dozen times. Theresa gave an involuntary shiver.

"Oh my God," she whispered.

Laura spoke again on the recording followed by a silent pause.

"Sooo pretty," sang the twins' soft voices.

Theresa gripped the edge of her desk in excitement. Laura's voice asked how she could help the girls and they gave their final reply.

"We've lost our mother."

"Doesn't that just break your heart?" Laura said.

"The poor things," Theresa said. "What did Doug say when he heard this?"

"He's not in the loop," Laura said. "I don't think any amount of proof about little girl ghosts would convince him. He's convinced it is all in my head. This project is for the two of us."

"So what's your plan, Ms. Ghostbuster?"

"We need a longer period of contact," Laura said. "A more detailed conversation that we can hear without having to replay a recording. For that, they need more energy, some power they can access easily."

Theresa thought a moment. Her face shifted from enthusiasm to concern and back. "I might have what you need." She left and pulled an odd-looking object off the shelf. It resembled a lamp, but where the bulb and shade would be, there was an opaque glass hemisphere. What would have been the lamp body was clear glass with two thin vertical metal rods inside. An electrical plug trailed from its black plastic base.

"And this escapee from a sci-fi movie set is…"

"A static electricity generator," Theresa said. "A science toy bought by some relative for a kid who no doubt never appreciated it. Turn it on and sparks fly from the half melon on the top. Touch it and your hair stands on end. Surely you had one of these in school in New York."

"Our school was lucky to have light bulbs," Laura said. "Let alone something like that."

"Well, if your spectral visitors need a power source," Theresa said, "you'll be hard pressed to find one as easy to tap into as this. Drain out all the juice you want and it just makes more."

Laura reached for the generator and Theresa pulled it just out of reach.

"I'm really torn up about handing you this," Theresa said. "I know how safe these girls seem. I heard their sweet voices. But my premonitions were strong and they are still unsolved."

"You are such a worrier," Laura said. "Be there for the show, then. What are you doing tomorrow night?"

Theresa gave her head a slow shake. "Had a little ex-husband issue this morning. Dustin and I had better stick together and close to the house for a few days."

"Anything I can do for you?"

"Nah," Theresa said. "It's under control. He's been worse. I guess you can do this by yourself. Who's better at handling kids than you?"

"Hey," Laura said with mock bravado. "I get paid by the State to handle kids."

Theresa handed her the generator with artificial reverence. "Then take this, sister. May it serve you well."

Theresa walked her over to the door. Laura glanced again at the lighter on the shelf. Theresa scooped it up and slipped it in Laura's pocket.

"Hey?" Laura said.

"Take it," Theresa said. "If it hasn't sold in two years, it won't sell. I owe you for all you've done for Dustin."

"Thanks," Laura said as she left the store. For some reason, having the lighter in her pocket felt reassuring. "I'll send the girls your regards."

"Be careful," Theresa said. "If the experience gets out of control, you pull that thing's plug, okay?"

"Right away," Laura said. "'Bye."

Through the shop's front window, Theresa watched Laura carry the generator to her car. She wrung her thin hands together.

It will be fine, she thought. She didn't have a premonition touching the generator. Of course that really didn't prove anything. She didn't get a premonition putting on her wedding ring for the first time, and how well did that work out? She wished she had told Laura to hold off until she could join her in the experiment. Theresa couldn't shake a nagging fear that something about the spirit girls was far from right.

Chapter Thirty-Nine

"Doug?" Laura called as she blew through the front door.

She tossed her purse on the kitchen table and saw the note. Doug must have been in a rush when he wrote it. The handwriting was kind of jerky and there was an odd backward slant to it. There were just two words—*Gone shopping.*

At the Moultrie Piggly Wiggly, the pimply teen at the checkout slid the last of Doug's spices over the scanner. The total rang up to $36.24.

"You must be making something special," she said.

"You have no idea," Doug said.

Laura was making notes in a history textbook when Doug rolled through the front door with the world's most expensive half sack of groceries. The refrigerator was nearly bare so Laura expected a bit more of a haul.

"I guess we're eating light," she said.

Doug gave the bag in his hand a glance. "Oh, no, I wasn't shopping for dinner. Just some spices and things."

"You brought home spices, but no food."

Doug breezed by her without a kiss hello. Laura realized it wasn't the first time. He pulled open the refrigerator.

"Son of a bitch," Doug said. "This thing's empty."

"I could have stopped for something on my way home," Laura said. There was an edge to her voice.

"No, no," Doug said. "I've got the home front. That's the deal. There's no problem here. We have rice as a starter and if a billion Chinese can eat it for breakfast, we can sure have it for dinner. I can mix something up."

"Forget it," Laura said. She closed the history book. "I'll find something if I get hungry. I've got work to do for tomorrow." She rose from the table.

"Are you mad?" Doug said. "Because I forgot to go shopping?"

"Hell, yes, I'm mad," Laura said. "But dinner's just a part of it. You're getting completely checked out. Moving here was going to be a new start for us. But I barely see you all week. You sleep in and then you're up there in that room all night."

"I'm writing," Doug said. His voice had an edge to it. "It's my job. It's what I'm here for."

"You can't do that during the day?"

"I have to write when the inspiration comes. It's not like churning out sausage."

"It's not just the time," Laura said. "Even when we are together, you act like I'm barely here. When was the last time you asked me about my day? When was the last time you kissed me without me forcing you into it? I'm your wife, not a roommate."

"Babe," Doug said. He moved behind her and put his arms around her waist. "I love you. You know that sometimes I get wrapped up in my work. It's nothing for you to be insecure about."

Insecure? Her blood came to a boil. She bit back the scathing response that begged to come out. Doug's arms around her had all the comfort of hospital bed restraints. She pried him away.

"Look, I do have prep to do for tomorrow and I'm already tired," she said.

She picked up her book and went into the nursery and slammed the door. Any ideas about testing the static generator tonight scattered to the winds.

The word still rankled her. *Insecure.* This was the same deflective crap he spewed with every problem they had. Somehow it was always her fault, always some defect in her personality that made life difficult. In college, *she* was too insular to appreciate his fraternity brotherhood and the time it demanded. In New York, *she* was too needy to understand the responsibilities of his job. After the miscarriage, *she* had to see the shrink because *she* needed to talk. Forget about *him* needing to listen. She dropped the heavy book on her desk.

He'd damn well better be in here with an apology in ten minutes flat. She cracked the door open a few inches to give him the hint.

But a half-hour later, she was still alone. She finished her work and went out in the hallway. The kitchen was empty. At the top of the stairs, a band of yellow light shone from under the closed door to the turret room. All that broke the silence of the house was the faint muffled click of computer keys.

Laura's heart fell. He really went back up there. Did their marriage mean so little? She shuffled off to the bedroom. It would be almost midnight by the time she fell asleep, curled up on her side of the bed, pillow damp with tears.

Chapter Forty

This time it wasn't a rabbit.

When Doug parted the tall grass around the trap in the morning the steel cage held a small fox captive. The little russet pup couldn't have been more than a few months old. She stared up at Doug through the mesh, ears drooped down, big brown eyes wide with fear, whimpering. With her tiny teeth, it wasn't likely that this youngster was long weaned from its mother. She was about to learn a harsh lesson about the consequences of curiosity.

Doug beamed at the thought of the larger project. The rabbit looked good, but the fox would look great. And with a little Egyptian voodoo tossed in...wow.

But first things first. This thing needed to die. Doug wasn't sticking his bare hands in the trap. The kit's teeth might have been small, but there were still a lot of them. Besides, her neck wouldn't snap like the rabbit's did. He needed a whole new approach that would still leave the skin unblemished. An idea came to him.

He pulled the trap from the grass. The kit let out a whelp and cowered in the far corner. She sniffed the air and shot desperate, searching glances from the swinging cage. But the mother that had rescued her so many times before was gone.

Doug crossed between the barn and the house and made his way down to the propane tank. He set the trap on the ground. The kit launched herself at the trap door to no avail. Doug pulled off his shoes and socks and pulled his jeans up above his knees. He grabbed the cage and headed for the pond.

The rank smell of stagnant water hung over the pond, a combination of dead algae and fish. Doug stepped in. The dark water was cool. The slick black muck oozed between his toes. A catfish heaved itself off the bottom and swam away in a charcoal cloud.

The kit let out a terrified scream. She threw herself at the sides of the cage, panicked by the water instinct taught her to avoid. Her paws flailed at the mesh in an irrational bid to somehow dig her way out.

Doug steadied the cage and lowered it an inch into the pond. The kit wailed and rammed its head against the top. Doug smiled and lowered the cage another few inches. Water sloshed against the kit's haunches. It looked up at Doug with pleading brown eyes and let loose another mournful yowl.

Doug pushed the cage underwater.

The water exploded in thrashing foam as the drowning kit struggled for air. Doug pushed down to keep the cage underwater. The shuddering of the cage grew weaker with the kit's waning struggle for air. The cage went still.

That same rush of power Doug felt while killing the rabbit flashed through him again, but this time it was many degrees stronger, as if the accomplishment of dispatching a predator was a greater accomplishment. A chill went up his spine and he smiled a little crooked smile. Doug watched the second hand sweep a complete revolution on his watch. He pulled the cage from the pond.

The kit lay dead. Her open glassy eyes stared through Doug. Her soaked, matted fur was tinged with the dark sediment her struggle had stirred up. Doug gave the corpse a concerned once-over. He breathed a sigh of relief. She hadn't broken her skin. He headed for the attic.

The skinning took much longer this time. Doug's work stretched into the afternoon, but not just because the fox was a little bigger. He took extra care with the beautiful coat. Each pass of the blade was a

163

labor of love, each peel of the skin like opening a gift. The kit would be a work of art.

Set up in the attic, he pickled the hide in denatured alcohol and was very gentle as he rinsed it clean in water and borax. As it hung to dry, Doug separated the entrails according to the instructions in the *Book of the Dead.* One container for the liver, one for the heart, one for the intestines. Her sprinkled each with the spices listed in the penciled translation and sealed the jars with wax.

The skull became an obsession. He extracted the brain as the text described and gave it its own jar. As he scraped the interior clean, he was inspired to use the skull in the fox. He'd fashioned a clay replacement for the rabbit's head. But wouldn't the fox deserve her true skull, to make the head perfect from within? He cleaned the bone with dental precision. He memorized the muscles he stripped and replaced them with clay. He was so engrossed in the skull, he barely heard the gravel churn under the Honda's tires as Laura came home.

He checked his watch. It was after five thirty. Where the hell did the day go?

"What is that smell?" Laura said. It hit her like an ocean wave as she opened the front door. Sharp, sterile and just a bit sweet. It reminded her of camping with her father, of the morning smell of the cook stove...

"Alcohol," Doug answered. He stood at the steaming sink, soap lathered up past his elbows as he rubbed a pot brush over his skin. "Just cleaning up a little paint project."

Laura knew garbage when it was delivered. Paint thinner cleaned paint, not alcohol, and all the paint they used was water-based anyway. Doug was breathing fast and his face was bathed in sweat. She caught him at something he thought he'd be finished with earlier. The "paint cleanup" BS was a Hail Mary pass because he wasn't expecting her to catch the alcohol scent. You'd think adults would lie better than kids, but they don't.

"Dinner's up in no time," Doug said as he dried his hands with a dish towel.

As usual, Doug had still been asleep when she left for work that morning. So their last conversation was the fight they'd had last night. He should have been crawling to her on repentant knees, but instead he was acting as if nothing had happened. The same way he acted whenever the shit hit the fan between them. Laura still had her book bag in her hand and she gripped it hard enough to feel muscles strain. She wanted to pound him with it.

"Dinner? After our fight last night and then ignoring me? After sleeping in this morning? You're going to stand there with that guilty look on your face and chat up dinner?"

Doug gave a surprised look. "You're still mad from last night?"

If she hadn't been, a comment that clueless would have rekindled the fire for sure. All the frustration of dealing with Doug's bizarre behavior and all the anger stoked by his constant condescension rushed up like welling magma. She couldn't stand to even look at him.

"I'm going out," she said. "I'm not sure where, as long as right now it isn't here. There's a thousand pounds of stress I'm carrying from work and I don't need to add you to it right now." She wheeled to the front door.

"Babe? I don't understand..."

Laura slammed the door shut on the last half of his sentence. She threw her bags in the passenger seat of the Honda and left a trail of spinning gravel as she raced down the driveway. She got on US 41 with no clue where she was going. She just had to get away from Doug before she really blew a gasket.

She slammed on the brakes as she entered downtown Moultrie and its thirty-miles–per-hour speed limit. It was after six and the uniformly nonessential shops around the courthouse square were all closed. With no area residents, the streets were deserted. She pulled into a parking space and yanked the car into park.

Well, now what was she going to do? The town had a gossip grapevine that ran 24/7 so if she went to one of the three local restaurants for dinner alone, it would be common knowledge in school first thing in the morning. Other than the Walmart at the far end of town, she doubted anything was open. She needed someone to talk to and sort this out.

She looked across the square and saw the Treasured Things storefront. Theresa's shop. Theresa! She whipped out her cell phone. Theresa answered on the first ring. Her invitation for Laura to visit was out before Laura could ask.

Doug pulled the phone from its charger. He really didn't understand why Laura was so angry, but whatever the reason was, he needed to fix it. They had had a few big fights before, mostly after the miscarriage, but neither of them had ever been mad enough to walk out of the house. Their marriage had to be at a new low.

Doug was about to dial Laura's cell when a vision of the fox popped into his head. The skull was almost ready. The skin would be pickled by now. He could get quite a bit done with what was left of the night and leave the Egyptian rites for morning when the powerful rays of the sun would fuel Osiris's power.

A powerful force stirred above him in the attic. A magnetic phenomenon that drew him upward to finish the fox.

Laura needed a little time to cool off anyway, he rationalized. She'd be back soon and then they could talk. All she'd do is yell if he spoke to her now. He could certainly make better use of the time up in the attic.

He dropped the phone back into its charging cradle and went back upstairs.

Chapter Forty-One

It wasn't until Dustin had been put to bed at nine p.m. that Laura had time for an adult conversation with Theresa. They sat in Theresa's living room, a small room furnished with a well-worn suite of brown starter-home furniture. Despite a workplace full of antiques, Theresa's home was stripped to the basics. Laura chalked it up to a combination of childproofing and cash flow.

"So," Laura asked. "Is getting him to bed always that much of a production?" Putting the boy in pajamas and between the sheets had been like trying to put toothpaste back into the tube.

"Oh, no," Theresa apologized. "Having you here supercharged him. It really says something that he'd be this excited to have his teacher over to the house."

"I think we've connected," Laura said. "He's going to pull through this rough patch he's in."

"How about the rough patch you're in?"

Laura squeezed her wedding ring and gave it a spin around her finger. "I wish I knew. I wish I understood what was going on. Since we've moved, Doug has really changed. He's distant, uninvolved. The way he sleeps in each morning, we hardly talk. Then when we do, it seems like he isn't listening."

"Well, if you're looking for someone to defend the male species," Theresa said, "you've come to the wrong place. My marital disaster produced only one good thing, and I just put him to bed."

"Maybe Doug's just obsessed with this novel he's writing," Laura said. "Some Southern saga of family warfare. He won't let me read it until he's done."

"He was never work obsessed before you moved to Galaxy Farm?"

"No." Laura paused. "Well, maybe. Life was so different in New York. Oh, wait. You aren't going to blame the house, are you? You saw the girls were no threat."

"I only know what I feel," Theresa said. "I've never shaken the feeling that there's something dangerous in your house."

"Well, it's not the girls," Laura said. "I was going to try the static generator tonight to see if I could contact them better, but then this mess unfolded. Maybe tomorrow."

"You can do what you want tomorrow," Theresa said. "But you're not going home tonight. You've been gone all night and Doug hasn't even called to see where you are." Theresa went to a hall closet and pulled out a blanket and a pillow. She tossed them on the couch near Laura. "You're staying at the Moultrie Hilton tonight. Let's give Doug a chance to see what he's missing."

Laura had been through too much that evening to resist. She knew she didn't have the energy to restart a battle with Doug that night. She could head back in the morning for fresh clothes before school. Then the two of them could sort the whole thing out in the afternoon.

"I'll take you up on that offer."

Theresa stocked the hall bathroom with a spare toothbrush and towels and bid Laura good night. Laura sat in the living room and contemplated the last year's chain of events that got her here, that journey from New York City to a friend's couch in downtown Moultrie, Tennessee. What events were going to unfold over the next year and where would they take her? And would she travel there alone? Despite all that had transpired, she hoped not.

Chapter Forty-Two

Uncle Mabron was still down there. Somewhere.

Vernon Pugh stood by the fence line in the moonlit night. The lights in the house below, *his* house, had gone out an hour ago. Only one car in the driveway tonight. The little Honda was gone. He wished he could count on that more often. Less people at home made him more inclined to continue his search for Sarah.

Vernon ran the stub of his index finger along the edge of the *No Trespassing* sign on the post. That bastard Locke had some balls posting this.

Coyotes sounded their mournful howl and the cool breeze blew in the stagnant aroma of the Galaxy Farm pond. How many nights had Vern walked the pond's edge, breathing in that algae-tinted scent and knowing he finally had a place to call home. That was the torture of his house trailer existence on the ridge. He had the same sights, the same sounds, the same smells, the same feel of being at Galaxy, but now overlaid with the emptiness of exile.

Theresa Mayhew-now-Grissom's Ford Explorer had been at the house one night. He remembered her from high school. Cute back then, a little strange around the edges, kept herself away from the crowd. Vern liked that about her, thought the two of them might go good together. But even she didn't want anything to do with "Nubs" Pugh. Ended up with Bobby Grissom 'til she tossed him out. Vern figured he sure dodged a bullet with that bitch.

Seeing the Explorer that night made him even angrier. Those Lockes were living in his house and even having other people over. The thought of strangers trespassing on his family land, setting up in the house he shared with his father, made his blood boil. But that was nothing compared to how it had to make the spirit of his uncle feel.

Since his father's death, and his discovery of the hidden passage to the attic, Vern had been in communication with his departed uncle, practically in communion with him. Vern missed the house. He missed the land. He missed the freedom of having a place he knew was his. But more than all that, he missed his uncle.

His father Alexander had taken him in, given him a roof over his head and food in his belly. He'd certainly done more than Vern's mother ever had in those ways. But there was always a distance between them, a chasm too wide for either to reach across. Perhaps it was the lack of bonding at an early age, perhaps the radically different social environments the two had. Vern thought he sensed a guilt that plagued Alexander whenever they were together, though whether it was for creating a bastard son or for something else, Vern could never figure out. Whatever the reason for the buffer between them, Alexander may have been Vern's father, but he was never Dad.

Departed Uncle Mabron was a different story.

Since Vern's first day at Galaxy Farm, Alexander had locked the turret room. After Alexander's death, it was the first place Vern needed to explore.

And Vern was heartily disappointed. The room was empty save a bookcase next to the door to the closet. The curtains had long tears in them where sunlight had obliterated the threads. No footprints traversed the dust and Vern realized that Alexander had locked the room to keep both of them out. He saw that the bookcase was not flush with the wall. When he slid it away, he saw it covered a second door, the closet door's twin.

The second door was nailed shut. The gap between the door and the frame was filled with red wax embedded with large chunks of salt. A red rose of extra wax bloomed in every corner and carried symbols that looked Egyptian. It sure didn't look like Alexander was trying to keep people out as much as he was trying to keep something in.

170

Vern grabbed some tools and went to work on the door. He cursed his stunted hands as the crowbar he took to the nails repeatedly slipped from his grasp. One by one, he pried the heavy nails from the door frame. Some carried a now-illegible inked inscription along the shaft. With a chisel, he gouged at the wax seal along the door frame, hampered by the poor control his misshapen fingers gave him. Piece by piece the brittle seal fell away. Chunks of salt hit the ground and exploded into dust. He scraped the last bit free of the hinges and turned the handle. The door was locked.

Now if you are going to nail a door shut, why lock it? he thought. And where the hell was the key? He looked over on the windowsills, but they were empty.

When he turned back to the door, the key protruded from the lock. A chill shot up his spine. His first instinct was to bolt out of the room, but curiosity checked the impulse. Something wanted him to open that door, was downright *inviting* him to do it.

He wiggled the key back and forth, and with a heavy *thunk,* the tumblers rolled over and the key turned. Vern pulled open the door. The hinges creaked and shards of wax in the posts scattered onto the floor.

A dark stairway led to the attic. Cobwebs thick as cheesecloth covered the entrance. They waved like a flag from the opening of the door. A smell of chemicals and corpses enveloped Vern.

A blast of frozen air rolled out of the stairwell and disintegrated the cobweb curtain. It enveloped Vern and he felt his skin tingle and contract. Then, as if two huge hands clasped him behind the back, it drew him up the shadowed stairwell.

Wondrous discoveries awaited him when he turned on the light. The mounted menagerie lined the attic walls, coated in a blanket of dust only decades could accumulate. He'd seen a few deer heads mounted at friends' houses growing up, but this collection was staggering. Animals he'd never seen, and animals he knew were protected species sat lifelike as could be. While he knew they were

Russell James

dead, he sensed something behind their glass eyes. The animals gazed at him as if he was a savior.

These had to be Uncle Mabron's. His father had inherited the house from Mabron, and Vern was certain that animal-loving Alexander would never have taken taxidermy as a hobby. But why stash all this in the attic? Why not throw it out when Alexander moved in?

Though the attic felt unnaturally cold, a rush of warmth filled Vern from within. It was a combination of familiarity and safety. He'd only had this feeling for fleeting moments with his mother, but he knew what it was, the way all people instinctively do. It was the feeling of "home". Whatever presence was here in the attic, and he was damn sure it was Uncle Mabron, was making sure he knew that this house, but more specifically this treasure-filled attic, was the family jewel and it was now passed to Vern's generation.

For the first time in his life, Vern felt unconditionally accepted. Not prejudged for the sins of his mother, not dismissed for his misshapen hands, not sheltered out of some pious sense of guilt. Just welcomed, and wanted, as family. He could feel the power that his uncle's spirit commanded and he wanted to taste that power.

Vern looked over the animals. A crested owl perched on a pine log caught his attention. The species had a white streak of feathers that circled from under its each eye and across its forehead like two glowing eyebrows. Its large yellow eyes seemed to bore into Vern. Even in the dim light of the attic, Vern could see that the bird had seen better days. There was a sunken spot in its puffed chest and one of its ears was bent. Still, he thought it would look good on the fireplace mantle, mostly because he knew it was illegal to have the rare species.

He carried the owl down to the turret room. The sunlight through the decayed curtains hit the bird and it shuddered in Vern's hands. Startled, he dropped the bird. It hit the floor and rolled face up, staring at him. Vern scooped it up and noticed an immediate difference. The owl's chest was puffed out like it was ready to hoot. Its two ears were both erect, and Vern could swear they were pointed more forward. He

172

stared into its big yellow eyes and there was a sparkle deep within, like a candle a thousand yards down a black tunnel.

By the end of the day, the entire ark of animals was back in the house. It was as if Vern knew where each one was supposed to go, where each one *used* to go, certain he was guided by Mabron's spirit, finally released from whatever prison the attic had become. By the end of the week, Vern had cataloged the rest of the attic, including the treasures within the great wooden chest. His hands would never master the taxidermy tools, but they had no trouble opening the locket to see the picture of his uncle and what had to be his beautiful bride.

And life at Galaxy Farm had been a dream for the months between then and the lightning storm. The night the propane tank exploded, so did Vern's world. Mabron came to him in a dream that night, the first time ever, and gave Vern a specific mission. Sarah, the locket princess was lost. Vern must find her by the pond.

So Vern spent every second of daylight searching the shoreline for the next few weeks, pushed by the recurring dream that plagued him each night. All other tasks fell by the wayside, and before he could explain what had happened, Galaxy Farm was no longer his.

So Vern failed. He failed to find Sarah's remains. He failed to hold on to Galaxy Farm. He thought returning all Mabron's treasures to the attic and hiding the door from the next owners would return him to his dead uncle's good graces. But no, he lost contact with his uncle's spirit. His last week before eviction there were no visitations in dreams, no more of that sense of being welcomed as family. Whether Mabron abandoned Vern out of profound disappointment or frustration, Vern could not tell.

All that will change, Vern thought. He would redeem himself in Mabron's eyes. He'd find Sarah. He'd get back the house. He'd make Mabron and himself one family, united forever. A couple of New York transplants weren't going to stop him. Step 1—Discourage any visitors.

Chapter Forty-Three

Across town an hour later, Vern pulled into the gravel parking lot of Slim's Place, a windowless concrete box of a bar along an empty stretch of Highway 41. Vern's headlights lit the peeling white paint. A silhouette of a thin cowboy leaning against a fence post passed as the only business identification since Carl Clemons wiped out the front signage during his third DUI. The lot was packed with pickup trucks sporting gun racks and the occasional rebel flag.

Vern knew Bobbie Grissom would be here. Bobbie wasn't a reliable employee. He wasn't a reliable husband. But he was a reliable alcoholic. And there wasn't a place that catered to drunks better than Slim's. Vern headed inside.

The joint reeked. The air in the bar stank of stale cigarettes. The rancid stench of spoiled beer rose from the sticky concrete floor. Each flap of the swinging men's room door delivered a fresh scented injection of vomit and piss. The dim lighting was a godsend, sparing any customer from seeing things they'd rather ignore.

A mournful ode to unappreciative women warbled from the jukebox over the rolling din of dozens of voices. The place was packed, every table filled with a knot of shaggy-haired men in baseball caps. Alone at the end of the bar sat Bobby Grissom, two upturned shot glasses in front of him and a longneck beer in his hand. He sat hunched over the bar with smoldering anger in his eyes. Vern knew his timing was perfect.

"Two Jacks," Vern shouted to the bartender as he sat on the stool next to Bobby. Bobby looked up with a slow look of recognition, followed by a derisive sneer.

"Nubs Pugh," Bobby said. "Ol' P.U. Pugh himself. What the fuck."

Vern gritted his teeth at the sound of his two most hated nicknames. The raw, open nerves in his molars sent a spike of pain into his jaw. He'd just as soon slit the throat of the worthless sack of shit in front of him, but there was a mission to accomplish. The bartender dropped two shots of Jack Daniel's whiskey in front of Vern. Vern slid one over to Bobby.

"Hey, Bobby," he said, fake grin framing his decimated teeth. "Have one on me."

Bobby stared him down through bleary eyes. "What's the occasion for you deciding to drink with me?"

"Word is the shit's been rolling down hill and you been catching all of it."

Nine times out of ten Bobby would have threatened to shove the drink so far up Vern's ass he could taste it. But being three sheets to the wind and depressed made this that lucky ten percent Vern planned on exploiting.

"Damn right," Bobby said. He threw back the Jack with one swallow. "Lumber mill cut my hours way back. Landlord won't fix the busted window in my shithole apartment. And some lawyer says I owe my ex-wife money."

"It's just a world full of assholes," Vern said. He slid the second shot in front of Bobby. Bobby eyed it and smiled. He gave Vern a punch in the shoulder.

"Fucking right," he said. He hammered back the second shot.

"Ain't right how Theresa done you," Vern said. "Especially who she's taken up with."

Bobby slammed the empty shot glass on the bar so loudly that the two closest tables went silent and stared. "Who's that?"

"She's doing that new guy, Locke, that moved into my house," Vern said. "Seen her truck there myself. Everyone knows."

Bobby's face turned beet red and his fingers balled into fists. "That bitch."

"Kind of makes you look the fool, her with an outsider, and a married one."

"That's what my child support pays for," Bobby said. "Whore needs to be taught a lesson."

"Ain't no one gonna fault you for doing it," Vern said. "People seen how she's been."

"Damn straight," Bobby said.

"And if Sheriff Dickhead Mears wants to know where you were tonight," Vern whispered, "I'll sure tell him you and me left here for a few drinks at my place until dawn."

Bobby smiled. "Then there ain't no time like the present." He slid his stool back from the bar and stood with a wobble. He put a hand on Vern's shoulder. "You're all right, Nubs."

Vern suppressed his revulsion at Bobby's offensive compliment and gave a satisfied smile. Bobby headed out into the parking lot.

The plan was in motion. Bobby was about to stir up enough shit that one way or another Theresa wouldn't have time to mess around at Galaxy Farm. That would be one less person to worry about when Vern made his next trip back home.

Chapter Forty-Four

Bobby's first inclination was to drive straight to her house, correction, straight to *his* house since he'd made years of payments until the judge tossed him out. He rolled up and saw a second car in the driveway, a Honda. Visions of Theresa screwing some guy in his former bedroom made him want to rush the front door. But even with his alcohol-stewed brain he remembered how ready the cops were to enforce that fucking restraining order the bitch had laid on him. So instead he wheeled his primer-black Dodge Ram into downtown Moultrie. He couldn't hit here where she lived, so he'd hit her where she worked.

Ever since the divorce, Theresa's life had been smooth sailing. She had more friends, joined the Chamber of Commerce, hell, even her stupid Explorer, which Bobby had slaved over every weekend to keep running, suddenly became reliable as sunrise. But the success of her store was the worst of it. The whole idea of reselling shit even the owners didn't want was stupid. But she was making more money than Bobby was now. He knew because his lawyer found out during his unsuccessful attempt to reduce his child support payments.

All that luck had to come from somewhere, and Bobby knew he was the donor. Since the divorce, all his news was bad. Lost jobs, broken U-joints, and an apartment with plumbing that backed up every time he took a dump. If all the miserable parts of his life were erased, he'd have no life at all. Well, the time had come to spread some of that misery around.

He killed the truck's lights as he rolled to a stop in the dim alley behind Treasured Things. The streetlight at the far end left the area in shadows. He kicked open his door and whirled to the rusting cargo box in the truck's bed. Inside he found just what he needed; a four-foot breaker bar and a can of the orange spray paint they used to mark trees targeted for cutting.

The back door to the place had *Treasured Things* stenciled on it in new white letters. He rammed the sharp edge of the breaker bar against the first *T* and gouged a valley through the letters. Then he slammed the bar into the crack between the door jamb and the door, just above the lock. The old spongy wood yielded easily. He heaved himself against the breaker bar and the door snapped open with a loud crack as the frame splintered.

The bar slipped out of his hands and hit the concrete landing with a clatter. Bobby ducked down and held his breath. Sweat beaded on his brow. It stank of beer and adrenaline. He waited for any indication someone heard the noise. Nothing. He picked up the bar and pushed the door open with it.

A shrill repeating beep sounded and a light on the wall alarm panel flashed red.

Fuck me, thought Bobby.

He ran to the panel and shoved the breaker bar between it and the wall. An idea made him pause. He tapped his son's birthday into the keypad and hit *Enter*. The alarm died and the light turned green.

"Can read her like a book," Bobby muttered.

He surveyed the store in the dim filtered light. Aisles of useless garbage. Vases and pictures and old broken toys. Nothing here anyone needed. But some sucker was going to hand his ex-wife money for it, just to make Bobby look more like a loser to everyone in town. Anger flushed hot in him again. No more of that was going to happen.

He gripped the breaker bar like a baseball bat, wound up and swung. A set of porcelain china exploded into a blizzard of white chips. The tinkling sound of the flying fragments gave Bobby a charge. Revenge was so sweet. He strode down the aisle, swinging and smashing. Each swing shattered hundreds of years of antiques. With

178

each pass, he imagined the look of horror on Theresa's face as she opened the door later this morning, and then the anger as she learned of his airtight Nubs alibi.

Bobby took a swipe at a standing full-length mirror in a rich walnut frame. The ancient glass splintered on impact. But the booze had his equilibrium on the run and all this wheeling around hadn't helped. He lurched right during his follow though and stumbled into the mirror. Shards of glass tore his right arm. Blood oozed and then ran in a stream. Bobby cursed and grabbed his arm. The blood felt hot on his fingers. The cut wasn't deep, but his night of homers in the shop was over.

He tossed the breaker bar out the back door and pulled the spray can from his back pocket with his injured arm. The laceration's pain made its first appearance through his alcohol-induced daze. He winced and cursed Theresa again since his decision to do all this damage was, after all, her fault. He steadied his arm as best he could and sprayed wobbly block letters onto the wall. Even in the dim light, the fluorescent paint glowed the word *Whore*.

He shoved the can back in his pocket and headed for the door. Then the growing pressure on his bladder gave him another brilliant idea. He turned, dropped his pants and sprayed a steady stream of hops-scented urine around the shop. He made an extra effort to soak the seat behind the cash register. As the last few drops dribbled onto his shoes, he surveyed the payback present he'd left his ex-wife.

"A job well done," he said with a laugh.

Chapter Forty-Five

Laura made it home before dawn broke. The house was dark and Doug's car was parked by the porch. He was asleep in bed by five thirty a.m.. Right on his schedule.

Laura crept through the house to keep from awakening him, but the act wasn't altruistic. She didn't want to talk to him now. She had a full day at school today and didn't want to start it off furious.

She pushed open the bedroom door. A sliver of light lit Doug's face. He looked peaceful, quiet. Normal.

Normal. None of that strange wisp of something that seemed to have imbedded itself in him recently. None of that feeling that Doug was a clock that was set just a few minutes off.

Listen to yourself, Laura thought. *Theresa certainly stirred up your imagination.*

Doug shifted underneath the covers. He pulled the blanket up over his eyes. Laura snapped off the hall light and plunged the room back into darkness.

No, there wasn't anything supernatural going on here. She just had a self-indulgent, self-centered husband. A husband so clueless he let her leave for the night and never checked up on her.

The idea of waking him up with a cold bucket of water crossed her mind, but she discarded it. Better he sleep and spend today as unaware of her frustration as he had been. She had a date tonight with Constance and Elizabeth and she could put off fixing her marriage until after that. She was certain that *he* could as well.

Hours later, Doug awakened like a bolt of lightning struck him. The bedroom was ablaze in sunlight. He was primed to finish the fox.

Doug had worked on her all night last night. He slipped into bed about four a.m., but Laura wasn't there. This concerned him, but something in him rationalized that she was probably just downstairs on the couch, or sleeping in one of the other bedrooms. As soon as he awakened, he returned to the turret room to finish his prize. He'd moved her out of the attic for more working room. In the light of day, the fox looked a bit cockeyed. The glass eyes were a bit askew, the seams a bit crooked around the hind legs. The excelsior stuffing did not do justice to the formerly well-muscled hindquarters. Doug had rushed the job and it showed.

But he hadn't hurried the tasks outlined in the *Book of the Dead*. The animal's organs were separated and seasoned exactly as demanded. The earthen jars were sealed with wax. Now they surrounded the mounted fox on the floor of the turret room, each at the tip of a precisely measured five-pointed star Doug had inscribed on the floor.

The windows were wide open to allow the unfiltered light of the sun god Ra onto the jars. Doug opened the *Book of the Dead* to the center, to the marked page where the phonetic translation for the *Taming of the Beasts* chapter began. He started to read aloud.

"*Haruch notak conig Osiris. Salut geriz cho vowatum.*"

A first he stumbled over the words, parsing each syllable. But a paragraph into the ritual, they became oddly familiar. His pace increased and a crooked little smile crossed his lips as he settled into a rhythmic chant.

"*Perko hasasam fidert gytutus.*"

Nonsense that made sense. He could *comprehend* the translation, though he could not translate it. He called on Osiris to tether the life force of this fox to its body, to capture its soul as the jars captured its organs.

181

The room got warmer. Beats of sweat broke out on Doug's brow. As he continued to read, the room grew brighter, as if somehow more powerful rays of the sun beamed through the windows. The jars took on a yellow, pulsing glow. They throbbed in unison, in cadence with the melodic chant Doug's reading had acquired.

Doug read the final page, a plea for Osiris to show favor on those who worshipped him, to grant this great request. The jars glowed white, pulsed twice and launched beams of brilliant energy at the fox. Doug squinted against the dazzling display.

The light disappeared and Doug was temporarily flash blind. As the room came back into focus, Doug checked the fox.

It looked magnificent. Every muscle in its body was perfect, every hair in place. The face fit the skull with precision and the flat black clay Doug had molded into gums had a luster it hadn't had before. Most telling were the eyes. The irises had depth, as if something lived beyond those glass windows. They had a rich, deep sparkle. Like the red-tailed hawk on his desk, or the bobcat in the corner.

The power that transformed the fox coursed through Doug's body. Every nerve ending tingled, every muscle bulged with strength. His mind raced at the speed of light. Killing the fox had been invigorating, but this...

Doug picked up the fox. The fur was warm, and Doug half expected to feel a heartbeat. He set the fox upright on all four paws. It could not have looked more alive. This was the tribute to life Doug had wanted to create. What better way to celebrate the essence of the animal than to give it eternal life on Earth? Doug scooted back and rested, exhausted and elated, against the wall.

He slid the *Book of the Dead* over and picked it up. *Mabron, you sly dog. Such black magic going on at Galaxy Farm. Did people marvel at your taxidermied collection back then? Did you laugh when they asked how you made them look so real?*

Doug thumbed through the next few chapters. The next to last one had only the title translated—*Preparing Spirits to Cross Over.* He recognized the glyph for Osiris throughout the text. He paged to the last chapter. The translated title read—*Binding Spirits on Earth.*

The translation explained that this offering was not to the god Osiris, but to his brother Set. Set had killed his brother to usurp the kingdom of Egypt and claim his brother's wife, Isis. But for that, and other evil acts, Set was banished to pull the boat that moves the sun across the sky for all eternity. Prayers to Osiris moved the human dead from their body to the final reward. Prayers to Set thwarted that journey and bound the soul to the mummified corpse.

Specific steps followed. As in the *Taming of the Beasts* section, internal organs were separated and preserved in earthen jars. The mummification process was outlined and Doug realized how similar it was to his taxidermy. All the same skills were in play. Then there were pages of special incantations with the burning of incense sprinkled throughout. It was about twice as long as the procedure he used on the fox.

How would this bound spirit manifest itself? All Doug could think of was a ghost, unable to pass on to the next life.

Mabron, Doug thought, *what temptations passed through your mind with this power? Did you want to get even with some of those hateful townspeople? Did you ever get the chance to try it?*

Doug could see the incantation's allure. He felt power snuffing the life from an animal. Controlling the animal's spirit was even more of a rush. But controlling humans beyond the grave? That had to be the ultimate. He closed the book, closed his eyes and imagined.

Chapter Forty-Six

The mess at Treasured Things was more than Sheriff Mears was used to seeing. There was some vandalism now and then in town, but usually it was a few high school boys smashing mailboxes or a rock though a window at one of the car dealerships. This looked like a tornado went through the store last night.

Theresa sat in an overstuffed chair near the front of the store. Her eyes were red from crying and the low morning sun through the front blinds cast shadows like prison bars across her face. She was a lot calmer now than when Sheriff Mears had talked to her an hour ago, but he knew how her emotions would progress. Shock and despair would soon upshift into rage.

"Any guess on the damages?" the sheriff asked.

"Hundreds," Theresa said. "Maybe thousands. I'll do an inventory."

Sheriff Mears nudged a few shards of blood-stained mirror with his foot. He pulled a plastic bag from his back pocket, bent over and dropped the pieces inside.

"Anyone you think might have done this?"

Theresa looked up at the sheriff with dull fury for asking such a moronic question.

"Sorry," Sheriff Mears said. "I had to ask. Didn't want to jump to conclusions. I'll head over to Bobby's."

As Sheriff Mears left, Theresa swept the floor in an aimless pattern. The shock of the destruction weighed on her, kept her mind from processing things at full speed. So much was destroyed, so much work undone. The spray paint, the pee. Bobby was a jackass, but what would set him off like this?

She flashed back to the morning at her house. She had sent him packing with his tail between his legs. In front of his son. He was drunk, but not drunk enough to forget that little incident. That's what made him do this. She pushed and he had to push back.

Despair filled her heart like a black ooze. She was never going to be rid of him. She avoided him and he didn't go away. She stood up to him and he came out swinging. He'd bond out of jail, if he even got arrested, and he'd be back at her again. There was no light at the end of this tunnel.

"Bobby!" Sheriff Mears yelled as he banged on the door. Bobby's apartment was on the bottom floor of a fading Victorian that had been subdivided six different ways. Flecks of yellow paint fell from the door with each impact of the sheriff's fist.

The door opened a few inches. Bobby squinted in the daylight, face haggard and unshaven. An unlit cigarette dangled from his lips. All he had on were a pair of shorts.

"Well, Sheriff," Bobby rasped. "Always a pleasure."

"Rough night, Bobby?"

"Nothin' a little hair of the dog won't cure."

"Where were you last night?" the sheriff asked.

"Down at Slim's 'til eleven," Bobby said. "Then over to Vern's 'til dawn." The answer came out way too fast. Bobby could barely contain a self-satisfied smile.

"Vern Pugh?" Sheriff Mears said. "When did you two become drinking buddies?"

"Hell, Sheriff, guy's a little misunderstood," Bobby said. "I can empathize."

Sheriff Mears had heard some stinking stories over the years and this one reeked. Plus only the guilty forget to ask "Why?" when a cop asked for an alibi. "You know I'll check that."

"Call the man, but he won't be in any better shape than I am."

Bobby had a wad of paper towels bound to his arm with masking tape. Sheriff Mears remembered the blood at Treasured Things. He pointed at Bobby's arm.

"Looks like you cut yourself pretty badly."

"Little scratch. Caught myself on a rake in the garage last night when I got home."

"Mind if I take a look?"

"Now I'm just touched by your concern, Sheriff. But I'm doing fine."

"How about I come in and take a quick look around before I go?"

"If you got a warrant."

Mears hated when someone with no respect for the law shielded themselves with it, like a deserter signing up for VA benefits. "Don't leave town, boy. We've got lots more to talk about."

"I'm thinking we're done," Bobby said. He slammed the door.

Mears knew he wasn't beat. He had Bobby's DNA on file from a previous arrest. He could match it to the blood at Treasured Things and then he had him. Of course, unlike TV, it would take time. He'd have to ship it to Nashville and get in line behind more critical crimes like murders, rapes and kidnappings. But Bobby wouldn't know that. And by mentioning the cut, Mears knew he'd planted the seed in Bobby's tiny brain. In an hour, the loser would be convinced that he'd left evidence at the crime scene, and would be doing something stupid to cover up his involvement that would only further implicate him.

But why wait that long. Bobby gave him a bogus alibi. Time to shake Vern and see what fell out. He could turn and Bobby would be behind bars before lunch.

Twenty minutes later Sheriff Mears' Charger was once more in Vern's driveway. God graced him this time and spared him a trip into the dank trailer. Vern sat on his front steps, sucking the life from a stub of a cigarette. He didn't look as worse for wear as Bobby. His eyes were clear and it appeared he'd taken the rare shower of the week.

"'Morning, Sheriff," Vern called. He waved with his cigarette between his first two fingers. "Had a premonition that you'd drop by today."

"Guilty conscience, Vern?" Sheriff Mears said as he approached the trailer.

"It's that charm that keeps getting you reelected, ain't it?"

Enough pleasantries. "Where were you last night, Vern?"

"Spent some time at Slim's," Vern said. "Then came home for a nightcap with Bobby Grissom. Hung out 'til the wee hours."

Again, a rehearsed story that answered all the questions Sheriff Mears would ask. And again, no curiosity about why.

"Didn't know you two were so close," Sheriff Mears said. "You two boys have a sleepover?"

Fire flashed in Vern's eyes, but he cooled it and didn't rise to the bait. "Just two buds sharing some Buds."

"This is the same Bobby that used to call you 'Nubs'? Once super glued your car shut?"

"Long time ago, Sheriff." Vern took a final drag on his cigarette. "A man can change."

"You understand the phrases 'obstruction of justice' and 'accessory to a crime'" don't you?"

Vern stared past the sheriff.

"I'll have some physical evidence that says your new best friend Bobby wasn't with you last night," Sheriff Mears said. "I know he was out busting up his wife's shop down on the square. When that evidence comes through, that will make you guilty of one or more of the felonies

I just mentioned. So before we get to that, do you want to rethink the story of last night?"

Vern mashed his cigarette out on the step. "Just two buds," he said, "sharing some Buds."

"Remember you had this chance, Vern." Sheriff Mears got back in the Charger and backed down the driveway. Vern just sat on the steps and watched the car depart. Sheriff Mears knew he was just waiting for the cruiser to pull out of site before he whipped out his phone. He'd be railing at Bobby, wondering what evidence he'd left behind. Bobby would mention the blood and they would both know they were screwed.

After that Sheriff Mears could only win. Either Vern would change his story to avoid prosecution, and he'd have Bobby. Or Vern wouldn't turn, the DNA would come back, and he'd still have Bobby but he could also nail Vern.

Police work took patience. Maybe not on TV, where everything had to wrap up in forty-two minutes, but in real life it took patience. Sheriff Mears had it in spades.

That sealed it, Vern thought. The plan was in motion.

Dumbass Bobby had probably left his driver's license or some other hopelessly incriminating evidence at the scene of his crime. Too bad for him. His role was over. Theresa wouldn't be out visiting the neighbors tonight. If she had any sense, she'd be holed up somewhere, fearing for her life. That meant an early night for the Lockes and a long night to find Sarah's remains by the pond.

Oh, and he'd find them. Somewhere out where that old oak got walloped by lightning, she'd be there. Finding her would get him back in Uncle Mabron's good graces. Then the two of them would get Galaxy Farm back. One way or another.

Chapter Forty-Seven

"What happened here?" Ruby asked as soon as she walked into Treasured Things.

It was four p.m., but even Theresa's full day of cleanup hadn't gotten things back to normal. There were two piles of damaged antiques against the back wall and Theresa was scrubbing orange paint off the wall with a green pad and some acrid chemical solvent. She wasn't crying now, but her bleary eyes confessed to a previous bout of tears.

Theresa gave Ruby a dejected look. "Hurricane Bobby made landfall last night. Category Four winds. Category Zero IQ. Believe me, the place looked worse than this earlier."

"The sheriff's on him?"

"Like a fly on shit."

"And, honey, that ain't just a metaphor." Ruby sat down next to Theresa. "You and Dustin okay?"

"Sure," Theresa said. "But we're going to my parents' house tonight if Bobby's not behind bars. Bobby might mess with my shop, but he won't tangle with Daddy's deer rifle."

"What set him off, anyway?" Ruby said.

Theresa gave a guilty shrug. "Me, maybe. He was around the house last week and instead of calling the sheriff and letting him handle it, I went out and told the shithead off. He probably let that simmer on low boil until..."

"No, no, and *hell* no!" Ruby said. She pounded a foot on the floor for emphasis and a nearby glass crystal lamp responded with a tinkling shudder. "You are not to blame for what he does, ever. You stood up to him, then good for you. About damn time. The man had any sense, he'd take his licks and move on. You got a court order and he needs to follow it. This ain't your fault. Uh-uh, no way."

Theresa cracked her first faint smile of the day. "It does sound stupid when you put it that way. You can sure cut through the crap."

"Honey," Ruby said. "That's what girlfriends do." She stood up to leave. "Don't think I'm not going to give the sheriff a dose of reality as well. Now, you don't worry about none of this." She gave the mess on the floor a wave. "I got some items I know you can move for me. They'll be in here tomorrow to fill this floor space."

Theresa stood and gave Ruby a hug. "Thanks."

Ruby headed for the door. "You know why men are like paper cups?" she said over her shoulder.

Theresa smiled again. "Because they're dispensable."

"Amen, sister." The door slammed with a jingle of bells.

Chapter Forty-Eight

Laura stayed late at school that evening. She completed tutoring class and then graded the day's tests in her classroom instead of at home. She had a plan to contact the girls, and the later she got home, the greater its chance for success.

It was pushing past seven p.m. when she walked through the front door. Doug had just stepped off the staircase. He'd probably been up in the turret room, waiting for her to come home before stopping whatever it was he was doing. She glanced into the kitchen and nothing was cooking. Perfect.

"Say, babe, long day?" Doug asked.

Not even a question about where she was last night. Avoidance-practicing jackass.

"You have no idea," Laura said. "TCAP tutoring is something else."

A month ago a vague answer like that would have triggered a probing question from her husband. No worry about that happening today.

"I didn't know what time you'd be home," Doug said. "What about dinner?"

No time to kill with that, she thought. The faster he scurried off to his writing retreat, the sooner she could get to work.

"I'm not too hungry," she said. She reached past him and pulled a couple of power bars from the pantry shelves and a bottle of water from the refrigerator. "I'm going to get some quizzes written up for tomorrow. Might as well get on it." She wondered if he'd grab the bait.

"Really?" Doug said with barely contained relief. "Same here. I'm in the middle of a chapter that begs to be finished."

Hook, line and sinker, Laura thought. He didn't care if they spent time together and if she gave him the opportunity to opt out of it guilt-free, he couldn't refuse. Self-centered son of a...

She forced herself to give him a kiss on the cheek. His hair reeked of alcohol. His clammy skin reminded her of washed-up seaweed. She suppressed a shiver.

"Write up a storm," she said with a pasted-on smile. That sealed it. Doug was upstairs before she had the door to the nursery closed.

After she was certain Doug was engrossed in whatever he was writing, she pulled the static generator out and plugged it in to the outlet next to her desk. She could reach the on switch with her foot and not startle the girls when they were in the room with her. Then if she was lucky, she'd see the two girls she dreamed about with her own eyes.

The sun set and she left only the desk lamp on as she opened the class science book. There was something about the night that drew the girls, and Laura knew they wouldn't show until then.

Laura faked perusing the book and her mind wandered to questions about her spirit visitors. Were they happy with one foot in this world and one foot in the beyond? Did they even know they were dead? They died eighty years ago, how did that much time feel? So many questions that she couldn't answer through EVP alone.

The tremor came. The little ripple in her consciousness that said "They're coming" made its evening debut. The air went cold and goose bumps sprouted on Laura's arms. Laura exhaled a little puff of vapor and rotated in her seat so her foot rested on the switch for the static generator. She grabbed the blue hand-exercise ball from her desk and tossed it up and down in one hand.

"Constance?" she said. "Elizabeth? I know you're here. Are you ready to play?"

Laura tossed the ball so it bounced against the far wall and back into the center of the room. It lay still and Lauren worried for a moment that they wouldn't touch it. She wanted a way to estimate their position, to know where to watch when she hit the juice, just in case the vision was fleeting.

The ball wiggled. Then in spun on its axis like a supersonic toy top. Laura tapped the switch.

The static generator hummed to life. Sparks arced up between the metal rods in the tube. The hemisphere took on a dull glow and the hairs on Laura's arms tingled and stood on end. The pitch of the generator rose.

The blue ball levitated and hovered a yard off the ground. Then in flew in a slow lob across the room, only to halt in midair again.

The generator whine maxed at a high-pitched thrum. Static charges like Lilliputian lightning spit from the surface of the hemisphere, a flickering uniform dance in all directions. Then the charges migrated to the side of the generator facing the girls. Combined into a more powerful stream, they reached out toward the floating blue ball like silver tentacles. The stream narrowed until it appeared to be one bright thin tendril. It shot out to the middle of the room.

Laura gasped. The energy vanished mid-flight as the spirits absorbed it. The two girls materialized; two fuzzy, transparent black-and-white apparitions. They wore long dresses with lace trim and high collars. Long blonde hair went almost down to their waists. They smiled at each other, unfazed and apparently unaware of their new visibility. They had a soft focus quality that made details indistinct, but nonetheless, Laura recognized them. These were the girls from her dream.

Laura yearned for contact, to physically touch the spirits who had already touched her emotionally. Her heart pounded in her chest until she thought it would explode. Laura went to her knees facing the girls and spread her arms wide.

"Constance, Elizabeth," she whispered. "Come."

The girls looked at her, and then shot a glance to the opposite side of the room. They smiled. One dropped the blue ball to the floor and they darted into Laura's arms. She closed her arms around them but stopped short of the outlines of their dresses, though she felt no physical boundary and was sure she could pass right through them. A kiss of warm breath brushed each of her cheeks and in her right ear she heard a soft, high voice from another dimension.

"Mother."

An unimaginable sense of completeness filled Laura. Tears welled in her eyes and she choked back a sob. Even on her knees, she barely had the strength to stay upright.

The girls disappeared. The static charge snapped back to dance around the plastic hemisphere. Laura bowed until her forehead touched the floor. Tears fell like raindrops against the polished wood. For the first time, she understood the true magnitude of what she lost five years ago in St. Luke's.

But it would be all right now. She could have what she was missing. The girls could have what they needed. Together, in this house, perhaps they could all find family.

Chapter Forty-Nine

Hours later, Doug needed to stretch. He'd been hunched over his laptop since dinner. Was it after two a.m. already? The love triangle between the brothers and the wife was reaching a climax and he'd been absorbed in the writing.

The bedroom was dark, as was the nursery downstairs. Laura had to have gone to bed. Great. She'd gotten over whatever had upset her last night. He figured she would. He crept downstairs in the dark.

A noise came from outside the house. It was faint, grinding and rhythmic. Nothing a wild animal would make.

Doug crept into the nursery and peered out the bay window. The night was bright with a waning moon high in a clear sky. Down by the propane tank a thin man probed the ground with a pole. The orange glow of a lit cigarette bobbed in front of his face. Vern was back.

Anger swelled inside Doug. Enough of this was enough. He felt none of the trepidation he experienced during Vern's last transgression. Just a boiling rage. What the hell was this scumbag doing on his property again? The sheriff said he had warned him. One warning should be enough.

On his way to the back door, Doug grabbed the iron poker from the holder in front of the fireplace. He rested the heavy round handle against his shoulder and slipped out the back door.

He kept the tank between Vern and himself and moved forward in a slow crouch. His feet moved silent as a snake across the grass, closer to the cadenced smack and grind of Vern's probing pole. He forced himself into longer, quieter breaths. When he reached the tank, he leaned back against it. He felt the cool steel of the tank through his damp shirt. His lips pursed into a little crooked smile.

As Vern prodded the ground on the other side of the propane tank, Doug crept around the far end. He raised the poker off his shoulder, point in his palms and the metal globe handle hanging in space. He slipped up behind Vern. The scent of Vern's stale beer sweat mingled with the stink of the stagnant pond. Doug wound up like a Hall of Famer and delivered a crushing blow to the base of Vern's neck. Bones split beneath the skin with muffled cracks. Vern dropped to the ground with a whimper.

Doug rolled Vern over. The dazed intruder sucked in short, shallow breaths. Doug would need to bash him again to finish him. But how long would it take to beat a man to death? And what kind of a mess would the blood make? It seemed an inelegant solution. He remembered the last time he made this decision in this same spot. He remembered the fox.

"Well, Vern, old buddy," Doug said. "Let's go for a dip."

Doug grabbed Vern by the shoulders of his shirt and dragged him down to the pond. Pulling the dead weight made Doug's back twinge in protest. He waded into the pond backward and his struggle eased as Vern's body went buoyant. Doug pulled Vern past him until he stood knee deep in the water at Vern's waist. Vern's face floated above the water. His mouth stretched as if trying to speak.

"See you around, asshole," Doug said.

He plunged Vern underwater and knelt on his chest. Vern's eyes shot open, two white, terrified orbs staring from the black water. He screamed and bubbles broke the surface with his garbled cry. He reached up and clawed at Doug's waist. His stunted fingers found no grip.

"Those stubby fingers aren't much good," Doug said. He felt a surge of adrenaline run though his body. "Life's a bitch, and then..." He pounded his knees into Vern's chest.

A massive air bubble burst from the pond, like someone had popped a balloon underwater. Vern went limp and his arms slid back beneath the water. Doug searched Vern's neck for a pulse. It was over.

Doug felt a nearly orgasmic sense of satisfaction. The power he felt killing the rabbit and the fox was nothing compared to this. He ended a human life, entered that elite club so few have the courage to join. He closed his eyes and sighed.

Doug stood up. Vern's corpse stayed submerged. Doug could leave him here, but he knew eventually the body would rise to the surface. Burial would be an exhausting, time-consuming event. Again he remembered the fox. An idea sprang to mind, fully formed to the finest detail, as if he'd already done each step before. He grabbed the corpse by the front of the shirt and pulled it out of the water. The head lolled to one side, mouth open, eyes pointing nowhere.

"Vern, my man," Doug said. "You are going to be a work of art."

Doug heaved the corpse over his shoulder and took it into the barn. He slung the body down on the grating over the old bathtub like a fisherman delivering the tuna catch of the day. He completely understood the arrangement in the barn he had once thought so bizarre. The waterless tub, the sink, the pickling barrel. The attic hadn't been Mabron's taxidermy studio. The barn had. At least after he graduated to larger animals.

It was after three a.m.. Skinning Vern wasn't going to be a quick event if he was going to do the effort justice. Laura would be up in a few hours and her introduction to Doug's latest hobby didn't need to be over a corpse in the barn. He needed to be back in bed *now*.

Thanks to watching too many police procedurals on TV, he remembered he had four hours before rigor mortis set in. Working on a stiff stiff would complicate things. He did the math and if Laura left on time for school, he could be back in time to avoid that complication.

A shipping box from the water treatment system was still in the barn. Doug slit it in half and covered the body with it. The cardboard tent covered the length of the tub. Doug gave it a pat.

"See you in the morning, buddy," he said. 'Don't go anywhere."

Chapter Fifty

Laura silenced her screaming alarm clock with a slap.

She sat up in the darkness and thought the bed felt wrong. She reached back and Doug's side was empty. She flicked on the bedside lamp. Worse than empty, his side was still made.

He might have been getting to bed late each night, she thought. But he was always getting to bed. Now what the hell? She tossed on a robe. She opened the bedroom door to the sight of Doug puttering in the kitchen.

"You didn't go to bed?"

Doug looked up with obviously feigned surprise. "No, you know I was in the groove and all of a sudden it's morning." He wasn't nearly rumpled and haggard enough to have pulled an all-nighter.

Laura nodded and went into the bathroom. It was a little too clean. The sink was cleared away and she was sure there were two blue towels on the rack yesterday, not the one blue, one yellow there today. A peek in the hamper found a blue towel stained with mud.

She rolled on the shower and slipped off her robe. Hot water surged out in seconds instead of minutes since it had just been running. She pinned up her hair and stepped in.

She let the warm water cascade across her face. Doug was even stranger than usual this morning. Whatever the hell he did last night didn't have anything to do with writing. And she was amazed to find that she didn't care.

She worked up soapy lather on a washcloth. She had too much going on to mess with his crap. TCAP was coming on like a freight train and she was panicked that she didn't have enough tutoring time to make an impact on her low achievers. And then last night she had that amazing experience with the girls. She'd invest time there before she wasted it arguing with her husband about whatever stupid task he'd undertaken.

Twenty minutes later she was dressed sharply in a calf-length black skirt, turquoise blouse, black jacket and heels. She strode by the kitchen, school book bag slung over her shoulder. She smelled eggs cooking.

"Breakfast in seconds," Doug said.

After weeks of sleeping in, she thought, *now it's room service time?* Another guilt-driven act. She didn't even break stride.

"Not today," she said with a disingenuous smile. "I've got a lot to do before classes start."

A month ago, that would have brought out a protest from Doug, or a probe about what work she had to do, or concern about her skipping a protein fix first thing in the morning. But now…

"See you tonight, babe."

Laura slammed the door behind her. When the TCAPs were done, she was going to fix this situation.

Chapter Fifty-One

Doug breathed a sigh of relief as soon as the door shut. He watched out the window until her car made the turn on US 41. Then he pulled the roll of taxidermy tools from where he'd hidden it under the sink and went straight for the barn.

The first thing he checked when he pulled Vern's cardboard tent off his body was rigidity. He raised one of the corpse's arms and it fell back with a slap like a side of beef. He wasn't too late. He unrolled the tools next to the bathtub. For the first time, he snapped on a pair of rubber gloves, a bright yellow pair previously relegated to bathroom scrubbing duty. Then he put a white apron over his head and tied it in back. Laura had given it to him as a joke when they were first married, during the every-night-chili era. On the front it said *Kiss the Cook* in black letters.

He grabbed a pair of scissors and cut away at Vern's wet clothes. He yanked away the shredded ribbons like a kid unwrapping a birthday present until Vern lay naked over the old stained tub.

He rolled Vern over onto his chest. He had been planning the cuts since he first flopped him on the grate. This was going to be a masterpiece, an opportunity to prove his skills with a large and complicated canvas. All the seams would be on the back of the body or under the scalp. Every finger, every toe was going to get its own underside seam. The book recommended skinning the leg from the top down, and rolling off the skin like a lady's stocking. But that meant a big seam at the hip. Doug was going to do it the hard way. When he finished, the skin would be one solid piece, like a suit someone else could slip on. From the front, Vern was going to look as lifelike as anything in the attic.

Then he'd throw in a little Egyptian black magic. If binding the fox worked wonders, binding a human soul would be amazing. He'd put Madame Tussaud's to shame.

Doug bowed his head and took a deep breath. He held it as he put the tip of a scalpel at the base of Vern's neck. Doug applied slight pressure and the skin stretched under the sharp blade. He worried that thicker human skin might need tools he didn't have. There was a tiny pop, and the blade sank into flesh. Doug exhaled and ran a perfectly straight incision down the length of Vern's spine. The skin separated along the cut and Doug thought it looked like a blooming flower. He smiled a crooked smile that was now more his than someone else's. He started the second incision.

Doug worked straight through the day, no breaks, no lunch, no thought of anything else that might be happening in the world outside the barn. He cut and trimmed and scraped, all the while he handled the skin with a reverence that matched the repulsion he felt when it covered a beating heart. He realized he was elevating Vern to a status he would never reach as a breathing creature. He would shed his imperfections and become a virtuoso tribute to the human form. Even those malformed fingers could be improved; straightened and shaped more naturally than Vern's stunted muscles could have done in real life.

The organs were dispatched to their separate jars in the same manner as the fox and sat on a shelf by the water treatment unit. The bones sat on the grate in separate piles, de-fleshed but not fully cleaned. The muscle and other now-useless material were buried by the wood line in a shallow pit. The idea of interring the remains in the graveyard that held his family did not even occur to Doug. Vern as Vern was nothing. It was only Vern as creative canvas that would be of value.

Doug went to the barrel where the skin was pickling. He reached in and grabbed the hide. It felt cold and rubbery and he had a hard time getting a good grip on it. He seized the shoulders and pulled. The skin lifted from the solution like a breaching whale. Doug dragged it along the dirt floor and over to the wall and a pseudo-clothes line he had improvised from some electrical wire. He flipped the skin over the line and pulled the edges tight. He clipped the edges to the wire with antique clothes pins he'd found in the attic. The he raised the head skin up and tied it to two nails in the wall by its hair. He brushed some dirt from the hide and stepped back.

Doug beamed with pride. It was Vern 2.0 up on the wall, spread-eagled and flat, a lot wider than he used to be. By tomorrow he'd be dry and ready to mount. Oh the agony of having to wait that long.

Chapter Fifty-Two

The three tutoring students she had that afternoon all went home earlier than usual since their baseball team had a game that evening, so Laura finally got out of school with enough time to get downtown before five p.m.. She had been dying to tell Theresa about her encounter with the girls' spirits for two days. But no one answered Theresa's home phone and her cell went straight to voice mail. Dustin had been out of school as well and that had made Laura worried. She hoped she could drop by Treasured Things and find out what was going on.

She walked in with fifteen minutes to closing and Theresa was alone in the back. She smiled as Laura came in.

"Laura!"

"Theresa!" They hugged like they were sisters.

"Looks like you have some new inventory," Laura said.

"I had an involuntary reduction," Theresa answered. She gave Laura a quick review of her ex-husband's visit to the store.

"And what did the police do?" Laura asked.

"Bobby's got a bogus alibi," Theresa said. "Until the sheriff punches a hole in it, he's still free. Dustin and I are staying with my parents until they can arrest him. I've kept him out of school in case Bobby tries to exercise his legal parental right to contact him."

"Well, I've got some news from the spirit world that might brighten your day," Laura offered.

"Oh, did the static generator work?"

"Like a charm," Laura said. "I saw the girls. Completely, head to toe. It was like Disney World's Haunted Mansion." She left out her more personal encounter at the end. "You've got to meet them. Why don't you come over tonight?"

"No, I really..." Theresa paused and thought. "Yes, I think I will. Dustin couldn't be happier being spoiled by Grandma and Grandpa, and I need an excuse to stop feeling like I'm being hunted."

"Perfect," Laura said. "Dusk is at seven. See you then?"

"You bet."

Chapter Fifty-Three

The jail door rolled shut with a clank. The sheriff had to admit Bobby looked damn good through a set of iron bars.

"I don't know how you can say that was my blood at her store," Bobby said.

"Because we have your DNA on file from one of your previous arrests," Sheriff Mears said. "Your blood was on the mirror at the crime scene, and you had cuts on your arm the next morning. Means, motive, opportunity. You got the big three covered, Bobby."

"Maybe someone got my DNA and put it in there," Bobby said. "She could be trying to frame me."

"That's the best you can do? Well, you tell that one to a jury and see if they buy it." Sheriff Mears left a deputy in charge of the jail and went outside to his cruiser.

He didn't have the DNA test results back from Nashville, but he did have his people at the local hospital type the blood. AB negative was a match for Bobby, but a match for only one percent of the population. That was good enough for the DA until the DNA check confirmed it without a doubt.

A great little benefit was that he had Vern dead to rights as well. Finally a good reason to haul his creepy ass into jail. Once he saw the inside of a cell, he'd sing for a plea bargain, testify against Bobby and still end up convicted of something. Some days it really paid to be in law enforcement.

Sheriff Mears fired up his cruiser and headed for Vern's. Fifteen minutes later, as the last red rays of the sun hit the horizon, be pulled into Vern's driveway. He was glad to see Vern's dented Chevy Celebrity in front of the house. That meant his quarry was home.

Even though it was dusk, there wasn't a light on in the trailer, which struck Sheriff Mears as odd, unless Vern was taking a nap. He donned his wide-brimmed hat as he left the car and approached the trailer slowly. He walked up the creaky steps and waited outside the front door. Silence. If Vern wasn't home, maybe he was walking the woods. At dusk? No way.

Sheriff Mears pounded on the door. "Vern, it's Sheriff Mears. Open up."

Still nothing. Mears repeated the process to no avail. He tried the door knob. Unlocked.

A second warning sounded in his head. No one left doors unlocked, especially Vern with his lifetime of unfriendly contacts. Sheriff Mears nudged the door open.

Warning sign three. The place stank. Not the usual unkempt reek from minimal housekeeping. Something in here was rotting. He pulled his gun and flicked off the safety.

"Vern, I'm coming in!" He flipped on the light. A mouse skittered across the floor and into a hole in the wall.

Sheriff Mears moved room to room and cleared the trailer. No one there, living or dead. He put a few worst-case scenarios to bed. He holstered his weapon and took his time walking back through.

The place was a mess, but not much worse than last time he was here. In the kitchen, he found the source of the stench. A bowl with the remnants of milk-sodden breakfast cereal sat in the sink. On the counter stood a half-finished bottle of beer. Sheriff Mears touched it. It was room temperature and flat.

Yesterday's breakfast in the sink and a flat beer on the counter from later in the day, or even the night. He guessed Vern hadn't been home for nearly twenty-four hours. But his car was here. Now where the hell would he head off to on foot?

"Shit, no." He looked out the front door and down the hill. Not Galaxy Farm. No, the Lockes would have called right away if he went over there. If Vern heard Bobby was arrested, he might have just lit out to the woods, knowing he was going to be picked up next. It would take the whole department to flush him out of there.

"Damn it."

Chapter Fifty-Four

An hour later, Theresa pulled up at the main house of Galaxy Farm. She had tried to make Laura think she was coming over to see the girls as a diversion. But her motivation was completely different. She hadn't forgotten the premonitions, the bad karma around Galaxy Farm, the mortal danger Laura was somehow in. Laura's enchantment by the spirits had only deepened her concern. Nothing had triggered a vision the last time she was here, and she hadn't had one in a while, but she knew not to let that lull her. No premonition that strong had ever gone unanswered. She was afraid she would get some of those answers tonight.

The lights on the bottom floor were on. On the second floor, only the two windows of the turret room were lit. Laura had the front door open before Theresa was out of her car. She wore a broad, excited smile.

"Oh, this waiting has been killing me," she said. "C'mon in and let's get started."

Theresa felt her first foreboding feeling as she crossed the threshold. Not a vision, just a hint, like catching the scent of smoke before you see the fire. She looked around the living room and across the kitchen for any source of the sensation, but nothing stood out. But it was touch that always brought out the talisman in an object.

"Is your husband here tonight?" Theresa asked.

Laura pointed up the stairs with her thumb like a hitchhiker. "Up there. Writing, he says. We won't disturb him. An earthquake wouldn't disturb him."

Apparently Laura hadn't settled much with Doug today.

Laura shut off the lights in the living room and guided Theresa into the nursery. The static generator sat on the floor by Laura's desk. Laura had put a dining room chair on the other side of the generator, assuming Theresa didn't want to spend her second encounter with the spirits on the floor again. How nice.

When she entered the room, Theresa felt the air in the nursery thicken. Whatever evil she felt in the living room, it doubled in here. But Laura didn't seem to sense it. She was still beaming.

"Now just have a seat,' Laura said. "They appeared here last time. I'm sure they'll be back. I can't wait for you to meet them."

Meet not *see*. The girls were more than ghosts to Laura, Theresa thought. What else had happened the last night she saw them to create that kind of a bond?

"Laura, you never felt any danger, any threats from these ghosts?" Surely Laura had to have a whiff of all the bad mojo wafting through this place, even just an inkling.

"Please! Never." Laura patted the dining room chair. "Now sit down and stop worrying. This is going to be fun."

Theresa took her seat. Laura sat and snapped on the static generator. A low hum filled the room. Sparks danced up the metal rods in the tube, electric soldiers marching to the half dome at the top. The hemisphere acquired an off-white glow. Laura turned off the main light but left on a small light on her desk. Its weak rays barely reached the far end of the room and gave everything a sepia tone.

Laura made no pretense of distraction, feigned no schoolwork. She faced the room from her desk and closed her eyes.

"Constance? Elizabeth? Are you out there?"

Another sign the relationship has progressed, Theresa thought. She doesn't wait for them. She calls them. But the room stayed silent save the hum and snap of the generator.

"Don't worry," Laura said. "Theresa is my friend. She wants to visit with you."

A moment later, Laura grinned and mouthed "They're coming."

Whatever comforting, benevolent force Laura felt approaching, Theresa felt the opposite. The air got viscous as motor oil. A fight-or-flight rush pumped though her veins. The room went ice cold in an instant.

"They're here," Laura cooed. Her breath came out in a puff of steam.

The static generator cracked like pine needles in a campfire. Sparks flew around the head of the unit and then coalesced on the side facing the room, pulled like iron filings to a magnet. The sparks braided into one beam that snaked outward. A few feet away it transformed into the shimmering shape of two little girls. They faced Laura, long hair streaming down their backs, high collars topping long dresses.

The girls looked with longing at Laura and stepped up to her. They held hands and then stretched their two free hands out to Laura. Laura took one of their hands in each of hers and they formed a triangle with two glowing sides.

The touching scene should have brought tears to Theresa's eyes. Instead she was terrified. The scene was so wrong. There was something about the girls' collars. They didn't seem attached to their dresses. Even fuzzy and indistinct, the textural difference was clear. And there was an evil in the room, an evil at odds with the two angelic faces that gazed at Laura with adoration.

Theresa pushed the base of the static generator forward with her foot. The arcing rope of sparks grew shorter until the generator touched one of the girl's arms. The energy loss over distance eliminated, the two girls flashed into bright, though still opaque detail. Every eyelash, every stitch of lace on their dresses was crystal clear.

But so were the collars. They were slave collars of pounded iron. Thick chains hung from them, running behind the girls like the support cables of a suspension bridge to hell. The other ends rested in the hands of a male spirit, thin, taller than the girls and in a suit coat and vest. He had a tangled mess of hair and eyes that glowed a dull red, though the rest of his translucent figure was a mixture of grays. His lips curled into a crooked smile. He seemed unaware that he was visible.

Laura's back stiffened when she saw the man behind the girls. She sucked in a breath to cry out.

Theresa knew he'd vanish and take the girls with him when Laura screamed. He was the source of whatever horrible future this place held for her friend. If she wanted that secret unlocked, she'd have to touch him.

Theresa fought through the fear and revulsion. She reached out and her hand passed through his shoulder. On contact, a look of shock registered on the spirit's face. His head snapped toward Theresa. His eyes narrowed to two burning slits.

Theresa's final premonition arrived. A blinding, terrifying, overwhelming rush of thoughts and emotions. Alien memories flooded in so fast she could barely sort through them. But she saw the plan. Clear as she had seen the branch destroy the family van years ago, she knew the fate planned for Laura.

"*No!*" she yelled.

She scooped the generator base from the floor and hurled it into the wall. It shattered with a sizzle like lightning. Sparks flew through the room and the stomach-turning smell of burnt hair filled the air. Laura shrieked. The three spirits shuddered like Taser victims and vaporized.

The link to the man broke and Theresa fell to the ground, drained as if the withdrawal of the alternate consciousness sucked some of the life from her. Laura dropped to her side and held her hand.

"Are you all right?"

Theresa nodded hazily.

"What was that? Holding the chains?"

Theresa rebounded fast, fueled by the panic her vision fired up. "It's Mabron Hutchington. And he wants you dead."

212

Chapter Fifty-Five

"Dead?" Laura said.

"Worse, actually," Laura answered. She jumped to her feet. "You know who Mabron was?"

"The girls were his nieces," Laura said. "They drowned in the pond behind the house. Their parents died soon after."

"You are missing a lot," Theresa said. "Who told you that much?"

"Doug."

Theresa shook her head. "Figures. The rest of the story is that the father died soon after, sick from trying to pull the girls from the frozen pond. Then months later, the mother commits suicide by hanging herself in the barn."

"Oh, God."

"But that's just the official version," Theresa said. "I just downloaded the real story through Mabron.

"He lived in the house with the family, nursing an unrequited love for his brother's wife. After the girls drowned, he saw an opportunity to get in her good graces, but in a horrible way. He had a book, a copy of the Egyptian *Book of the Dead* that contained black magic to bind souls to the Earth. Before the undertaker took the girls away, he performed a perverted rite on them. He kept their spirits bound here at Galaxy Farm."

"The chains..." Laura said.

"The chains keep them with him, but the spirits are still bound to their bones here," Theresa said. "So with the girls' spirits here, Mabron thought he'd started some twisted family. His brother had to go, then. The 'heart attack' the brother suffered was really suffocation, smothered by a pillow by Mabron.

"Now in Mabron's diseased mind, Sarah, the widow, should come running to him, the man she secretly longed for. She rebuffs his advances and he decides he will have her, dead or alive. He fakes her suicide and binds her soul here with the girls. When Mabron passes on, he doesn't need any black magic to stick around. He wants to stay and spend eternity with the 'family' he's ensnared."

"Where's Sarah, then?" Laura asked.

"Sarah's gone," Theresa said. "Mabron didn't bury her in her grave. Couldn't stand the thought of her being beside her husband, He buried her out by the pond, where he could sit by her grave under the shade of an oak without the rest of the headstones reminding him of the past. The lightning storm that fried the old oak and blew up the propane tank somehow freed her soul."

"Fire," Laura said. "The ghost hunter website said burning the bones, preferably with a healthy dose of salt, releases the spirit to move on. The blast must have cremated her."

"And now Mabron wants you to take her eternal place," Theresa said. "He's duped the girls into making the idea enticing, to build up your relationship. He thinks you'll join him willingly."

"Like hell I will," Laura said.

"As the generator exploded and the ghosts vanished," Theresa said, "I sensed dizzying confusion, like getting a concussion. I think the overload sent Mabron reeling. That gives us a window to hit him while he's out of it."

"If fire sent Sarah packing," Laura said, "then let's torch Mabron. Everything we need is in the barn. Let me get Doug."

Theresa grabbed her arm. "No! It's got to be us. I've got a feeling it's got to be us. I don't know why, but trust my intuition."

Laura paused. She gave a short nod. "Nothing I trust more right now."

Theresa followed Laura out of the nursery. She glanced up the stairway at the closed door of the turret room. A fan of light spread out from under the doorway. A shiver ran down Theresa's spine. She lied about going on intuition. She had seen Mabron's plan. She knew who Mabron planned to complete his handiwork in this world. Laura didn't need to know about that now.

The low moon on the horizon wasn't going to deliver much illumination. The air was crisp and a light breeze blew the compost-like stench of the pond up across the backyard. The open space felt good compared to how claustrophobic the evil had made the house. Laura flew to the barn with Theresa one step behind. Laura yanked at the sliding door and it grudgingly rolled right. She flipped the light switch on and screamed.

The flayed skin of Vernon Pugh swayed from the makeshift clothesline. Flies buzzed in and out of the empty eye sockets. Stray bits of dried flesh hung from the grate over the tub. The barn reeked with the stink of coagulated blood and decaying flesh. Theresa's stomach roiled and she covered her nose.

"Jesus Christ," Laura said. She stared at the skin unable to process this act of butchery hanging in her barn. "Who the hell..."

Theresa blocked her view of the clothesline. She cupped Laura's face in her hands. The stink of the barn swirled back up her nose and she fought back rising bile. She stared Laura in the eyes.

"There's no time," she said. "We'll worry about this later. Mabron first. Think, Laura. What is out here we need?"

Laura's eyes came into focus. "Salt," she whispered. Then in a stronger voice. "Salt. fifty-pound bags by the water treatment system. Paint thinner. A gallon can on the shelf by the..." She pointed at Vern. "Shovels in the corner."

Theresa turned Laura away from the body and towards the pallet of salt bags. "Go."

Theresa went to the shelf. She reached for the square can of thinner and a puff of wind flicked Vern's leg skin across her arm with a repulsive caress. She jerked her arm away and nearly dropped the can. She grabbed two shovels from the corner. Theresa met her at the door. A sack of salt teetered on Laura's shoulder.

"You okay?" Theresa asked.

Any trace of shock or confusion was long gone from Laura's face. Her green eyes blazed with determination.

"That bastard's toast," she said.

Chapter Fifty-Six

During the school shooting, Laura had been afraid, even terrified at some points. But as soon as that gun shattered the window in the door, her fear turned into fury. Her kids were threatened and she was going to take whatever steps were necessary to keep them safe. She would have twisted the barrel right off that gun if she had the strength.

Mabron had pushed that same button. Enslaving those girls' spirits, manipulating them. Assaulting their mother while she mourned the loss of her children, a loss Laura knew was near unbearable. Rage boiled inside her. The fifty pounds on her shoulder felt like nothing as she slogged through the field to the Hutchington graveyard. The uneven ground tried to throw her off balance at every step.

Then there was Doug. What the hell had Mabron done to her husband that would make him skin a man? God knew what other sick crap was going on upstairs in the house.

She entered the graveyard and the sensation was the opposite of her last visit. In the dark, what had felt like a cathedral now reverted to crypt. The stark headstones were bone gray. Furtive creatures scurried through the dead leaves, motions hidden by inky shadows. That light sense of the presence of the twins was gone. In its place was a thick, black malevolence that struggled to stir to consciousness.

Laura and Theresa swapped a quick knowing glance. Theresa felt it as well. Laura guessed Theresa probably felt it more strongly with her gift. If that thing revived while they were out here, there was no telling what it would do. The girls had lifted the charm from around

Laura's neck and tossed around the blue ball. If Mabron could move things in the real world, what would he be capable of?

"Let's fry this son of a bitch," Theresa said. She slammed the shovel into the ground in front of Mabron's tombstone. She launched a spade full over her shoulder.

Laura set up their defense. She tore a corner off the salt bag and poured a ring of white crystals around the gravesite. The website said this would protect them. Had the writer ever faced something with Mabron's power? Had the writer ever even seen a ghost? Here she was placing her life in the hands of an anonymous internet source. Good plan. She dropped the bag by the headstone and grabbed the second shovel.

"How much time do you feel we have?" she asked as her shovel bit into the soft earth.

"Not as much as I'd like," Theresa said. "This place is ripe with bad mojo. I'm afraid to touch anything but this shovel."

The earth gave easily, the top layer being mostly decomposed leaves. The original grave diggers had dug through the usual collection of Tennessee stones the first time through and had added them to the enclosure wall. Piles of dirt formed outside the ring.

A low moan sounded from within the graveyard, a subdued bellow like an angry bear awakening from hibernation. A pile of leaves shifted outside the salt ring. The women were not alone.

The women doubled their speed. Blisters rose on Laura's palms. The shovel blade sang with each scrape of the earth. Laura's back felt the strain.

Footsteps sounded in the leaf clutter around the salt ring. One , two, three. Slow at first, as Mabron's invisible spirit tested the salt ring perimeter. Then they came faster, a tangle of shuffled steps back and forth around the gravesite, as the frustrated spirit found his access blocked.

Theresa drove her shovel into the ground and jumped onto the edge of the blade. It sank a few extra inches and there was the muffled hollow echo of metal hitting wood.

"Got it!"

Mabron's spirit spun into a frenzy. It raced around the gravesite so fast that the footsteps became indistinguishable. He plowed through the leaves at whirlwind speed. The grave was like the center of a forming tornado. Some of the salt-covered leaves began to wobble.

The women uncovered the center of the coffin. The wood was soft from years underground. Laura prayed there would be no metal liner and brought her shovel down at one sagging point. The blade broke through. She pulled the shovel out and tossed it aside. She dropped down on the coffin and yanked at the rotten wood. A wide strip came up from the center. Laura pulled a book of matches from her pocket, matches that she'd been drawn to carry and collect since her first week here. She lit a match.

The weak yellow light barely lit the recessed space beneath her. Mabron's bones lay in the coffin, white skull facing skyward. He wore a black suit that was years out of style when he was buried in it. Save a few wisps, his hair was gone but all his teeth were still in place. The lower jaw hung open as if he was mid-laugh. Laura looked at the gleaming teeth and had a flash of that strange crooked smile Doug had acquired lately. Her skin crawled.

"Salt!" she said, but Theresa already had the bag on the way down. Laura grabbed the bag and poured pounds of it into the coffin, straight into Mabron's gaping maw.

Outside the ring, the tornado had become a hurricane. A rush of dry debris whipped around the ring. A low, furious roar rumbled from all directions. Salt crystals hopped on the vibrating leaves and threatened to disperse.

Laura jumped out of the hole and Theresa poured paint thinner into the cracked coffin. The stream dissolved the salt crystals into a white lump that coated the skull. She ran the rest of the can up and down the exposed coffin top. Despite the maelstrom outside the gravesite, the air within the salt ring was dead still and the overpowering fumes from the thinner made Laura's head reel. She lit a match.

Outside the ring, the wind scoured free a buried tree limb. It grabbed the knotted end and the limb wiggled back and forth. Its other end ran under the salt ring. The salt-covered leaves on top of it bounced and slid to one side. The storm rushed the gap.

"Now they'll be free," Laura said. She dropped the matches into the pit.

The coffin burst into flames. A roaring scream of pain echoed through the grove and the churning wind stopped its clockwise spin and burst out in all directions like the blast ring from an explosion. The graveyard went silent, the only sound the crackling of the burning copse and coffin.

Laura and Theresa looked at each other, afraid to say what they dared hope true.

"Do you think we did it?" Laura finally said.

Theresa reached down and touched Mabron's tombstone. She smiled.

"Not a twitch here," she said. "Where did we send him?"

"The burning separates the spirit from the bones," Laura said. "With no vessel to hold it, the spirit moves on to whatever is next after this life."

"Let's hope it's filled with just punishments."

The women watched the flames consume the coffin and the last remains of Mabron Hutchington. When all that remained were embers, they walked back through the field to the house, Theresa walked behind Laura.

"So what do you think happens to the girls?" Theresa said.

"Without him to hold them here," Laura said, "I hope that they can pass on and be with their mother again."

"That would be—"

A loud *thunk* cut Theresa's sentence short. Laura heard a heavy thud on the ground behind her and whipped around.

Doug lunged out of the darkness, black fireplace poker held over his head like a deranged samurai. His mouth was twisted into a lopsided smile and the pupils in his eyes burned ruby red.

Before Laura could scream, the heavy globe at the poker's end crashed down on her head and the world went dark.

Chapter Fifty-Seven

Sensations.

It had been so long since Mabron felt them. The stretch of air filling lungs. The comforting scent of decomposition wafting off the pond. The weight of Laura's warm body across his shoulder. The sting of cold iron from the poker in his hand. None of this ever happened in the half-living state of being a ghost. Mabron reveled in the feelings.

He'd been afraid when the two meddling bitches had brought the seeds of his destruction to the graveyard. When they vaporized his bones, he was sure his time on this plane of existence was over. But there was another vessel to enter. Dear old Doug was ripe for the picking. Mabron had rooted around in his mind more than enough to know how to successfully storm it. And now that he felt the quantum leap of power from influencing Doug and possessing him, Mabron wished the unconscious woman on his shoulder had set his remains ablaze earlier.

He wouldn't let Laura's actions upset the plan. He'd worked far too hard to rebuild his family. He had it all under control before the lightning storm. Vern released him from Alexander's attic trap and Sarah and the girls were still here with him, bound for eternity. But after the storm cremated Sarah's body and set her free, the girls had become a handful. They were increasingly difficult to control without the undercurrent of calming maternal care.

Vern, the poor bastard, wouldn't be any help. His twisted hands would never complete the rituals needed to bind a new woman's soul to his. A fortuitous foreclosure put Vern out on his ass. The next owners fit the bill. The Lockes were perfect.

The plan would have Doug sacrifice Laura and perform the old Egyptian ritual to keep her soul here. Mabron had worked him up to it through the rabbit and fox. Vern, making his last contribution to the family cause, would have been the warm-up for the main event. But now there was no need for practice. Mabron's skills would flow unfiltered through Doug's hands. When he was done, Laura would be perfect.

Mabron had nursed a hope that Laura would make the sacrifice willingly. He'd let the girls enter her dreams. He'd allowed them to create those touching moments in the nursery. Mabron himself had shaped the saccharine scene in the cemetery where the leaves fell on Laura's hands. He had hoped for the sake of the girls, she would choose to share eternity with them, only meeting her afterlife husband when it was too late.

That scenario would not play out, but no matter. The binding need not be voluntary, it was just stronger if it was. He would still win.

Inside the barn, he flopped Laura down on the grill over the bathtub. She let out a soft moan. Mabron removed her shoes and dropped them to the floor. The taxidermist kit lay rolled open on the workbench. Mabron grabbed a scalpel. Starting at her feet, he cut away Laura's clothing with slow, precise incisions. Socks. Jeans. T-shirt. He marveled at Laura's beautiful skin, so soft and without a single scar. Quick snips removed her bra and panties. His pulse quickened. He was tempted to touch her, to caress her for his own gratification. But he held back. Not yet. Not while she was still warm and breathing. Sarah has been perfectly satisfying after mounting. Laura would be the same.

Mabron bound her hands and feet to the grill with short lengths of rope. He slipped one more strip around her neck and positioned it to expose the carotid artery. It thumped away beneath her white skin. She'd bleed out quickly from there and he could easily repair the incision when he worked the skin.

He breathed in the familiar scent of dried blood and pickling alcohol and sprouted a twisted smile. This was going to be magnificent.

Chapter Fifty-Eight

Laura shivered herself to consciousness. Her head pounded. The cold steel grid pressed into her back and buttocks like it wanted to cube her. Where was she? Where were her clothes?

The light hurt her eyes as she forced them open. The double vision passed and she made out the barn's roof rafters. She had a partial view of the barn interior over the lip of the tub. How did she...

She remembered. The graveyard. The fire. Theresa attacked. Doug wielding that poker in the darkness. She tried to sit up and choked herself on the rope at her neck. She flexed her feet and hands with no better result.

Doug appeared from the side and looked down on her. But she knew it wasn't Doug. The smile, the expression, above all the red irises, all said someone or something else was inside pulling the strings. She knew that instant Mabron had not passed over.

"Where's Doug?" she said.

"Doug is gone." Mabron polished a scalpel with a faded red cloth. "It's just the two of us tonight."

She searched the face above her for a trace of her husband, some clue that he might be inside trying to get back. Nothing.

She should have been scared, lying naked, bound and defenseless. But instead she was furious. The girls, her husband, her friend were all taken by this bastard. She would not be next. She struggled against the bindings. They held fast.

"Now first," Mabron said, "I'll need to bleed you out." He placed the unsharpened edge of the scalpel against her neck. She felt the cool steel pulse against her artery. "A little slice here and you'll gush cleanly into the tub. You'll get tired and pass out. It will be a peaceful, lovely way to go." Mabron pulled the knife away from her neck and returned to polishing it.

"Then I'll perform the binding ritual. Doug had everything I need ready for Nephew Vern, but he won't be necessary now."

Vern, Laura thought. The skin on the wall. The previous owner of Galaxy Farm.

"Your body will become a permanent tribute to your mortal life. Don't worry. When I mount you you'll be so lifelike...you will be forever young in the eyes of the world. But only mine will have the pleasure. The two of us will move into the turret room."

Laura shuddered at the repulsive thought.

"I'll bind you here with Constance and Elizabeth. They need a mother. They've been distraught since they lost their first mother. You'll need to help them. You've seen how much they care for you."

"Under your manipulation," Laura spat. "Who knows how they really feel."

Mabron stuffed a rag into Laura's mouth. She gagged and tried to spit it out.

"We'll have time to talk later," Mabron said. "Plenty of time."

"Doug! Don't move!"

Sheriff Mears stood in the open barn door, pistol leveled at Mabron's head. His eyes flicked to Vern's flayed skin on the drying line and then back to Mabron. "Put your hands up and step back from the tub."

Mabron grimaced, but did not look back at the sheriff. The red in his eyes dulled back to brown. He tucked the scalpel into the corner of the grill.

"Thank God!" he cried. He turned to the sheriff with a convincing look of panic on his face. "I've got to get Laura free. Vern is crazy!"

Sheriff Mears dropped the weapon an inch. Mabron fiddled with the ropes tying Laura to the grate. Mears took one step closer. Laura attempted a muffled scream, but Mabron choked it off with pressure on the rope at her neck.

"Doug," Sheriff Mears said. He strung the name out and it sounded a bit like a question. "Step back from the tub."

Mabron punched his panic up a notch. "No time. He's coming back. Help me get her free. He'll kill her!"

Mabron had positioned himself to consistently block Mears' view of the tub. Mears dropped his weapon to point at the ground. He stepped around Mabron's right side and closer. Too close.

Mabron's eyes flashed red. He spun around and his hands moved like lightning. He grabbed Sheriff Mears at the collar with both hands and yanked him forward. The sheriff's head hit the side of the tub with a crack. Blood gushed from a jagged gash at his hairline. Mears crumpled down below Laura's sightline.

Mabron hunched down below the rim of the tub. There was a metallic click. The bark of the sheriff's 9mm broke the silence. Mabron rose back into view. He stared at the floor like an artist appraising his work. He stepped over to the barn door, rolled it shut and threw the bolt to lock it. He returned back to the tub. He bent over so his eyes burned inches from Laura's.

Mabron grabbed her head at the temple, strong as a clamp. She tried to yell but only coughed against the choking rag. Mabron bent closer.

"Now, without further interruptions…"

The icy scalpel tip traced a practice incision against her skin.

"In a few minutes," Mabron said, "you'll be mine in both dimensions." His eyes burned like two blacksmith's forges.

The blade's pressure on her skin increased. Then Mabron's hand jerked away. The scalpel clattered against the grill and fell into the bottom of the cast iron tub with a ping. A look of utter surprise crossed Mabron's face. He snapped straight up. The tip of the fireplace poker

227

stuck out of his chest. Blood ran down around the front of his shirt like a pulsing waterfall. His lips moved in indecipherable silent words. The flames in his eyes extinguished and Mabron dropped to the ground.

Behind him stood a shimmering spirit, more distinct than the girls had been, even with the static generator. A beautiful young woman with a face lovely as a china doll, hair cut close just below her ears. Her white ruffled dress was immaculate. There was no mistaking Sarah Hutchington.

Sarah reached down through the grill and grabbed the scalpel. She pulled it back up and slit the rope that bound Laura's right arm. She placed the scalpel in Laura's freed hand.

Laura wanted to thank her, to tell her that her children were free. But the gag in her mouth kept her from it.

Sarah shimmered, like TV reception that was about to head south. She leaned down in and whispered in Laura's ear.

Tears formed on Laura's eyes. She nodded her head to say "Yes, I understand."

Sarah looked down on her with a sad smile and faded away.

Chapter Fifty-Nine

Two hours later, Galaxy Farm was bathed in the flashing blue lights of a half-dozen police cruisers. The barn was roped off with a mile of yellow crime scene tape. Police radios crackled and spat from all over the property. The wind brought a whiff of the graveyard fire back to the house, but the swarm of officials were too preoccupied to notice. The sheriff was dead in the county's first triple homicide.

Laura had put on an old college sweatshirt and a pair of jeans. She had applied a few streaks of her husband's blood to the sweatshirt. She stood by an ambulance stretcher and held Theresa's hand. Theresa's face was pale, but she had a grip like steel.

"It's just a little concussion," she said. "I don't see why I have to go to the hospital. I can just go home..."

"Absolutely not," Laura said. "You're going to get fully checked out. Your father is already waiting there for you." She glanced around to be sure she wasn't overheard. "You know your story?"

"Please," Theresa said. "We've been over it a dozen times."

"Perfect," Laura said.

Two paramedics arrived at each side of the gurney. Theresa gave Laura's hand a tug. She locked her eyes with Laura's.

"It's over now," Theresa said. "I'm sure of it."

"I'll hold you to that."

As the paramedics loaded Theresa into the ambulance, a tall black man in a rumpled charcoal suit approached Laura. A frayed toothpick stuck out of the left side of his mouth. He pulled it out with his two forefingers to address her.

"Mrs. Locke, I'm Detective Williams. Are you up to answering a few questions?"

Laura nodded and led the detective to the front porch. They sat on the stoop.

"I'm sorry for your loss," the detective said. "Can you tell me what happened?" He popped the toothpick back in his mouth.

"Theresa came over for a visit this evening," Laura began. "I hadn't seen Doug since I got home, but that wasn't unusual. After an hour or so we went to the barn to look for him. We rolled open the door and surprised him arranging something that looked like a human skin on the wall. Doug had a crazy look in his eyes. He came after us with that old fireplace poker.

"He hit Theresa first, then he hit me. He knocked me out and I woke up on the floor of the barn to the sound of shouting. The sheriff and Doug were in a fight. There was a shot and the sheriff was dead. That's when I ran Doug through with the poker."

Detective Williams rolled the toothpick to the other side of his mouth and waited to hear more. Laura wasn't playing that game. She used silence to get her kids to keep a story going all the time. She'd change tack instead.

"Was that really human skin on the wall?" she asked.

"Yeah," Detective Williams said. "Vern Pugh from next door. You know him?"

Laura shook her head.

"You notice any strange behavior from your husband lately?"

"He was distant, spent a lot of time by himself," Laura said. "I just thought he was writing his novel. Nothing like..." she pointed at the barn, "...that. What was the sheriff doing here anyway?"

"His car is parked at Vern's. He went there to pick him up. We guess he couldn't find him and the trail led him here, where your husband had already killed him."

Detective Williams sighed and stood up. She could tell that Williams had ruled her out as anything other than a woman defending herself. He spit the tattered toothpick from his mouth. He pulled another one from his pocket.

"Wrong week to quit smoking," he said. "We'll have the barn sealed off for a while for the investigation. We'll be in touch with any information we uncover. Again, I'm sorry for your loss."

"And I for yours," Laura said.

The detective nodded and went back to the barn. Laura leaned back against a post. If Theresa could be as believable, she would pull this off, and be able to keep her promise to Sarah.

Chapter Sixty

"Are you sure about this?" Theresa said. Three months after the terrible night at Galaxy Farm, Theresa was fully recovered. She was dressed in coveralls that had dirt stains from the knees down.

"A promise is a promise," Laura said. She wiped her filthy hands on her jeans.

It was near midnight and they both stood on the porch of the house, the house that Laura had thought was so beautiful the first time she saw it. It wasn't beautiful anymore. She had explored the turret room after the police left that awful night. The dread she felt in the turret room had departed with Mabron's spirit. She had found the cache of taxidermidied animals in the attic, the box of sick mementos and texts. The depth of Mabron's depravity became apparent, as well as the extent that Doug had joined him in it. No house that ever held that much sickness could ever be anything but black.

She had also found Doug's manuscript for his novel. Hundreds of pages of random letters, not a word among them. Whatever he thought he was creating, it wasn't there. How far Mabron had burrowed into his mind, and what seeds he had laid there, she would never know for sure.

"You coming in with me?" Laura asked.

Theresa gave her head a shake. "Nope. It's all yours."

Laura entered the house and passed by the new collection on the living room floor without a glance. She went straight to the nursery, sat at her desk and closed her eyes.

Since the night Mabron was finally exorcised, the girls had come to Laura every evening. They might have been controlled by Mabron, but they did not pass over to the other side when his spirit was banished. They were glad he was gone but happier still that Laura was there for them. Every night they came to play with their new mother. In their eyes, she was the only mother they had ever had. They had somehow melded Laura and Sarah Hutchington into one being. Their bond was so close that Laura could summon them now.

Laura cleared her mind. "Constance. Elizabeth," she called. The back of her neck tingled instantly. The two girls appeared at her feet, hazy full-body apparitions. Without Mabron draining their energy, they could coalesce without the boost of the static generator, though Laura could not hear them when they spoke. They came to her smiling and put one head on each shoulder.

Laura would not deny how she loved seeing them each night. Some evenings they would play simple games together; rolling a ball, building with blocks, playing jacks. Other nights she would just watch them play together, just the way any mother would her children. Freeing them from Mabron had only enhanced the maternal bond she felt.

But this was not how they were supposed to be, half living, half dead. And it wasn't how Laura was supposed to live, nurturing a family that would never grow. She had put off fulfilling her promise long enough.

"Girls," she said. The two raised their heads from her shoulders. A lump swelled in Laura's throat. "You know that I love you both very much."

They both smiled and their translucent lips mouthed, "We love you."

Tears welled in Laura's eyes. "Something scary will happen tonight. Something that might hurt and confuse you. But when you feel lost, listen. Follow the voice you remember and trust."

The girls looked at each other in fear. Their lips moved too fast for Laura to understand, but it made no difference. Tears rolled down

233

Laura's cheeks and she headed for the living room. The girls followed close behind, mouthing questions Laura could not answer.

Laura and Theresa has spent the afternoon and evening creating the collection on the living room floor. It had taken that long to excavate the twins' graves and exhume their remains with any level of respect. Now the girls cream-and-gray bones lay in a pile on the floor, two skulls on top.

Laura cut open a bag of rock salt, salt from the water system the house had never needed. But Sarah had convinced Laura's subconscious it did, so that a ready defense from Mabron would be available. Laura poured the salt around and over the bones.

Then she picked up a can of barbeque starter fluid and squirted it all over the bone pile. Some of the salt melted into slag on contact. The twins tugged at her arms, demanding answers.

Laura slid a locket from her pocket. It was the one from the attic. Laura had torn out Mabron's picture and replaced it with one of the two twins taken just before they drowned. She popped it open and laid it on top of the bone pile.

Laura pulled out the lighter, the slim gold model Theresa had given her. It was the one Sarah had tricked her subconscious into desiring, like the books of matches she'd been obsessed with carrying, so that a spark for Mabron's immolation would always be available. She flicked it and a flame ignited.

"Go your mother, girls," Laura sobbed. She dropped the lighter on the wet pyramid of bones. An inferno whooshed to life as the starter fluid ignited.

The girls screamed, and this time Laura could hear the high-pitched wail. Their bodies wavered and they grabbed each other in panic. Light as a butterfly, they rose in a slow counterclockwise spiral around the fire, crying in terror.

Constance stopped screaming. She put her hand over Elizabeth's mouth to silence her. As they floated around the flames, they both cocked an ear upward.

On the ceiling, a pinhole of blinding white light appeared. It stretched open until it was several feet wide. The girls looked up into the brilliant void and burst into smiles of ecstatic recognition. They raised their arms and were sucked through the shimmering disc. In an instant, the disc shrank to nonexistence. The girls were back with Sarah.

Laura stared at the empty space on her ceiling in a mesmerized rapture. Only a searing feeling on her leg brought her back to the real world.

The living room floor was engulfed in flames. Black smoke rolled along the ceiling. Orange runners licked at the walls and the curtains were already ablaze. In seconds her escape route would be gone.

Laura leapt through the front door and raced to where Theresa stood a hundred yards from the house. Theresa reached down and beat a few stubborn flames from Laura's pant leg.

"You have to cut it so close?" Theresa said. She looked back at the house. "Promise kept?"

"They are reunited."

The women sat and watched the flames consume the desiccated wood house. The turret room went ablaze and the two windows glowed like Mabron's eyes staring out from Doug's face. Then the dome above it collapsed and crushed the dreaded room into a pile of flaming splinters. The women turned to walk to Theresa's car.

"Now you're sure Dustin doesn't mind having his teacher live in the same house with him?" Laura said.

"Are you kidding?" Theresa said. "He already painted me a picture of all of us at the dinner table together."

About the Author

Raised on Long Island, NY, Russell James joined the Army after college graduation. After a tour flying helicopters with the U.S. Army's 101st Airborne Division, he became a technical writer. He has published several short stories, but this is his first novel.

While he did live for six years in a small Tennessee town *much* nicer than Moultrie, he and his wife now reside in sunny Florida.

Visit his website at www.russellrjames.com or drop him a line at rrj@russellrjames.com.

Can true evil really die?

Sacrifice
© *2012 Russell James*

Thirty years after graduating high school in Sagebrook, New York, Bob Armstrong calls five friends home for a long overdue reunion. They have not had any contact with each other since the horrible events the weeks before graduation, when they took on the murderous entity they came to call the Woodsman. The Woodman's prey were the children of Sagebrook, but the friends fought back...and barely escaped with their lives.

As soon as they arrive, death stalks the six once more. They band together again, forced to relive the terrifying ordeal of their past while they battle nightmarish dangers in the present. But thirty years have taken a physical and mental toll on them. Can they overcome their psychic scars and keep the children of Sagebrook safe? What will each of them have to sacrifice to once again keep the Woodsman at bay?

Coming soon in ebook and print from Samhain Publishing.

Enjoy the following excerpt from Sacrifice...

June 1980

Lightning arced across the night sky. In its flash, the Sagebrook water tower stood like a gleaming white beacon above the trees on the hill. Ten seconds later, thunder rolled in behind it, the way every event has an echo that follows.

Five figures scurried along the catwalk around the tower, one of the old-fashioned kinds, where a squat cylinder with a conical hat sat on six spindly steel legs a few hundred feet in the air. A newer tower served the people's water needs, but the old girl was an icon for the Long Island town, so the trustees kept it painted white and emblazoned with the "Sagebrook-Founded on 1741" logo to remind themselves of their heritage. Once per year, the logo changed to celebrate the graduation of the Whitman High senior class.

The boys on the catwalk were going to see that this year it changed twice. These seniors had committed more than their fair share of pranks; stolen street signs, a tap into the high school PA system, swapping the state flag in front of school with the Jolly Roger. But this stunt would top them all

They had all met in the sixth grade, where their teacher had dubbed them "The Dirty Half Dozen" due to their inseparability and penchant for trouble. The title had stuck. They hadn't done anything as dangerous as tonight's foray, but anything worth a good laugh was worth doing.

"Who's got the red?" Bob whispered, though no one but the boys could be within earshot. He crouched at the base of the new banner that read "Congratulations Class of 1980" with "Go Minutemen" painted underneath in red letters. Bob was rail thin with an unruly head of brown hair that consented to a part on the right and little else. An unlit cigarette dangled from the corner of his mouth.

"Right here," Paul said. He handed Bob a can of red spray paint. Paul stood several inches taller than the rest of the boys and his broad shoulders made the narrow catwalk a tight fit. He wore his Minutemen football team jacket, though Dave had told him the white leather sleeves would look like two glow worms crawling across the tower at night. His hair was cropped close and he sported the shadow of what he euphemistically called a moustache.

A blast of cold wind hit the tower. The snaps on Paul's jacket hit the metal railing with a reverberating ping.

A third boy, Jeff, hung over the catwalk railing. He had a long face with ears that had stuck out just enough for a good round of elementary school ribbing. He held his New York Mets ball cap tight as he looked down at the perimeter fence. A ten-year-old Olds Vista Cruiser station wagon idled near the hole in the fence. There was a slight lope to the modified V8's rumbling exhaust through the turbo mufflers. The headlights were off, but the parking lights lit the edges of the car. Jeff spoke into a cheap Japanese walkie talkie.

"Dave," he said. "What the hell are you doing with the lights on?"

"Damn," Dave answered from the Vista. "Sorry man." The marker lights in the car went dark. "It's clear down here."

"At two a.m. it had better be," said Ken, a red headed kid with a rash of freckles across his cheekbones. He slipped behind Jeff to join Bob and Paul. He brushed against Jeff's butt as he squeezed by.

"Watch it, homo," Jeff said.

"It's your ass," Ken said. "It's so enticing. We're here in the dark..."

"Hey," Bob snapped. "You girls want to shut the fuck up and start spraying?"

Twin lightning flashes lit a big cloud like a floating anvil-shaped lantern. Thunder crackled across the sky five seconds later.

Marc, the last boy on the tower sat at the opening where the access ladder met the catwalk. His feet dangled through the opening. Both hands gripped the catwalk rail. He was the slightest of the gr and he had to brace himself against a renewed gust of wind that rocked his thick curly black hair back and forth. There were only four cans of paint, so he could have stayed in the car on watch with Dave. But there was something to prove by climbing the tower, though he wasn't sure if it was to the others or to himself. The journey did enlighten him about one thing. He was definitely acrophobic.

"We better hurry," Marc said. "We don't want to be up here in the rain."

"You said we'd have clear weather," Paul said to Ken as Ken handed him a can of white spray paint.

"No," Ken said. "I said there was a twenty percent chance of a shower. When I have a few free hours, I'll explain probability to you, Jockstrap."

"There's a one hundred percent probability I'm going to throw you all off this fucking tower if you don't shut up," Bob said. The spray can in his hand started to hiss. "If we don't do this tonight, they'll have time to paint over it before graduation. Let's go."

"All for none..." Paul said.

"And none for all," the group finished. The teen's unofficial motto, in its sarcastic denial of camaraderie, completely represented theirs.

Paul, Jeff and Ken joined in and the side of the tower sounded like a den of spitting cobras. The "G" in "Go" lost a few of its edges. A "B" took shape on the tower's side.

Another bolt of lightning arced from the anvil cloud to the ground. This time the thunder reported only a second after. The smell of rain wafted in on the breeze. A spray of fat drops splattered against the tank like machine gun fire.

"Hey, guys," Dave's voice said from the walkie-talkie in Jeff's belt. "It's starting to rain down here. Is it raining up there?"

"No," Ken answered to himself with a roll of his eyes. "It always rains from the ground up."

Jeff gave a quick look at the peak of the tower, then at the approaching cloud. "This thing is one hell of a conductor. We should—"

Lightning split the sky above their heads. The thunder was simultaneous and sharp, so loud that the boys could feel it rumble.

"Hang on, wussies," Bob said. He gave the tower one last blast from his can. He stood up and leaned back against the railing. "Go Minutemen" had been transformed into "Blow Minutemen."

Paul gave his "L" one final shot of red. He appraised his work with an admiring stare. "How did Ms. Kravitz ever give me a D in Art?"

Marc stood at the ladder, one foot on the first rung. "Let's go!"

The air around them seemed to come alive, as if the molecules had decided to dance in circles around each other. The hair on the boys' arms stood on end. Jeff's walkie talkie buzzed like a cicada. A freezing downdraft swept the catwalk. Five heartbeats went into overdrive.

"Lay flat!' Jeff shouted.

The boys dove for the decking. Marc, already on the ladder, just hung on.

A white light blinding as the power of God enveloped the tower. Deafening thunder blanketed the boys and the air turned hot and dry. Uncountable volts pumped through the tower as the lightning bolt ripped from the spire on the peak to the ground below. Jeff's radio exploded in a shower of sparks and melted plastic. The boys' bodies jittered against the catwalk decking, belt buckles clanging against the steel. Clothing smoked and there was the disgusting smell of burnt hair. The split second seemed to last forever.

Life on Meditrine Island is luxurious...but brief.

The Lamplighters
© *2011 Frazer Lee*

Marla Neuborn has found the best post-grad job in the world—as a 'Lamplighter' working on Meditrine Island, an exclusive idyllic paradise owned and operated by a consortium of billionaires. All Lamplighters have to do is tend to the mansions, cook and clean, and turn on lights to make it appear the owners are home. But the job comes with conditions. Marla will not know the exact location of the island, and she will have no contact with the outside world for the duration of her stay.

Once on the island, Marla quickly learns the billionaire lifestyle is not all it is made out to be. The chief of security rules Meditrine with an iron fist. His private police force patrols the shores night and day, and CCTV cameras watch the Lamplighters relentlessly. Soon Marla will also discover first-hand that the island hides a terrible secret. She'll meet the resident known as the Skin Mechanic. And she'll find out why so few Lamplighters ever leave the island alive.

Now available in ebook and print from Samhain Publishing.

First things first. Vera put the handset in its cradle and headed for the kitchen. She walked over to the huge range in the centre of the room and ignited all four of the gas taps. Then, crouching on her haunches, she turned the oven on full blast. The expensive smoked glass oven door afforded her a look at her own reflection. Only a month on Meditrine Island and already she looked five years younger. Amazing. Gone were the dark grey shadows around her eyes - even her signature brittle dry hair had a new luster. Berlin could take care of itself, thanks very much. The island really was like a fountain of youth, she thought as she rose and crossed to the patio door.

Unclipping the latch, Vera had to use two hands to slide the glass behemoth open. Whoever owned this house had a serious heavy glass fetish. Stepping out into the night, her senses were flooded. The island's fresh air was like no other; an intoxicating blend of jasmine and ocean spray. When she went back to the city, she'd have to remember to bottle and sell it.

Click.

Her quiet moment was suddenly blasted with fifteen hundred watts of raw security lighting as she stepped in front of the infrared sensors. She cursed the light for blinding her as she picked up the watering can, blinking away the white-hot glare. The light had brought the mosquitoes a-calling too. They whizzed around her as she dashed back into the kitchen.

Vera filled the watering can with cool, clear water at the bath-sized sink. This was the least tedious of her tasks - the plants were going to drink their fill tonight. Amidst such fabulous wealth, such meticulous order, it felt good that a mere backpacker could decide the fate of items so precious to their millionaire owners.

Millionaires? Billionaires, more likely.

She remembered Jessie's sardonic voice from the first time they'd out together, gossiping about who owned these mansions; this But Vera didn't really care who the owners were. That they were handsomely to do a few chores was all she cared about. And the most strenuous chore was watering the plants. Easy money. "The job's a doozy," Jessie had giggled. 'Doozy Jessie' been working on the island longer than Vera and seemed to be going a little stir crazy...

As the water rose closer to the brim of the watering can, the security lights clicked off suddenly. *Like everything else on the island they ran to a tight schedule,* thought Vera. As she did so, milliseconds before the light bulbs faded, Vera saw something outside.

A figure.

She blinked twice, slow and firm. The ghost imprint of the blinding bulbs still there, forming crescent shaped black holes in her mind's eye. Was there someone out there?

Vera blinked again, then swore furiously as liquid spilled onto her feet. Soaked, she closed the faucet and let the watering can rest in the sink unit. *Shouldn't have smoked that joint before coming up to the house,* she thought, sounding for all the world like her mother. Scatterbrain, she used to call Vera whenever she lost the power to function normally; everyday tasks becoming impossibly hilarious missions. She still wondered if her mother had known her daughter was stoned, or if she simply believed her child was missing a neuron or two million.

The old clumsiness was really kicking in now, as she left little pools of water on the tiled floor on her way to the patio. Putting the can down (yet more spills) she grabbed the door handle and pulled with all her might.

Swoosh.

The glass giant slid open easier this time. Vera bent down to pick up the can — then the smell hit her.

Something had invaded the envelope of jasmine and surf, corrupting the very night air with its presence. A hospital smell, harsh and synthetic, like the way her dentist smelled. She'd hated the dentist since she was a kid. Had he followed her here, to paradise, tracking her down after all these years to do all that work she had chickened out of?

To tut and frown disapprovingly through his paper mask, noting her cannabis-stained enamel and ugly overbite?

She leaned out into the night air, her nostrils searching for the source of the stifling smell. It was mixed with something else now, like ripe leather.

Click.

He was standing right next to her, impossibly close. Vera's heart blasted into her mouth, choking her scream. The source of the smell regarded her idly, his black eyes like camera lenses. Cold. Unforgiving.

Before she could react, Vera heard a swooshing sound. The smell of rubber gloves perversely filled her nostrils, pushing all the way back into her throat as if someone really had jammed two fingers up her nose. The intruder's dark form was a monolith, burned into her eyes by the security lights.

Click.

Swoosh.

The bulbs faded once more. Vera's senses imploded as the sliding door crushed her skull against the alloy doorframe.

Crunch.

Swoosh, as the door slid back again.

Crunch.

Vera's body jerked uselessly then fell still; her brains spattered across the cool, thick glass.

www.samhainpublishing.com

Green for the planet.
Great for your wallet.

SAMHAIN

PUBLISHING

It's all about the story...

Romance

HORROR

www.samhainpublishing.com

CPSIA information can be obtained at www.ICGtesting.com
Printed in the USA
BVOW071433260112

281468BV00002B/16/P